MAGICAL ECHO

MAGICAL ECHO

LINDA KAY SILVA

SAPPHIRE BOOKS

SALINAS, CALIFORNIA

Magical Echo
Copyright © 2013 by **Linda Kay Silva**, All rights reserved.

ISBN - 978-1-939062-03-1

This is a work of fiction - names, characters, places, and incidents are the product of the author's imagination or are used fictitiously. Any resemblance to actual persons living or dead, business, events or locales is entirely coincidental.

All rights reserved. No part of this publication may be reproduced, distributed, or transmitted in any form or by any means, including photocopying, recording, or other electronic or mechanical methods, without written permission of the publisher.

Cover Design by Billie Tzar
Editor Kaycee Hawn -

Sapphire Books
Salinas, CA 93912
www.sapphirebooks.com

Printed in the United States of America
Second Edition – March 2013

Dedication

This one is for my Dad.

He taught me how to bunt a baseball, shoot a basketball, play tennis without a backhand, swim, use tools, and be myself no matter what.

He showed me that laughter is the best medicine, that brains are better than brawn, and that family is everything. When I was 14, my dad sat me down and told me, "Sweetheart, it's time you started wearing a shirt. You're not a boy." When he realized this was news to me, he smiled and said, "You're way better."

When I told my very Christian father that I was gay, he hugged me and said, "I don't care, sweetheart. I will always love you."

And he does.

Even in the grips of dementia, when my dad laughs, I am magically transported back to a time when he was teaching me how to bunt, shoot, swim, and be proud of who I was and who I would grow up to be.

Every minute I get to spend with my dad is a gift.
This one is for you, Dad, for
Ron Silva
Uncle Ronnie
Ronnie Sonnie
Ron
and the gentle man who raised doves,
my hero.
I love you.

Acknowledgements

I want to, once again, thank Team Storm for their tireless dedication and attention to detail when helping me birth my baby. I can't thank you all enough for your help, guidance, problem solving, and hard work.

Sandi Morris, who types faster than I can speak, and who proofs with the eye of an eagle.

Isabella, for not just being my publisher, but also my friend. You're big fun.

Billie Tzar, for your creative genius, your endless patience, and your amazing technical skills. You make my life easier.

Lucy who warms my lap, smiles at me when I come home, and loves me all the time.

Kat Warner and Beth Burnett, my two favorite stalkers who tell everyone about my books.

And of course, Lori Major, who does all those little things (and big things) so that I have time to write. Thank you, love.

When we landed in the suffocating heat of Las Vegas, a black Lincoln Navigator SUV with tinted windows was waiting for us like a big, black bug on the scorching pavement. The heat rose in waves off the blacktop of the runway while a huge no neck Guido-type in a blue Armani suit with Rayban sunglasses stood next to it, hands folded in front of him as if this heat wasn't melting the sole of his shoes. He was rocking back and forth on the balls of his feet, looking like an extra on *The Sopranos*. He was clearly waiting for us.

I turned to my best friend, Danica Johnson, and punched her in the arm. "Damn it, Dani. Really? You went to Nick Harper for a car? Nick *The Thug* Harper? You didn't really have a security meeting with him, did you?"

Danica nodded her head. "I did, and no, I didn't go to him for just a car...a car and a super cool place to stay if we need it...and who said I was done with him? We're...buddies with bennies." She waved her hand dismissively. "Do I need to explain that or do you get the picture?"

All I could do was glare at her. "Funny. I suppose I could have figured that one out, but a gangster will only muddy the waters."

Bailey, our resident animist and shaman, had been napping in the back but snapped her head to when she heard this. "You seem to have a lot of *buddies* like that, Dani."

I laid my face in my hands and groaned. We'd come down to Las Vegas from Marin, California to find a murderer. The last thing we needed was Scarface and his merry band of henchmen in our back pocket. "Please tell me you're kidding. I know we need help down here, but damn it, he's a *gangster*."

Delta Stevens, an ex-police officer we had hired on as part of security, looked hard at me, as I knew she would. Working with a thug was not in her character. She was the straightest arrow I'd ever met. "A gangster? You never said anything about meeting up with hoodlums."

"Come on, you two Pollyannas." Gathering her purse and bag Danica shrugged. "Nick's a good guy to the right people and a font of information where Vegas is concerned. He can steer us in the right direction so we're not chasing our tails. This is a big city and we don't have time to waste."

She had a point. We flew here from the San Francisco Bay Area to help out with *a situation*. Danica had all the right connections to accomplish that, lawful or otherwise.

We had been asked to come down because a young magician's assistant had been murdered, and the group that oversees all things supernatural, the Others, charged me to see what was behind it.

The Others wanted me to check it out and get a lid not only on the murder, but on the paranormal beings who were using their powers for professional gain—a no-no to the Others. We were not supposed to use our powers to make money or for other wealth. Doing so brought too much attention on us and we were...well...still in the closet.

My name is Echo Branson, and I am an empath. I have the ability to feel what other people around me are feeling. I can tell when someone is lying and when someone withholds the truth. When I was Cinder's age, a tender fourteen, my powers first kicked in during a moment of fear, and they scared the crap out of me. I nearly killed a classmate for coming at my best friend, Danica Johnson, and was sent to a loony bin, where a *spotter* found me and shipped me to New Orleans.

A spotter is a super whose job it is to find and grab those of us she or he spots before the authorities or doctors or the government can get their hands on us. Big George, an orderly at the nuthouse, who immediately knew I was one of them, spotted me. He helped me escape before I became a drooling lump of flesh who didn't know how to keep everyone's emotions at bay. That was the fate for those of us who were not trained in building psychic shields to protect ourselves. I know. I saw it firsthand, and it wasn't pretty. So, Big George got me out of the hospital and made arrangements for me to get to New Orleans to one of the best supernatural mentors in the western hemisphere.

In New Orleans, I trained for four years with my mentor, Melika, way out on the furthest reaches of the Louisiana bayou. Melika took me in and showed me how to protect myself from the onslaught of emotions I felt from everyone around me. She taught me how to use the energy I was born with to project a defensive energy outward. She had taught me more in four years than all other adults combined in the whole of my childhood, and there had been many of those.

For the first fourteen years of my life, I was a kid in the foster care system. A kid whose name was Jane

Doe. Can you imagine your name actually *being* Jane Doe? Well, it was, and for a reason I wouldn't find out about until I was almost thirty.

As a foster child, I was in and out of foster homes so often, the kiddie home considered installing a revolving door. It wasn't that I was unmanageable—I was just different.

Then I got out and to the bayou, where I wasn't just understood, I was loved and nurtured. Those were the four best years of my life because it was the first time in my life I'd had a real family. My family had consisted of Jacob Marley, a necromancer, Zack, a telekinetic—or mover—and the woman who would eventually become my lover, Tiponi Redhawk, a level five telepath. These people gave me the strength and wisdom to live in this world as part of the regular society. They taught me everything I would need to know in order to survive and be happy.

Now, I am the mentor and the head of my own family, of which Cinder is a large part. No longer on the bayou, I'd moved my charges to a chateau in Marin County; to gorgeous rolling hills with one hundred and fifty acres of vineyards surrounded by the best security system money can buy. I had moved, in part, because I couldn't imagine being that far away from Danica…a city girl, and my best friend for more than half my life.

Danica had been my confidante forever, and I couldn't imagine living without her, so we compromised. She bought the land and built the chateau for me, knowing it would keep me nearer to her while also keeping my students safe.

I reluctantly agreed to come down hoping to get in and out without an investigation dragging on. I had recently moved into a new place and had barely spent a night there. I didn't wish to be away any longer than necessary. I had students to teach and a life to live.

"Okay, but we're staying at the hotel—not his personal residence," I said.

"Of course. I got us a sweet suite at the Pentagon. It's all the rage here these days. His rooms are just Plan B, in case it's needed. You know how important a Plan B is."

I did.

The Pentagon was a brand new hotel on the strip that had all the major United States monuments inside it. I'd never seen it, but was sure it was as gaudy as the rest of Vegas, a place of which I was not a fan, and not just because it was called Sin City.

I am an empath.

I was born with the ability to read people's emotional state. Before I learned how to control it, people's emotions could batter my own around. A place like Vegas is poison to an empath like me because emotions run either really high or really low, and the two conflicting feelings can short circuit your wires pretty quickly, even with good blocking skills. I had excellent psychic shields, but even in a place like Vegas they could get worn down, especially in the casinos where more people lost more than they won.

"And we have a meeting with Nick in—" Danica checked her ultra thin Rolex. "Half an hour. I briefed him on the particulars of weird activity or people of interest, that sort of thing. He's a good source. You'll see."

"A gangster, Dani?" Delta asked. "Can he even be trusted?"

Danica looked Delta in the eyes: the only woman I knew who was tall enough to go toe to toe with the nearly six foot tall ex-cop. "You don't need to trust him, Storm. You need to trust *me*."

Grabbing my bag, I stuck my head in the cockpit of the plane Danica purchased for the paranormal school I'd started back home. Danica had made her first million before we'd graduated from Mills College. She now owned Savvy Software, a company that produced cutting edge software and apps. The plane was a present and I had already gotten used to having a private plane at my disposal. It rocked. "We need you back at the chateau, Sal," I said to the pilot. "We'll call when we're ready to come home."

The little redhead in green army fatigues saluted and grinned. "You got it."

We thanked Sal before stepping out into the heat and into the cool Navigator.

Guido introduced himself as Mario, and informed us he would be our driver for the duration. I had to hand it to her, Danica's money and connections always made everything so much easier.

"Mrs. Harper will meet you in conference room A. She set out a spread and asked that you feel free to eat your fill."

"Thank you, Mario." Danica fiddled with the seat and I could see her Glock lying in the interior pocket of the Coach purse she'd had altered just for the gun. Danica loved that gun. She loved guns in general. That was the ghetto girl in her. Born and raised in Oakland, Danica could go from software genius to bitch from the 'hood' in two point two seconds.

Danica had been my best friend for more than half of my thirty years and had used that Glock more than once to protect me and my charges. She thought nothing of pulling the trigger, and I thought everything of her for doing so.

Even after I told her what I was, we remained the best of friends. So good, in fact, that, along with the private plane, she had bought me a beautiful home in Marin, California so I could teach other young supernaturals how to wield their powers. She was generous that way, and had recently thrown in the plane as a bonus. Danica Johnson did nothing half ass—hence the plane and the bodyguards.

Looking across the tarmac, I watched as the heat continued to rise off the pavement like it was alive. The weather was typical of the desert almost year round, and I was thankful Mario had the air conditioner on. It was a nice, cool ride through the bustling, tourist trodden streets of Vegas, which was crowded year round.

When we got out at the Pentagon, the air felt much hotter, like we'd just stepped into a tanning booth.

We thanked Mario, who reminded us he would be just outside if we needed anything. When we checked in, we were shown to a suite bigger than the one thousand square foot bedroom Danica had built for me. This suite was more like a house. A really big, really elegant house.

"Oh. My." Walking in, I stared at the opulence of a room with one whole wall of windows overlooking the Vegas strip with its flashing neon signs and array of lights and fountains. New and old neon signs alike mingled together to create a skyline unlike any other. "What an amazing view."

Danica tipped the bellboy a crisp Ben while Bailey, Delta, and I stared slack-jawed at the enormity of the suite. One side had a small replica of Jefferson's library. There were three big screens mounted on a wall in a step-down living area with a large U-shaped black leather couch. The lines were clean, the ambiance not the least bit tacky or gaudy like so much of Vegas. There were four large bedrooms with the same clean lines—very modern, sleek, and over-the-top expensive. I shuddered to think of how much money Danica had dropped on this suite.

"Pays to know someone in this town," Danica said, closing the door and handing each of us a gold key card. "Quite a spread, huh?"

"Incredible," I said, taking the key from her. "I'm very impressed. Not old school tacky like a lot of Vegas."

"What can I say? Nick has good taste...and good connections."

We saw more of that good taste in the conference room, where there was enough food for the Oakland Raiders—good food like waffles, Eggs Benedict, lox, and cream cheese. There were four different carafes of coffee, three different juices, and four kinds of breakfast meats. Bailey was in heaven. That girl could eat her weight. While she loaded up a plate, Delta, Danica, and I sat down with coffee and a bagel.

"Anything...else...we need to know about you and Nick?"

Danica grinned. "Besides that he's great in the sack and has a schlong the size of—"

Delta held her hand up. "Uh uh. Too much for my lesbian ears. No talking about schlongs, Johnsons, or any other penile sobriquets."

Before Danica could offer up more, there was a buzz at the door and after Delta let him in, Nick Harper entered the conference room wearing the same kind of suit Mario wore, only he had on a pink silk tie and some spicy cologne that wafted in behind him. His hair was a soft brown with flecks of gray that gathered at the top of his sideburns. He was slightly shorter than Danica's six feet and had the lightest blue eyes I had ever seen. That was when I knew what attracted her to him. Powerful men with light blue eyes were her Kyptonite.

Striding into the room, he made a beeline for Danica and hugged her to him in a way that confirmed they were more than friends.

After all of the introductions were made, he sat across from us and folded his hands on the table. He made eye contact with each of us, his eyes lingering a little longer on Delta's emerald eyes. "So, what can I do for you?"

Delta took the lead. "We know you casino owners have your own network of information. We need to tap into some of that intel for a job we came to do."

Nick looked from Delta to me and back to Delta. "You a cop?"

She smiled, revealing two deep-set dimples. "No, I'm not."

He squinted and leaned closer. "You sure seem like one."

Her smile never wavered and her pupils narrowed to pinpricks. "I've been told that."

Danica laid her hand on Nick's arm. "No one's out to bust you, babe. We need what you know. Information, pure and simple."

As if soothed by her touch, he relaxed immediately and sat back. "What do you want to know?"

Delta leaned back as well, her eyes never leaving his face. "There's a group, perhaps three or four young gamblers who are winning...not a lot...not enough to make anyone notice...or be worried, but—"

Nick held his hand up. His fingernails were polished and well manicured. "I know exactly who you're talking about. We've been tracking them for a few days now, but no one found anything." He shrugged. "Buncha college kids screwing around. They got lucky, didn't get caught, and probably moved on. Haven't seen them in a couple of weeks at my place, but I know they just took the Silver Dollar for a few grand. Why? What's this about?"

"Are they still in town?"

Nick pulled out his phone. "I can find out for you easy enough."

"Excellent. Have you heard of anything...strange going on with any of the illusionists?"

"The magicians?" He laughed, displaying perfect rows of veneered teeth.

Yeah. I understood now how he had become one of Danica's bed buddies. He was incredibly handsome and well dressed.

"Why are you laughing?"

"Are you kidding me? Those *are* the strangest group of performers in Vegas. People don't mess with them. They're spooky and creepy with all those swords and body parts." He shrugged. "They spook people."

"Then that's a no?" Leave it to Delta to cut to the chase.

Nick shook his head, and at that moment, he reminded me of Richard Gere. "This one's all business." He hooked his thumb over to Delta.

"We all are, Nicky. We're not playing here." Danica leaned closer. "What can you tell us about Max Rhodes?"

Nick's poker face caved right away. "He's even creepier than that weird dude, Angel. No one knows how he does half the shit he does, either. Rhodes's show is like no other. Not as edgy as Angel's, but impressive nonetheless. The guy does things that even Copperfield envies. Is this about *him*?"

"Maybe. We're not sure. This is all fact-finding for now." Delta wrote down a few notes. "We really need to get a bead on Max first."

Nick pounded the table with an open hand. "Done. My guys'll find him before the end of the day. What else?" Nick winked at Danica. "Because once we get the business out of the way, this place is pure pleasure."

Delta looked to me, so I chimed in. "Those young kids, the ones making bank off the house. When you see if they're still around, let us know when and where ASAP, okay?"

"Absolutely, but like I said—they're not winning enough to get on anyone's radar. They win some here and some there, but they're smart enough not to win too big that anyone would have them removed. Still, I doubt they've gone far. Kids never really know when enough is enough."

I nodded. "Good. We need them not to know."

"I've got my best guys on it. What do you want me to do when we find them?"

"Nothing. Yet. I just need to make sure we can get to them when the time is right."

"I'll have my best guys tail one or two. How's that?"

Danica nodded and laid her hand over his. "More than we were asking for, thank you."

Nick's eyes softened as he looked at her. Oh...

he had it bad. I'd seen that look before. "This must be important to drag you away from the city, and what's important to you is important to me." Nick turned from Danica and leaned forward toward Delta. "The big silent type one of yours?"

Delta glanced over at Bailey, who had been uncharacteristically quiet. "Maybe. Why?"

"I pay well. Really well, but I don't poach."

Danica and I exchanged worried glances.

Poach?

"Bailey is a free agent," I said, turning to her. Her facial expression never changed, and that told me Bailey was absorbing the energy in the room and trying to figure Nick Harper out. Her shamanistic ways were not as strong as my empathic ones, but if I had to hazard a guess, I'd have guessed she didn't trust him.

"Thank you, but I am happy where I am," she said coolly.

Nick clearly gauged Bailey's reply before laughing a little too loudly. "Of course you are. I just seldom meet such beautiful bodyguards."

Bailey didn't even offer up a smile. Just a slight nod. "Like the Brazilian Wandering Spider, I am easy on the eyes and deadly as shit."

"Bailey."

She shrugged. "I'm just saying."

Rebuffed, Nick turned from Bailey and rose. "Well, ladies, I hope you find our accommodations here amenable. If you need anything—anything at all, call or text Mario and he'll make it happen. He's your concierge for this trip, so don't hesitate to use him."

"The food was lovely," Danica said, hugging him and kissing his cheek. "You're a peach."

Checking his watch, Nick moved to the door.

"Well, this *peach* has pressing appointments, love. I'll get back to you as soon as I know something."

When Nick was gone, Delta pushed her notes over to us. "I'm not used to working with such a high profile criminal element, ladies, but it'll save us legwork having him on our side." Straightening her jeans, Delta leaned over and pointed to her notes. "I'm going to the Vegas P.D., then the hospital, and then the morgue. I won't be back for dinner, so don't wait around."

"What if it wasn't reported?" I had a gut feeling this may not have gone outside our kind yet, and hoped we could get a handle on it fast.

"Then I'll do some digging around Max Rhodes. If it really was his assistant who was killed, we have to assume he knows something about it and is first on our list. Always go with the obvious first."

I nodded. "Do what you do best, Delta. We're going to see an old *friend* and see what she can tell us about all of this. You want to take Bailey with you?"

Delta shook her head. "Not necessary. This is just a fact-finding mission. I'll see you back here after dinner."

We parted ways, with Delta heading to the police department while Danica, Bailey, and I hopped into the Navigator and went to Jasmine's Flower Shop.

When we pulled up to the florist's, I told Bailey to stay in the car and took Danica with me. There was bad blood between Bailey and Jasmine—a history that wasn't yet water under the bridge. I didn't need any tension between them right now. We needed answers, not a catfight, and though Jasmine wasn't one of my favorite people either, this wasn't a personal call nor was it time to settle a personal vendetta.

"Dani, please curb your natural desire to verbally

dismantle her, okay? She's paid for her transgressions. Big time."

Danica made a harrumphing sound and folded her arms across her chest. "Transgressions? You kidding me? Jasmine used her powers to get in between Bailey and her lover. If that wasn't bad enough, Jasmine nearly killed Bailey when she came after her to see what the fuck she was thinking. And finally, when you—"

I held my hand up to stop her. "Danica, do you need to stay in the car?"

She stood up straighter, her eyes narrowing. She was simmering. "Like you could keep me there."

She had me there. "Come on. Promise me you'll keep the claws sheathed until we get what we came for. That battle is over. Bygones and all that crap."

Chuffing, she shook her head. "I'll try, but the woman nearly cost Bailey her life. Bad enough she stole her girlfriend, but to go after her like that? Sending ghosts to shove her off a cliff? And you want we me to just let it go? Oh hell no. Jasmine's lucky to be alive, that fucking ghost whisperer."

Jasmine was a necromancer—a being capable of talking to the dead. Apparently, she had convinced a couple of them to try to shove Bailey off a cliff. She had almost got away with it, too. Since then, she'd done her due diligence. Bailey made sure of that.

Opening the door, I put my arm out to stop Danica. "I mean it, Dani. Behave."

"Pfft." Reaching into her bag, she pulled out a snub-nosed revolver—not her usual weapon of choice. Dani was Glock all the way. "Take this. Nick thinks every one of us should be packing, and I don't trust that bitch." She pushed the gun at me. "I'll behave if you take it."

I stared at the little gun and pushed it back. "Packing? Who are you? Tony Soprano? Please tell me you're kidding."

"I'm not." Danica dropped the gun in my bag and pushed past me, walking into the florist's, eyes scanning the room. "Ding, ding, ding. Customers!"

Jasmine came out from the back and stopped dead in her tracks, staring slack-jawed at Danica. "Aren't you—"

I stepped into the cool room. "She is." I cut my eyes over to Danica, who stared open-mouthed at Jasmine's face.

It was quite a sight watching the two of them staring at each other.

When Jasmine betrayed Bailey, Bailey exacted the best revenge she knew how. She ended Jasmine's pipe dream of having her own television show by tattooing Jasmine's face with Maori markings, successfully curtailing her run at a show featuring a necromancer. It was a story my ex-girlfriend, Tiponi Redhawk, had told me, and I wasn't sure I believed her. To see it in person was pretty amazing. Her whole face was marked with dark ink in a pattern of swirls and swooshes that reached down her neck.

"What the fuck?" Danica looked at me and back at Jasmine. "Dude...your face..."

"If you don't mind—" Jasmine said, stepping closer to Danica. "You staring at my face makes the spirit guides nervous."

Danica bridged the gap. "*I* oughtta be making *you* nervous, bitch."

"Danica, please," I cautioned.

"Echo," Jasmine tossed out, nodding at me and extending her hand. "Thanks for coming."

Breaking eye contact with Danica was just what we needed.

"I understand you agreed to help with the issue of the independents," I said.

Jasmine nodded. "In my attempt to get back into the Others' good graces, I told them I would keep an eye out on the Indies. They're causing a lot of trouble down here and are bringing a lot of unwanted attention to our kind. I had no idea it would get this bad."

Suddenly, Danica burst out laughing. "Oh shit, Clark. I know what happened here! Bailey did this to her face, didn't she? That's why you wanted to leave her back home, huh? She tatted up the bitch's face!"

Danica had been calling me Clark for nearly half my life. Ever since I'd told her about my empathic powers, and right after I had worked for the college newspaper, she had called me Clark, after Superman's Clark Kent. She was dumb that way.

My real name is Charlotte, or Charlie. My orphan name was Jane Doe. My chosen name was Echo. Danica called me all of them, depending on the situation. Right now, she was being randy, so it was Clark.

"Dani...hush."

The tattoo on Jasmine's face was black, dark against her caramel skin. It started symmetrically at her nose and curled around her temple and onto her forehead. It was thick like black smoke. Then it ran down the sides of her mouth. It would have been an amazing tattoo for someone living in Australia who wanted it. Jasmine hadn't, but she *had* to pay for what she had done to Bailey, and since her dream was to be famous, Bailey had chosen to take that away from her instead of her life. It was a just consequence for her actions, and one the Others sanctioned.

"Don't shit on my life anymore, Echo. I've had—"

The smile dropped from Danica's face and she immediately stepped into Jasmine's space, going nose-to-nose with her. You didn't speak poorly to me in Danica's presence without her getting her up your grill. "Watch how you speak to Echo, tattoo girl. You're lucky I don't fuckin' bust a cap in your very full trunk for what you did to—"

Lightly touching Danica's arm, I stepped back so she would. I should have known she would jump in Jasmine's face the first chance she got. Danica and Bailey had become tight in the last few months, and Danica didn't appreciate anyone threatening those she loved. "Dani, please."

She ignored me. "You know all those dead folk you talk to? Well, you'll be seeing them *in person* if you step out of line. You talk to Echo with respect or I'll be all over your tattooed shit. Are we clear here?"

Jasmine threw her shoulders back. "Back off. I pay for that mistake every goddamned day of my life. Your *boss* is safe from me."

Danica sneered. "Oh, I know that. But *you* are *not* safe from me. I just want to be certain we are clear."

"Crystal."

I stepped between them now. "Dani, I'm sure Jasmine learned her lesson. If not, Jazz, then Dani's right. You're not long for this world. Lower your shields." It was a command I seldom asked others supers. It was invasive and intrusive, but I needed to know. So, I waited as she did what I asked, and lowered mine as well. I needed to read her intent and make sure everything was on the up and up. While I could not and did not read minds—that was left up to telepaths—I *could* read whether someone was being authentic, and that was what I wanted from Jasmine at this moment.

Honesty.

Giving Danica a warning look, I turned all of my attention to Jasmine. "Are you working for Genesys or anyone else who would harm me or my people?"

Sighing loudly, she shook her head. "No, Echo, I'm not. I'm really trying to clean up my act. I made a lot of mistakes when I was younger, but I'm trying. I really am."

She was telling the truth, but it felt...different than what the truth usually feel like. It wasn't an out and out lie, because a lie vibrates energy differently than the truth. This particular skill is what made me a great journalist. I couldn't put my finger on it, but there was something in the mix that didn't feel right. She was telling the truth, but...I shook my head. "Now that—" I stopped and cocked my head. I felt something coming, and Danica, who knew me almost better than I knew myself, was already reaching inside her purse for her Glock.

"Who else is here?" I demanded.

Jasmine blinked.

"Who *else*, Jazz? It's a super. That much I know. What in the hell is going on here?" I started toward her back room, and when she reached out to stop me, she found Danica's Glock pressed against her cheek.

"Don't fucking move, bitch."

Jasmine stood still, eyes wide.

"Move an inch and I'll paint the wall with your minimal brains. Are we clear?"

Jasmine nodded. "It's...it's Max Rhodes. He's scared and needed a place to stay. I swear to God, Echo,

I'm trying to do the right thing here. He doesn't know who he can trust."

"So he came to *you*?" Danica asked.

I nodded to Danica, who hesitated before lowering the Glock, but did not put it away. In all our years together, it had taken me a long time to come to understand that a girl from the 'hood kept that feral part of herself locked up like a genie in a bottle. Once freed, there was no telling how long it would be before she would return, and no telling the damage she would wreak. Oddly, it had been more of blessing than a curse in my life.

"Max is *here*?" I stopped at the door and turned around. "What's he afraid of, Jasmine? What do I not know that I ought to know?"

Jasmine shrugged and looked away. "*Them*."

"Who are *they*?"

"That damn group of misfits from Atlantic City. The Conjurer met with Max two weeks ago asking for help starting a show here in Vegas. Max was willing to help, but The Conjurer wants more than help. He wants Max's show."

Danica replaced her gun with the Vidbook, a checkbook-sized phone and computer that had a crystal clear webcam display, a GPS, and apps no one else had heard of yet. "You're kidding us, right? *The Conjurer*? What's this guy's real name?"

"Townsend. Townsend Briggs."

Danica made eye contact with me before calling the boys back home in the Bat Cave. The boys were Roger, Carl, and Franklin, three brainiacs who had not only invented the Vidbook, but security software and holographic games that had brought in millions. Those three technogeeks had made Danica a very rich woman.

When Carl's face appeared on the screen, Danica went right to the heart of the call like she always did. No beating around the bush for that girl. "We need intel on one Townsend Briggs, two gees, formerly of Atlantic City. Goes by pseudonym "The Conjurer"."

Carl nodded, his big face in the monitor. "All over it." He made a motion with his chin to one of the other guys before returning his attention to the screen. "You guys okay, Boss?"

"We are. I need that intel ASAP, Carl. Leave no stone. Lives could be at stake." Danica snapped the Vidbook closed and returned her attention to Jasmine. "So let me get this straight. Townsend Briggs, AKA The Conjurer, wants Max's show, so he killed his assistant? That's a little extreme, don'tcha think?"

Jasmine shook her head. "We don't know he was the one who murdered Isis, but someone did. She's dead and the word on the street is that Townsend had something to do with it." Jasmine slowly eased away from Danica and grabbed her pruning shears.

"Her name is Isis?"

"Stage name," Jasmine said, rolling her eyes as she started deadheading roses.

"Where is she? The body, I mean."

Jasmine lowered her voice as she deadheaded more flowers. "A freezer someplace."

I cocked my head. She was beginning to irritate me. "Someplace?"

She stopped deadheading and tossed the heads into the trash. "Look, I don't need any more trouble, Echo. Not from you, not from your gangsters, not from the Others. I am merely trying to put some goodwill in the bank. I'm not looking for trouble, and the way you look at me out the side of your eyes…" she shook her head.

"I'm thinking trouble finds you," Danica growled. "Answer the goddamned question."

"Look, Danica," Jasmine shot back. "I have no beef with you. Back off."

"You may not have one with *me*, but with those I care about, so it might as well be me."

"That was a long time ago, and I'm pretty sure I paid the price." She pointed to her tattooed face. "*Big price.*"

"I'd heard someone tattooed you—"

"Not *someone*, Echo. *Bailey*." Bailey's name dripped off her tongue like acid. "She ruined me, and though I wanted retribution, wanted to kill her myself, I let it go. She needs to let it go as well. Now, all I want to do is to fly under the radar and live my quiet boring life. I've been touring the—"

I held my hand up. "Where is she?"

She motioned with her chin. "The freezer downstairs."

Danica groaned. "Shit. That doesn't bode well. So, Max is in your back room hiding with a dead chick?"

"I didn't know what else to do. He showed up with her. What was I supposed to do?"

Before either Dani or I could answer, the Vidbook buzzed.

"That was fast," Jasmine said.

"Danica hires only the best."

Carl was on the other end. "That's what you pay us for, Boss. Here's what we've come up with. Townsend Briggs has spent the last seven years in Atlantic City under the tutelage of a magician by the name of Zero. When Zero wouldn't cut Briggs in or give him a bigger role, Townsend made a fuss and Zero fired him, but not before Zero ended up in the hospital with some bizarre ailment no one had ever heard of. It's all in that article from *Magician Monthly* I've emailed you. That's the gist of this guy's bad mojo."

"Thank you, Carl."

"We'll keep digging."

"Do that." Danica hung up.

I turned to Jasmine. "And what about Townsend's powers? What do we know about this guy?"

Jasmine continued deadheading. "The guy's no slouch in the magic department. His specialty is making things disappear, of course."

"Oh brother," Danica said. "*Power*, Jasmine, what does he *do*?"

Jasmine looked at me as she answered. "He has TK powers he uses in his show, along with telepathy. The book on him says he is very good at his craft, but Zero wasn't having it, so things fell apart. There's not a lot more, except that he has a girlfriend who is an assistant. She left Atlantic City with him, but other than that, that's about all we know."

"What do we know about the girlfriend?"

"Sadako Takimami is a low end empath who'd been off the grid since she was twelve. Popped back up as Townsend's assistant, but not much is known about her. Word has it there are three to six other low-level psions traveling with them, but there's no book on any of them. I have a call in to the librarian on the island to see if we know anything about the Atlantic City supers." Jasmine walked over to her desk and checked her notes. "One last piece—but there's no confirmation on this—word has it they might be traveling with a precog."

Danica cursed.

I nodded, then picked up on something from Jasmine I had missed earlier. Jasmine wished she was anywhere but here. Her fear was palpable, but it wasn't of me. It wasn't of Danica. She was afraid of these people...these misfits.

"That's all I have for now, but I'll keep my ear to the ground." She set the clippers down.

Danica put her Vidbook away and eyed Jasmine, stepping up to her.

I knew she felt it, too, though just not on the level I was. Danica's inner dialogue was often as on as mine.

"You'd better start coughing up what you know, girlfriend. We don't have time for any of your bullshit." She got right into Jasmine's space.

Ghetto on ghetto was like being between two snarling pit bulls. I backed away a bit.

"First of all, I am *so* not your *girlfriend*. Secondly, I've told you everything I know. Max came to me in a panic with his assistant a bloody mess. Dead. Very dead. Don't get in my face, *girlfriend*, unless you want to see just how badass I can be if pushed."

Danica went nose-to-nose. "Consider yourself pushed."

"That's enough, Dani." I stepped between them. "Jazz, have you tried *reaching* the deceased?"

Jasmine shook her head, her eyes never leaving Danica's. "I tried, but I couldn't reach her. New deaths are harder to corner. Not that you'd have any idea what I am talking about."

"Couldn't reach her?" I shook my head. Although Jacob Marley was one of my best friends, I knew very little about the inner workings of necromancy. To be honest, it kind of scared me a little, but I wouldn't trade his often timely astral appearances for my weight in gold.

Jasmine stepped away and picked her clippers back up and continued deadheading. "People who die of trauma like that can be difficult to reach for quite some time. Murder victims can stay away for years."

"Have you kept trying?" Danica asked.

Jasmine glared at Danica. "No, I haven't, but I'm not going to explain all that to…you…a natural. What do *you* know about necromancy?"

I put a hand on Dani's shoulder to keep her from lunging after Jasmine. "Take it easy. She's paid her debt, Dani. Give her a break."

Reluctantly, Danica backed away. She had been protecting me for over half my life and I was used to her ghetto ways, but now was a time for diplomacy.

"What did Max say when he brought her to you?"

"That she'd been murdered, that he didn't know by whom, and that he was scared shitless. He asked if he could hold out in my back room until he could get a solid plan. That's all I know."

"And what was *your* plan?"

"Plan? I have no plan. I have a dead chick on ice and a scared shitless magician in my back room. I should have known they'd send *you* to save the day, Echo. It's what you do. I just wish you could have left Bailey and this pit bull here home."

I shot a warning look at Dani, who caught it and said nothing.

"Is there anything else you think we should know before talking to Max?"

Jasmine tossed a few more heads in the trash. "He's skittish, scared, and desperate. I've heard he can vanish at the drop of a hat. Nenshas do that."

"Nensha?" Danica asked, looking at me as if I knew what one was.

I didn't.

"*Nensha*," Jasmine explained like we were stupid, "is Japanese for sense copying. We call it projected thermography. Your illusionist has the ability to actually burn images of his mind onto surfaces or even *into* the minds of others. That's why Max Rhodes is so gifted. He can make an entire auditorium see things that aren't there. That's something Townsend Briggs will never be able to do."

"An entire auditorium?"

Jasmine ignored her. "He's an illusionist in every sense of the word, Echo. The guy is amazing. He's really good. A comer. Well...he was. This murder might take him completely off the grid."

"Any advice on how to keep him from bolting?"

"Typically, Nenshas are also paranoid beyond the norm because they get to a point where they can't separate fact from fiction in their own minds."

"Oh dear."

"He's an Indie for a reason and probably always will be. He just wants to be a magician."

"Any advice?" I repeated.

Jasmine shrugged. "Looks like he could use a friend right about now. Who knows? Maybe that friend is you."

"We'll see. I'm not here to make friends. I'm here to put an end to whatever the damn Indies are up to. Show me where he is."

"Last room on the right. Be careful, Echo. You can't trust what you think you see with a Nensha. Remember that he makes a living pushing his thoughts into other people's minds. It can be...disconcerting at first. Keep your shields up."

Nodding, I looked at Danica and then at the door. She nodded in understanding. I would never fully trust Jasmine. How could I? She had so angered Bailey that she'd had her face tattooed. That wasn't something she was likely to get over, but Bailey had sent a message to the rest of the paranormal community that messing with her was not a wise thing to do. Bailey could have terminated her but that wasn't her style. The tattoo sent a loud message to her and everyone else. Bailey may have trimmed the tiger's claws, but she still had teeth. Danica understood that as well, which is why she hadn't let her guard down.

Walking to the back room, I knocked on Max's door and waited. I'd never known an illusionist and had no idea what to expect.

I'd heard of telepaths, telekinetics, empaths, clairvoyants, necromancers, technopaths, and a slew of others. I had never heard of a Nensha. Was there no end to the amount of supernatural issues I *didn't* know?

Armed with that piece of Nensha intel, I lowered my shields and threw open the door to Max's room. I knew what Jasmine said about keeping my shields up, but I needed to read him first, which is what I did the moment I walked into the room.

It was a regular little guest bedroom with a twin bed, nightstand, and white shabby chic armoire that had seen better days. A small mirror hung over a pedestal sink, but other than the dorm room-like interior, it was empty. There were no shoes on the floor, no suitcase, no books, nothing.

I smiled.

Indies probably weren't used to dealing with

higher-level supers. Max mistakenly believed his Nensha powers trumped my empathic skills.

Boy, was he wrong.

I stepped into the room and closed the door. With my shields lowered, I could feel his fear and panic, but they were second to his astonishment that I'd entered what appeared to be an empty room. He was good. I had to give him that.

But not good enough.

Leaning against the door, I crossed my arms. "You're not playing in the sandbox anymore, Max. I'm a big leaguer and your talents, while impressive, do not cancel my powers out. I've not come down to collect you or even to offer you refuge. I'm here to sort out what the hell is going on between you and Townsend Briggs and put a stop to the shenanigans of the Indies before they bring too much attention to us."

The room suddenly dissolved into reality, and there was Max, sitting on the edge of the bed with his hands folded in his lap. "There's nothing to sort out. That fucker had my assistant killed as a warning to me, only it's worse than that because he made it look like I did it."

Well, that explained a lot.

"Did you?"

He looked up at me with blue-grey eyes. He was a cute young kid, maybe twenty-four, with a mop of curly black hair and cool blue eyes. "Of course not."

Well, that registered as the truth, so that was good. I'd feared he would try to lie or bluff. "Okay. That's good to know."

His expression changed. "You believe me?"

"I'm an empath. I know truth from lies, so yeah, I believe you." I watched as the rest of the room returned to normal. "Nice trick."

He shrugged. "Comes in handy."

"I'm sure it does." I reached my hand out. "Echo Branson."

He rose and shook my hand. He was even more afraid than I'd originally realized. "Max Rhodes. I've heard about you somewhere, but I can't really remember from where."

"I used to date the woman who tried to collect you a few years ago."

"Tiponi Red something. Jesus, she's a scary one."

"Yes, she is. Speaking of scared, want to tell me what the hell is going on down here?"

He studied me a moment and I felt his hesitation.

"Look, I don't blame you for not trusting me. You don't know me from Adam, but you're in a corner here and I may be the only one who can help."

"Why would you help me? You don't even know me."

"You Indies have no clue about the complex system of organizations the rest of us belong to. When you all get too close to being revealed or outed, it's up to one of us to make sure that doesn't happen."

His hand went to his mouth. "Oh fuck me. You're the one who did that to Jazz's face."

I shook my head. "Not me, but one of mine, yeah."

I could see him weighing his options. "That tattoo was harsh, man."

"The alternative was far worse. Believe me. So tell me, what in the hell is going on and why is there a dead body in Jazz's freezer?"

He blew out a breath. "The body is one of my assistants. Her name is…was…Hannah, though she went by Isis on stage. She's...she was a telepath."

"Your assistant was a telepath. Is that all?"

"I don't think she had any other skills."

I bristled at the word skill. "I meant was there anything else between you besides a work relationship?"

He rose and paced across the floor. "Uh uh. Hannah was single. Didn't date much...or at all. Hooked up with me because she was one of the few chicks not afraid of the saws and daggers. Everyone thinks we're together, but we're not."

"How was she killed?"

He looked down. "Daggers."

"Ah." The light went on. "That's how someone made it look like you did it."

"Yep. My daggers. My backstage. I was the last person to see her alive. Everything points to me."

"Pretty strong circumstantial evidence." Pulling out my Vidbook, I called Delta and left her the address of where we were and that there was a special delivery in the refrigerator for her.

Hanging up, I looked at Max. He felt defeated. The loss of his assistant was secondary to how he felt about losing his career or his freedom for a crime he didn't commit. And though I knew he didn't commit the murder, his lack of remorse or loss bothered me. It didn't endear him to me.

"So tell me what happened. All of it. From the time Townsend Briggs whooshed into town until the moment I stepped into this room. Leave nothing out. It's important I have all the information."

He sighed. "Briggs got to town and came right at me. Started giving me all these reasons why I needed to help him get his groove on, but the truth was, I didn't see anything in his show that could even come close to mine. Boring shit, really. I mean, come on! Between Copperfield and Angel, if you're gonna get on a Vegas stage, you'd better bring it." Max shook his head. "And he didn't. I totally got why Zero fired him. He didn't want to learn and his base skills sucked."

There was that word again. "So what happened?"

"Nothing much. I simply told him he needed to step up his game and look me up when he did."

"Ouch."

"Hey, man, the stage favors the innovators—the edgier players, and magic is no different. Think Siegfried and Roy would have been successful just parading around with their tigers? No, they were geniuses. Cutting edge. Briggs has a lot to learn about showmanship. A lot."

"So, you rejected him. What happened then?"

"Then he resorted to intimidation and threats. Met me backstage a few days before Hannah was killed and told me I would regret not including him in bigger and better plans."

I flipped open my Vidbook. Roger answered. He had mustard on the corner of his mouth. "Sorry to disturb you, Roger, but I need data on a Hannah…"

"Olivier," Max supplied for me.

"Hannah Olivier," I said. "Everything you can get."

"I'm all over it. We looking for something… um…special?"

"Yeah. Like me. Get back to me when you can." Hanging up, I saw Max tilt his head as he stared at the Vidbook.

"Cool gadget."

"I have the best tools to do my job. So…" Before

I could finish, there came a loud crash and the sound of breaking glass from outside the door. The sound caused me to look, and when I looked back, Max was gone. Well, not gone. Just no longer visible.

Nensha.

Before I could say anything, I heard Danica shout and I felt her anger to the core of my being. Not fear. I don't remember a time when she was ever outwardly afraid. And she wasn't scared now…just super pissed.

Then I felt the reason why. There were three supers in the shop with Danica and Jasmine, and they weren't there buying flowers.

"Max, can you cover us?"

"*Cover* us?"

"Someone just blew out the window of the shop. Those assholes out there mean business. Cover us!" Throwing open the door, I bolted down the hall and saw Danica just as she withdrew the Glock. It was scary how quickly that woman could draw that weapon.

"I've faced way stronger supers than the likes of you punk-ass bitches." As Danica's Glock cleared her purse, I sent a wall of energy at the three women entering the building, knocking them back.

"No, Dani," I said more calmly than I felt. "They're just rookies."

"No shit." She aimed the Glock at their kneecaps. "But I'm not gonna stand here while they take pot shots at us."

Suddenly, all three young women stood at the door just staring in confusion. One glance over my shoulder told me Max had stepped into the game. Max projected into their minds whatever those young women thought they saw.

Nensha.

I was becoming a fan rather quickly.

"Come on!" Jasmine yelled as she headed out the service door. All three of us followed her, only to run right into a tall man standing with his hands on his hips.

"Well, that was easy," he said, sneering at Max. The man raised his hands at us but I beat him to the punch. As a low-level mover, his energy bounced off the defensive shield I'd placed around us. When he saw the Glock in Danica's hand, his eyes grew wide. "A natural? You brought a knife to a gun fight?"

Danica moved faster than I thought possible, and shot between his legs. He jumped back so quickly he was off balance, and Max took care of the rest by shoving a bunch of boxes on top of him.

"This way!" Bailey yelled, whipping the car around the back of the shop as we all jumped in. "Get in! Get in! Get in!"

"Don't run those bitches over," Danica growled as the three girls made their way down the alley. "We couldn't explain—"

"They don't see us," Max said. Then louder. "They don't —"

Bailey slowed down.

Leaning out the window, Danica fired a shot ahead of us. "Get the hell out of the way!" she yelled at the women, who looked stunned to see us coming. "Fuckin' outta the way!"

All three jumped out of the middle of the alley and pressed themselves against the dirty brick wall as Bailey floored it and pushed the car out into traffic. As she quickly maneuvered through the traffic, I called Delta and told her we had trouble. Then I called the Others and asked for a clean-up crew. We *had* to get

Hannah's body out of the shop before it became a burden too heavy for us to explain away. We had to figure out why the hell those women thought they could attack *us*.

Us!

That took some nerve.

Some kinda nerve, for sure.

As Bailey weaved in and out of traffic, I thought back to the weeks before coming here and how much I had not wanted to come down here.

It was a lot.

༄༅༄༅

Two weeks ago

The heat emanating from fourteen-year-old Cinder was blistering, and I felt the soles of my Nikes soften as they melted. She had gone super nova on me, and the air around us crackled with her heat and energy. She was becoming stronger every day and it was only a matter of time before she outgrew my paltry tutelage.

"Concentrate, Cinder. Use more focus and hone in. You're letting the heat control you, when *you* should be controlling it." I watched carefully as Cinder focused on a huge block of ice perched atop a tree stump. We'd been working all morning on her directional capabilities so she could use her powers more accurately. I didn't want super nova. I wanted pinpoint accuracy.

Accuracy is vital to a creature such as her.

Cinder is a rare human being known as a pyrokinetic, or PK: a fire starter. She was one of my students who came to me to learn how to control her innate paranormal abilities. It was vital for a fire starter to have *complete* control over their powers or they could do serious damage to themselves and those around them. Today, however, she'd been incapable of retrieving the small marble encased by fifty pounds of ice, and I could tell she was becoming frustrated. It was etched all over her teenage face.

"I know you're frustrated, Cinder, but you can do this. You have to believe you can do this."

Narrowing her eyes and furrowing her brow, Cinder pointed at the block of ice with her index finger and concentrated. A line much like a laser pointer came from her finger and carved one side of the ice, like finger painting from a distance. She was doing really well, until something caught the corner of her eye and she turned, cutting the block of ice in half.

"*Shit!*" The voice in my head was Cinder's.

I stifled a smile. When I'd first met Cinder, she did not speak. She still didn't. She could, she just chose not to. "Language. That's good for this morning. You can go."

She looked hard at me. Cinder loved our lesson time and hated when it ended early.

"I know you're frustrated and brain weary. It's a good time to stop. We'll continue in the morning." I looked at my watch. "Almost time for math."

"*I'd rather set my head on fire.*"

Putting my arm across her shoulders, I walked her through the vineyard that surrounded the chateau we called home. Nestled in the hills of the Marin Valley, we lived on a luscious vineyard away from the prying eyes of the rest of the world. *We* are a large contingency of supernaturals—or supers—who live and train here in Marin. We are not the only beings who live under the watchful gaze of the grapes. I employ several naturals, and we all come together to help young supers not only learn how to wield their powers but how to *be* in the world—in a world that denied our existence and would have been afraid of us if they knew we did—a world that would have hunted us down or experimented on us.

We taught them how to comport themselves in a society that would either shun them or use them for monetary gain. I guess we taught them a great deal because it was a hard row to hoe being closeted.

I knew.

"I'm sucking in math."

Cinder still communicates with me telepathically and we're not sure why. We all handle the onset of our powers in different ways, especially pyros. Most PKs don't make it through puberty because they often implode, not even aware of their powers until it's too late and they are burnt to a crisp from their own powers. Cinder became aware of hers, only she didn't implode…she burnt someone else to a crisp. We got to her before she hurt herself or anyone else.

"If you think you can or can't, you're right."

Cinder groaned. *"Spare me."*

I pulled her closer and hugged her to me. When she first came to us, we thought she was about ten years old. She had been living with her aunt and uncle who were unsure of her birthdate, and because she was small in stature, thought ten sounded right. We had done some digging and discovered she was actually a few months over twelve when she first landed in our care. Cinder had just celebrated her fourteenth birthday, and was in that eye-rolling stage all teenagers go through. "I need you to be the example for the other kids. They look up to you, you know? Time to step up."

I wished I'd bitten those words back. Cinder had stepped up more times than I could count—if killing someone who meant me harm was stepping up—she'd stepped up and over more than once. She was just being a typical teenager.

"The triplets act as if they think I'm going to set them on fire, and Tack and I giggle too much whenever we get together. I am nobody's role model, Echo, even on my best day."

We stopped walking and I looked at her. She had grown up so much since we'd met. I supposed blasting bad guys to ashes will bring on premature maturation, but she was also blossoming physically as well. We stood almost eye-to-eye and she was at that stage where it seemed like she got taller every day.

"They don't think that, Cinder. Their language barrier makes them shy. Be patient with them."

We'd been back from our Alaskan adventure for a little over two months now. My ex-girlfriend, Tiponi Redhawk, or Tip, had traveled to Russia to collect these three young supers whose powers amazed me on a daily basis. Boris is a mover, Alexei is a thinker, and their little sister's powers are still unknown. What we do know is that when the three of them hold hands and focus, they can bilocate. Bilocation is the ability to send your energy far away and actually see and remember what it is looking at. I had only scratched the surface of their powers, and since we got back from Alaska, I had learned a great deal about their abilities. They were amazing little people and the more time I spent with them, the more I fell in love with them.

Alaska had something else, and we had barely

managed to get out of alive.

"*Alexei tries to get in my head all the time.*"

"He's just practicing, Cinder, really. Cut the kids a bre*ak, okay?*"

"*I like Nika. She's sweet.*"

We continued walking. She was right about Nika, but so far, I was batting zero trying to discover what power she possessed. It was possible only the two boys were psions, but not likely…not with shared DNA and all.

"Wait."

Cinder stopped. We both stood very still. The main rule everyone knew was no one could come out to the training ground without texting me first. That was possibly the best way of being toasted like a marshmallow or battered into the creek.

But someone was near. That much I knew.

"*Probably one of the Slavs.*"

"What did I tell you about calling them that?"

As an empath, I can feel people's emotions. I know when someone intends me harm. I can read through even the strongest telepath's emotional shield, but today, all I knew was that someone was curiously poking around the vineyard.

I kept my eyes on Cinder's hands just to make sure no fireballs were forming. She could form fireballs in the blink of an eye and she had a fastball few college pitchers could match. We both instinctively knelt down. I could hear someone approaching us, light on foot…too light. I only knew one person who could walk through a room like a Ninja or silently across dried leaves, and the moment I read her, I knew I was right.

"It's Taylor," I said, rising.

Sure enough, here came Taylor, dressed in a

leather cat woman suit, wearing a huge smile on her face and a twinkle in her eye. Taylor was a natural who worked for us and was currently dating Bailey. "Sorry to interrupt, but there's a package for Cinder back at the house and it can't wait."

Cocking my head at Taylor, I asked, "What do you mean it *can't wait*?"

She shrugged, but her eyes gave her away. They were literally sparkling. She was trying to keep a good secret from me. "All I know is the Boss told me to come get you and if you gave me any sh—uh—flack, you could take it up with her."

The Boss was what everyone called Danica. Fifteen years ago, when I first became who I am today, I shared *what* I was with Dani, the only "natural" person who had ever truly loved me. She had never told another person. She kept my secrets fiercely guarded, and though I had recently left Officer Marist Finn because I could not tell *her* the truth, Dani had backed me one hundred percent. It was one of the hardest decisions I had ever had to make, but the secret was simply too big to go on.

"Oh, did she now?"

Taylor put her arms around both our shoulders and we started back toward the chateau. She was one of the three of us who never complained about the walk. The way I figured it, we lived in California, where the sun shines eighty-nine percent of the year and everyone could afford a little exercise out to the small clearing by the river bend.

Well, I call it a river. It's actually a man-made creek Danica had put in to remind me of my home. See, Danica made a killing off a security system she named after me. As CEO and owner of Savvy Software, she landed on Style's "Who to Watch" when we were attending Mills College. Whoever had watched that show got to see a mixed African-American woman ascend like a rocket as she blew the doors off every software security company out there. Danica was that good.

So, when my mentor, Melika, told us she was dying, she requested that I take her place. Well, I like to think it was a request. While I was debating whether or not I could become the matriarch and teach young adult supernaturals, Danica was secretly building me a home and a school, and just about anything else I needed. Dani was nothing if not generous, and she built everything as far as the eye could see because of a debt she felt she owed Melika.

"How did you manage to get so close without making a sound?" I asked Taylor. Taylor had once been a jewel thief who'd turned in her diamonds for more…legal activities, and not long ago, she'd come to help work out the kinks in our new security system.

"Gotta stay in shape, but damn it, E, I have yet to get within ten yards of you before you know I'm coming."

I smiled at this. The other naturals who lived at the chateau, or in the three cottages Danica had recently finished adding to our compound, knew we were different, but had no clear idea just how different. Again, revealing who we truly were and what we were capable of doing would put all of us at risk. Imagine what any government could do if it employed just one telepath. No one's secrets would be safe. We could go anywhere and know what the other world leader was planning. What a coup that would be for any leader. No, it was best if we revealed our own secrets only after long and careful consideration.

"*A package for me? Come on!*" Cinder tried to pull ahead, but Taylor wouldn't let her.

"Uh uh, little one. You're staying put. You walk right here with us."

As we walked along a bark-strewn path, Taylor texted someone to let them know we were on the way back.

The chateau was an amazing construction brainchild of Danica. The lower half had the kitchen, media room, classrooms, and a security room manned by one of the strongest women I'd ever met. Sal was part woman, part boy, and all military. I'd never seen her out of military fatigues, and her reddish blond hair stuck out of her army cap like straw. Sal was an electronics whiz who made sure our peace and safety were nearly unbreachable. Hired for her security sense, Sal eventually moved into a teaching role as well, showing my charges the ins and outs of computers, cell phones, iPods, and anything that was battery-operated. When she wasn't in the security room watching the dozen or so monitors of the vineyard, she was teaching somebody something. She'd been an important addition to our growing family and lived in one of the cottages on the property.

When we neared the front steps, Taylor turned to me, her blue eyes twinkling happily. Short, dark hair wisped around her face in a devil-may-care attitude. She reminded me of a fairy.

"Stay out here with her."

"Where are you going?"

Shaking her head, she laughed. "Oh hell no. This messenger ain't about to get shot. This here is Danica's show."

Uh oh.

"Dani? What's going on, Taylor?"

But she was gone as fast as she'd come.

Looking at the front door, I watched Danica slowly descend. All legs and ass, Danica was the perfectly statuesque black woman found in any magazine. She was stunning in every way. Whether she had her hair cut short or wore corn rows, Danica Johnson turned heads wherever she went.

"Dani, what have you done?"

She smiled at me, her right eyebrow arching in a wouldn't-you-like-to-know manner. And yes, I would.

"Firefly, you stay out here, okay?"

Cinder nodded, her entire being quivering with excitement. Leaning into my ear, Dani whispered, "Sometimes, Clark, when you want a kid to be responsible, you have to give them a responsibility."

"What are you talking about?"

"A couple of weeks ago you said you wanted Cinder to be more responsible where the other kids were concerned."

"Yeah, so?"

Dani moved us away from Cinder. "So, we have to *teach* her what that looks like. You keep getting frustrated because she's not leading the triplets, when you haven't really *shown* her what it *means* to be responsible for something."

I jammed my hands on my hips. "And?"

"Well," Dani cupped her hands to her mouth and yelled, "Bring her out!"

Bailey, our resident shaman and animal empath, walked out the door holding a bundle of fur the same color as the Huskies we had met in Alaska.

For a moment, Cinder wasn't sure what she was

looking at.

In Alaska, we had used sled dogs, and Cinder had fallen in love with them. She'd never had a pet, and the beautiful and strong Huskies and Malamutes so enamored her, she could barely take her eyes off them.

As Bailey reached us, she held the little fur ball out to Cinder. "Cinder, you have grown so much and worked so hard that we all decided it was time you were rewarded for that."

Cinder's eyes watered as she looked from the puppy to me. *"Really? Please don't be kidding."*

I blinked, feeling tears in my eyes and wishing I had been the one to think of it. "Really. She's all yours."

Faster than the naked eye could see, Cinder gathered the puppy in her arms and let it lick her tears away. She was giggling and laughing, and I have to say, I'd never seen her happier than at that moment.

Cinder, like most of the supers I knew, hadn't had an easy life growing up, and now, here she was, big sister to young triplets who spoke passable English, and a member of our security team who could fry any threat. Dani was right: she deserved the puppy.

"Before you get all love struck," Dani said, producing two books on raising dogs,

"You need to realize she's going to be a lot of work. You'll need to—"

Bailey was shaking her head. "She's not listening. She's in love."

"Can I go play with her? Have the triplets seen her? Does she need to eat? Should I—"

"Go play," I said, reaching over to be puppy-licked. There's something about puppy breath that makes people grin, and all of us were grinning.

"Does she have a name?" She was looking at

Bailey as she thought this, but Dani answered. "The Inuits named her Shila. It means Flame."

Cinder couldn't have smiled any brighter than right then, and I, too, was suddenly in love with the little fur ball.

"The triplets are still in class, so why don't you go show her to Tack. He's helping William at the barn."

Cinder put Shila on the ground and ran into Danica's embrace before taking off toward the barn, the little pudgy fur ball racing after her. Soulmates in an instant.

When she was out of earshot, I turned to Danica and Bailey, arms across my chest. "I should kick both your asses. You know that, right?"

Danica held a hand up. "Would you have said yes if we'd asked?"

"Well…"

Bailey stood next to Taylor who stood next to Danica—solidarity between them all. They clearly had ganged up on the matriarch. "Better to ask for forgiveness than beg for permission," Taylor said.

"Are you asking?"

Danica shook her head. "Oh, *hell* no, Clark. Look, remember last week you were worried that the people she's blasted might have affected her psyche."

"I remember."

"Bailey and I were talking about it and we decided what better way to balance the death in her childhood than by giving her some life?"

"A life she needs to nurture and care for, E," Bailey added. "You won't be sorry. Cinder *needs* something to balance the incredible power burning inside her. She needs—"

I held my hand up. Looking from one to the other,

I sighed loudly. "You're right. She deserves something that makes her little heart sing. You did well."

All three smiled at each other.

"But, from now on, you run something like this by me first. I don't like being ganged up on by you yahoos."

"Hey, who you calling a yahoo?"

I ignored Danica. "How long has that puppy been here?"

"I picked her up at the airport yesterday when…" Bailey stopped, her eyes wide.

Uh oh. There was more. "When what?"

Danica started laughing. "It's okay, Bailey. Not like we could hide something like that forever."

"What's okay? What are you up to?" I'd been so busy worrying about the puppy, I hadn't felt the secret they were all sharing.

I was feeling it now.

Danica started back up the steps. "Oh, nothing. I just bought us a plane and I took Bailey and Delta to see it yesterday. Gotta go."

"Oh no you don't. Get back here."

"I don't think so." Danica disappeared into the chateau, leaving Bailey holding the bag.

"She bought a *plane*?"

Nodding, Bailey looked away. Her long blond hair had gotten lighter in the California sunshine, and her long limbs cast a bronze hue from being in the sun. Bailey had an uncanny and often frightening ability to communicate with nature. I had once seen her send a wild boar to devour a grown man, which it did rather loudly. She was also a shaman—a healer—who could make hundreds of potions, salves, and unguents from life around her.

When we first met, I didn't care for her. I think I was jealous or something stupid. I can't really even remember. Over time, however, she became one of my dearest friends, and she was now second in charge of the chateau: a job she took seriously.

"Dani was bothered by us having to use Malecon's jet to get to Alaska, so she got home and started shopping for a plane." She shrugged. "She got the plane and hired a pilot."

Malecon was our mentor's twin brother who had started off against us, but had done a one-eighty and was now desperately trying to help Melika conquer her brain cancer.

"She hired a pilot?"

"Nope, we already have one. I just added her to the roster."

"Who?"

"Sal. Apparently, she got her pilot's license a couple of years ago. So now, it looks like we have wings, a pilot and—"

"I'm gonna kill her." I started up the steps when Bailey reached out and stopped me.

"No. You're not. You're going to say thank you. You're going to appreciate the effort, and take her out for a pedicure." Bailey put her arm through mine and started walking toward the barn. "That woman adores you, E. If she wasn't so goddamned straight, I'd think she was in love with you." She held her hand up to silence me. "I'm just saying—your happiness is really important to her and, well, to be honest, we sorta needed one. With all your hobnobbing around, we need a plane. It will just make things easier. That's what she does: makes things easier for you. She saw to it and made it happen. Do not shame her for being so generous."

Tapping my finger against my lips, I nodded.

"She wanted to surprise you, but that's kind of hard."

Chuckling softly, I nodded. "Not really. You all seemed to do a great job with the puppy. So we got paws and wings all in one day?"

Bailey's eyes lit up. "We did. Did you see Cinder's face?"

Who could have missed it? She was radiant when she realized Shila was hers. "I never thought about balancing her life for her, Bailey. It's a brilliant concept. Was that you or Dani?"

"Actually, neither, though we would like to take credit for it. It was Connie. She was talking about balance in the Native American culture and said we needed to right the scales before Cinder came to see herself as a purely destructive being. Danica may be bright, but that Connie Rivera is off the hook genius material."

I shuddered, remembering my mentor's face as she explained to me what a pyro was all about. Cinder was the perfect weapon. She could get through any metal detector. She looked harmless enough, and the power she wielded...well, let's just say I'd seen her on more than one occasion light up the sky with her power. She was that powerful. My job was to help her get better control of it. So far, I wasn't so sure I was very successful.

"Well, Connie was right. Cinder needs to know the side of her that is caring and nurturing as well. I'm just sorry I didn't see it. Thank you guys for seeing it for me."

"Don't thank me. Dani made it all happen. I just

placed a few calls. The Inuit boys were more than happy to trade." Bailey flipped her hair over her shoulder and sniffed the air like a rabbit might.

Sometimes, I think she was more animal than human.

By *Inuit boys*, she meant the two lovely gentlemen sled drivers who had driven us all over Alaska and shown Cinder true puppy love. We had made quite a few friends while in the frozen tundra, so it came as no surprise that they sent a puppy to Cinder. What did surprise me was the notion that they traded.

I looked at her. "Trade?"

"Well, they wouldn't take Dani's money, so she offered to buy a few computers for the school."

My right eyebrow rose in question. I knew what that meant. "*A few?*"

Bailey shook her head and then leveled her gaze at me. "You know how she is."

"Thirty?"

"Close enough. The guys are expecting three."

"They don't know her very well."

Bailey knelt down and drew in the soft dirt. I wondered what it was she had on her mind, but as a creature, I knew she was communing with something other than me, so I let it go. "She adores Cinder, and vice versa. I don't know what it is, but I would fear for the person who hurt either one of them." Rising, Bailey shielded her eyes from the sun and watched an eagle before locking eyes with me. "You're still sure you don't want to go after Genesys?"

We continued walking. "Yes, I am sure, Bailey, we're not ready—not until Cinder has more control over her powers and the others know the extent of theirs. We need time to regroup, time to breathe. I know some of you think we should have gone after Hayward, but I won't enter into that battle until we are absolutely ready, and we're not." I hesitated. "*I'm* not. I am tired. It feels like I haven't had a second to myself, to breathe, to figure out where we're going and what I want to do."

Bailey nodded. "Fair enough. Any luck reaching Sonja?"

Sonja Satre was a fire starter we'd met briefly in Alaska. She was a rogue psion who worked for the highest bidder. I wanted her to train Cinder, but so far had had no luck locating her. Apparently, she'd left Alaska for a warmer climate. Or she was dead.

I voted on the latter.

"No one knows where she is."

"I bet she's with Genesys."

"I don't know. She seems pretty independent, not really the Genesys type."

Genesys was a supernatural's version of Hell. A for-profit organization our government privately funded in secret, it hunted down younger, impressionable supernaturals in an effort to see if they could either duplicate or restructure our DNA for their own use. What they wanted to construct was the ultimate soldier—the ultimate fighting machine. To do so, they needed us. Problem was, most of us didn't survive their experimentation techniques. So Genesys was our version of a medieval dungeon…only worse. Torturing children in the name of experimentation was against all Geneva Convention Laws. We had battled them twice already, and the second time, in Alaska, we fairly crushed them…still, not enough to make them shut their doors, but enough to put them on notice: We weren't messing around anymore, and when we were ready, we were going after them.

That day would come.

But not now.

Now, I had my hands full as matriarch to kids who needed to learn how *to be* in the world before donning armor to face the likes of Genesys.

"It's just as well. I don't like Sonja, nor do I trust her, but Cinder's going to need a mentor. I am a poor substitute."

Bailey hung her arm across my shoulders and stopped walking. In the distance, I watched Cinder laughing and playing with Shila; a girl and her dog, oblivious to anything but each other.

"Something tells me, E, that girl is going to be just fine."

As far as I could tell, the triplets could communicate telepathically with each other, but not with anyone else. Whoever had been their first mentor had taught them the rudimentary shield-building skills. A supernatural must know how to build a psychic wall around his or her mind in order to stay sane. If I couldn't stop from feeling everyone's emotions around me, I would go batshit crazy. I'd seen an empath once who hadn't learned how to block that emotional noise. She was a drooling shell of a person rocking back and forth, unaware of her surroundings, of the walls closing in around her. Unaware of anything, I would imagine. The sight of her scared me to death. I would never forget that image. So, just like Melika showed me, I was teaching the triplets how to create shields, and it wasn't easy.

First off, there was a language barrier; they were getting better with English, thanks to Connie Rivera, our resident linguist. She'd managed to come every Tuesday and Thursday to help with the lessons, but on Monday, Wednesday, and Friday, it was slow going; me fumbling for simpler words, them chattering amongst themselves in an attempt to translate my directives.

Right now, Alexei, the oldest of the three, was focusing on erecting shields to keep his brother, Boris, from reading him. Boris was a telekinetic, or TK, otherwise known as a mover. Movers were incredibly powerful supers capable of using enough mental energy to move objects. Some movers were so well-trained, they could knock people over. While I wasn't training him to do that, I was feeling out their powers to see their limits. So far, Alexei's powers were the strongest of the three, but he was lazy. Boris was a pleaser, a real sweetheart, but he lacked focus and drive.

Then there was little Nika. Her blue eyes never left her brothers. All tow-heads, all blue-eyed, they were identical triplets—a rarity in the natural world and ever rarer in ours. Nika, the youngest and smallest of the three, was also the most thoughtful, the most mindful of her actions, but I couldn't seem to break through to her. No one had. She stuck to her brothers like glue, as if gauging her own reactions through them. Even Cinder had been unable to get in.

"You're tired. Hungry. You want dog, too," Boris said softly.

Alexei opened his eyes and sighed. Boris had read him, again.

"Why don't we take a break?" We'd been at it for a couple of hours. The boys took off like a shot toward the rope swing over the bend of the river. Nika started after them, but I put my hand out to stop her. "Mind keeping me company?"

She looked up at me with those eyes. She didn't like not being with her brothers. I could feel that from her even with my shields up.

Sitting on one of the eight large rocks surrounding a campfire ring that was the middle of our training grounds, I patted the space next to me. Nika sat down, her eyes still trailing after her brothers.

"How are you doing, Nika? Are you happy here?"

She didn't want to turn from the boys but managed a nod.

"How happy?"

She hesitated, choosing her words carefully. "Better than home. Warm."

A weather report wasn't quite what I was looking for, so I let her go play with the boys. As I watched them drop from the rope swing into the water, I thought back to the wonderful times I'd spent on the bayou with my own classmates. I'd spent four years on the river with some of the greatest people on the planet—one of whom wasn't with us anymore. I still felt Jacob's loss every day of my life, and out here without him and Zack, I sometimes felt this pit of loneliness reminding me that I was all grown up now and we all had our own lives to live.

All grown up.

We worked so hard to get here as kids, and once we get here, it's too late to go back.

"Dollar for your thoughts."

Looking up from my reverie, I saw Danica standing between two rocks.

"I know I'm supposed to text before coming, but as you know, I've never been any good at following the rules." Sitting on a rock next to me, she reached for my hand. "Your empathic abilities must be rubbing off on me. I could feel you struggling all morning. Want to talk about it?"

Looking over at her, I felt the weight of the world on my shoulders. "Am I over my head here? I'm just an empath. Do I have what it takes to train these kids?"

Danica looked over at the triplets on the rope swing. "I believe you do. You. Not Melika."

Cocking my head in question, I asked, "What does that mean?"

"Mel was old school...you know...repetition, drills, etcetera. You're still trying to teach using *her* as the model, but you're not her." Rising, she motioned for me to come with her. "Melika had a brother growing up. She knew something about boys. But you? You're gay through and through. A purebred lesbian, as it were. What you know about testosterone you can dress an ant in. Watch and learn." Walking over to the kids, she knelt down. At six feet tall, she struck quite an imposing figure. "You guys love this swing, don't you?"

They all nodded.

"Good. I'm glad. Tell you what. Boris, you guys can keep swinging for another fifteen minutes *only* if you pull the rope to your brother using only your powers."

Boris looked over at me. The kids had all been told they were never to use their powers around naturals...except Danica. She knew what we all were.

"Go head, Boris."

He turned to the rope, which was a good ten feet away, and closed his eyes. At first, it looked like nothing was happening. Then, barely noticeable, the rope twitched and began moving toward him until it was within Alexei's grasp.

Nika clapped and Alexei beamed. When Boris opened his eyes, he high-fived Dani and hugged his sister.

As Dani and I returned to the rocks, she sat down and grinned at me. "And *that* is how you train boys. Make a game out of it. Make it a competition. Make it fun, but find *your* way of teaching, Clark. Once you do, everything will fall into place. You'll see."

I watched the kids laughing and playing, my heart filling with motherly joy. "When did you get so smart?"

"I run with a higher level of intellects," she said, laughing. "You're going to be fine, Clark, trust me. You've got this."

And for the first time since we'd moved into the chateau, I believed that maybe I really did.

One Week Ago

After checking on the triplets and Tack, I peeked into Cinder's room. She was on her back with Shila curled in the crook of her arm. Both were lightly snoring. She'd had Shila a week, and in those seven days, I'd never seen Cinder happier. She was more patient with the triplets, more serious about her studies, and generally just happier. It was wonderful to see and I had to hand it to my crew: they knew what they were talking about.

"The kid's all heart," Bailey whispered over my shoulder.

"What are you doing up? I thought you and Taylor had a date."

"Oh my God. What are you? Eighty? We haven't left yet. Jesus, E, you really do need to get out more. You sure you don't want to join us? You could use a good night of dancing and carousing while the Big Indian is away.

Taylor and Bailey had hit it off a few months ago and were "dating." Nothing exclusive, but they spent enough time together to make me wonder. "Third wheel is never fun, so I think I'll pass. I need to finish up my Alaska article anyway."

"You work too much."

"You sound like Dani."

"She's a smart woman. You oughtta listen to her."

Before I could reply, Shila made that adorable puppy grunting sound as she switched positions, her back paws staying in contact with Cinder.

"Poor little pup is exhausted," Bailey whispered. "Tripod kicked her ass this morning."

Tripod was my three-legged Siamese cat who had decided he liked the outdoors of the vineyard more than being cooped up inside. Tri was definitely not down with sharing space with an enthusiastic puppy.

"Oh? How come?"

"Shila romped over there, as puppies will do, and Tripod's front paw smacked her little nose so hard, she took off yelping."

"Ah yes. The cute puppy routine never really works with cats."

As we both walked down the hall, I double-checked the security room to make sure Sal had gone home. I wasn't the only one who worked too much.

"Enjoy your date," I said when I reached my room. Danica had spared no expense on my suite. My bedroom alone was over one thousand square feet, complete with computer desk, flat screen television, a fireplace with two Queen Anne chairs in front of it, and an entire wall of bookshelves. The wall opposite was all window, with sliding doors opening to a balcony overlooking the vineyard.

When we were teenagers, Danica and I had made a scrapbook of all the things we wanted in life. She wanted two things: to travel around the world, and to give me the bedroom of my dreams.

She'd managed to do both.

As a foster kid, I'd never had my own room, so I pasted a photo of my dream bedroom into our book. Danica recreated that room for me as a way of paying back the supernaturals who had foretold of her mother's cancer. As a result of this knowing, we had chosen to attend Mills College so Danica could spend as much time with her mother as possible before she died.

The vineyard and the chateau were Danica's way of balancing the scales, and she spared no expense on my incredible bedroom as well as the rest of the mansion. As much as I appreciated the effort it wasn't my beloved bayou, but I would never admit that to her. The truth was, I missed it.

There's something alive about the bayou. The scents, the creatures, the way the water laps at the shore. I'd never felt more alive, more energized than when I was there. So yeah, I missed it. A lot.

Sitting in front of the laptop, I re-read my article. Not long ago, I'd made a big splash as an investigative reporter for the *San Francisco Chronicle*. I wrote a major story that made me a media darling. After that, I did a couple more articles of merit before all hell broke loose in my real life and I had to choose between a full-time position as a reporter and my position in our supernatural family, which needed more and more of my time and energy. I thought turning in my full-time career would be a tougher decision than it was...but it wasn't. I had come to realize that my career was a crutch. It had been my feeble attempt at being normal... at finally feeling like I fit into a world in which I would never truly belong.

Oh sure, I could fit in—and had. I was successful, whatever that meant. But things happened, and I realized I had a greater duty—a more important calling. So I went to my boss and asked if I could freelance. He said flatly, "No." He thought his answer would mean his golden girl would choose to stay. I did not. By the time he reconsidered, I had already submitted my resignation. Now I was truly a freelance journalist writing about everything from Alaska to Zimbabwe. *The New Yorker* had picked up my last piece. It was about the ways Alaskans travel from village to city and the importance of sled dogs to the indigenous people. Now, I was doing a follow-up piece on the Inuits I'd met. I liked what I had so far, but my mind had been elsewhere lately.

My mentor, Melika, the only mother I'd ever known as a child, was dying of brain cancer. She and her brother had gone to Switzerland with Tip to check out options the American medical community didn't offer. I supported the trip because we were that desperate, and we wanted to exhaust every option before just throwing in the towel. Anything that gave Mel hope was worth exhausting, and Malecon was spending his millions doing just that. I had to hand it to him, he was certainly going above and beyond for a guy who had recently tried killing us all.

I desperately missed both Tip and Melika to the point of heartache. I could not imagine my life without Melika in it, and losing her would rock my very core. I would never recover from that loss, and I knew that. So did she. Maybe that was why she had Danica give me a home and a family to fill it...because having a purpose would give me the strength I needed when that day came.

Walking out to the deck, I looked up at the stars. When we were a couple living apart, Tip and I used to communicate mentally with each other while staring at the moon. It gave us both a sense of unity to know we were at least staring at the same thing. It was as silly as it was romantic, and truth to tell, I missed it. I missed her, but she was so angry at me. We hadn't spoken since I left Alaska, but oh how I wanted to. Next to Danica, Tip knew me best. Older and wiser than me, she had often been a source of comfort and wisdom, but we were not in that place anymore. I still loved her very much, but we were the kind of couple who were better off friends.

"I'm looking at the moon," I whispered, a long pause as I tried to tear myself away from my moon gazing. *"Talk to me, Tip. Tell me how Melika is. Tell me how you are? How is your new love life? How are you? Please...talk to me. Say something. Anything."*

Suddenly, big stinging tears filled my eyes. *"I'm just an empath, Tip, with a fire starter, a mover, a thinker, a techno, and an unknown. I barely know where to begin. I need you. I need you to stop being so angry with me. It's not like there's an instruction manual for* all this."

Actually there is, but I had left my training with the Others before I could uncover it.

The Others.

The Others were a group of supers who had retired from real life to live on an island away from society. An aging super eventually loses control of his or her powers, thus becoming a danger to themselves and others. So they retire and sit in judgment over the rest of us and often, as I've seen, bailing us out when we needed it most. I had been invited to the San Juans for some training, but I left early. It just didn't feel like a fit.

"I miss you, Tip. I wish you would talk to me."

I went back inside and flopped down on my bed. I didn't want to miss Tiponi Redhawk, but I did. I didn't want to miss Officer Marist Finn, but I did. While I didn't mind sleeping alone, I did miss having someone to cuddle with at the end of the day. I longed for that. I longed for what Taylor and Bailey had, even if it wasn't exclusive. Sometimes, it's hard to find balance without someone's arms around you. Everything about my life had changed in the last couple of months. Everything. I'd discovered who my real parents were, that I had a sister, that my mentor was dying, that I couldn't be with a natural, and finally, that my father worked for the organization that hunted my kind down. So yeah, I was slightly off-kilter in my new role, in my new house, in my new life. Even with Dani and Bailey around, and all I had to do at the chateau, I still felt so very alone.

When the front door opened to the beach house, Tricia's face broke into a grin. "Charlie! Come in. Come in."

I was born Charlotte Hayward to this woman, my biological mother. She and my father had handed me over to the state when I was five in order to save my life and protect me from Genesys, the company they worked for. They also had my memory erased so Genesys couldn't find me, and that proved to be problematic. I had no idea who I was or what my past looked like. They had dropped me off at the state home and I had no clue who I was, who my parents were, or why they had left me. I had never been so lost.

Following Tricia in, I watched her grab two lemonades and we headed out to a deck overlooking the Pacific Ocean.

"It's so good so see you," she said, sliding a frosted glass over to me. For the last twenty-eight years, I had wondered what it would be like to have a mother. Now I had one and I hadn't the foggiest idea how to negotiate that relationship. Tricia was very sweet and didn't push herself on me, but I felt like there was more I ought to be doing.

"Everything okay? I thought I'd see you once you returned from Alaska."

Watching the surf lap lazily at the sand, I sighed heavily. I hadn't realized how emotionally drained I was. I hadn't wanted to see Tricia because I knew I would have to explain to her that her presumed dead ex-husband was alive and well, and working for the company that had destroyed our family.

So that was what I did. I told her everything I knew. She remained quiet and still the entire time I was talking, and she handled that news with a grace and dignity I hadn't expected. I don't know what I expected, but it wasn't the calm acceptance Tricia had displayed.

"He's alive." Tricia whispered, shaking her head. "Bastard. He left me in that sanitarium for nine years. Nine long years." She looked away. "I am so sorry, Charlie. I wish there was something I could say."

"You don't need to say anything. You are not responsible for him, Tricia. He made his choices, and now, he is going to have to live or die by them. I just need you to know that it is the latter that is on my agenda for him. If you have an issue with that, you need to say something now and we can be done."

Tricia locked eyes with me. "Trust me when I say this, Charlie." Her voice was cold steel. "Kill the son of a bitch."

I nodded slowly and watched as two sea gulls wrestled for a piece of bread. "I plan on it."

We sat in silence for a while before she said, "Enough about him. How are you doing?"

"The new place and the triplets are really taking my time. I thought I'd find a moment to take a breather, but I couldn't until today."

Sipping her lemonade, she nodded. "It's going well?"

"It's...out of my comfort zone. I'm working my ass off, though. I've got these charges, none are empaths, and I am beginning to doubt my teaching ability."

Leaning closer, Tricia brushed a stray hair from my forehead. "You look tired, Charlie."

"I don't have time to be tired. There's so much to do." Turning to her, I frowned. "Any word from Kristy?"

Her eyes spoke before her lips. "Not a word."

"I'm surprised. I thought—"

Trish shook her head. "It didn't sound like she had forgiven me for leaving you, Charlie. You have no idea how distraught she was when your father and I told her that we were sending you to be with Santa."

My jaw dropped. "Santa?"

She nodded, her eyes sad at the memory. "She wouldn't stop crying. She loved you so much. Broke my heart when she said goodbye to you. That girl watched over you like she was afraid someone would..." her voice became softer, "take you away from her."

"I wish I could remember. I had no idea she cared so much. It's not like we're playing for the same team now. She's so damn angry all the time."

"What that poor girl has had to endure." She shook her head, her eyes tearing up. "That bastard put her through hell. I shudder to think of the pain she experienced at the hands of those monsters."

My father had handed my older sister, Kristy, over to Genesys in exchange for a job. He bartered her life for a goddamned job. As a result, my sister was a scion, which is short for grafting. In supernatural terms, Genesys had "grafted" powers onto my sister's already unique DNA, making her a genetically altered super whose powers were artificially created. Before Genesys got their ugly hands on her, she was just a telekinetic. Now, she was a lightning rod capable of processing lightning through her body and out her fingertips, eyes, and anywhere else she focused her concentration. She'd barely escaped from Genesys with her life, but the daughter Tricia had once known would never be the same. She had left there an angry and resentful young woman, and still was. I wondered if anything could ever bring her back.

"She fights for our cause, Tricia. I may not agree with the methods they employ, but I secretly root her on in her effort to burn Genesys to the ground."

"Is that what she does? Is that how my oldest daughter lives her life? Focusing her energy on destroying her father and some ridiculous laboratory?"

"Pretty much."

"What...what's she like?"

I watched a man walking his pit bull and decided against using the dog as an analogy. "Angry. Bitter. Focused. Very powerful." I shook my head. "*Very* powerful."

"Is she...insane?"

Something like a chuckle escaped my mouth. "Some might think so, but no, she's not. She has... issues. She could afford to take an anger management course."

She thought about this a moment. "When you told me you two had seen each other, I really thought...I don't know, I guess I thought she'd call me. I thought maybe, maybe we could actually be a family again someday."

"Trust me. Kristy has dedicated her life to one thing and one thing only—destroying Genesys and everyone involved with them. Think of her heart in terms of the Grinch's...only smaller and blacker."

"What a sad life she must lead. Do you know anything else about her?"

"Not really. Our...interactions have never been outside a battlefield. We've spoken briefly, but she doesn't recognize me as her sister. I'm more of a... competitor."

"Oh my. Is it really that bad?"

Standing, I leaned against the railing with my back to the ocean. "Tricia, Kristy belongs to an elite group of supers who track down young psions before Genesys can get to them with the aim to turn them into soldiers who fight the good fight. I, on the other hand want to turn them loose to live their own lives. It's a race of sorts that can and has gotten ugly."

"And you? What is *your* role in all this?"

"My role." I watched a couple walking their dog and thought about Bailey and the many times she'd called on dogs as backup. "I have spotters in various places around the country. Once they are sure they've found one of us, they contact me and I send a collector. A collector holds a very special position. It isn't easy going after these young ones. You have to get to them, earn their trust, and then figure out a way to remove them from their environment and to a safe house. Once they get to me, I train them. I teach them how to use their skills, and then I'll send them back out into the real world, hopefully better able to live more peacefully with their abilities and skills."

"Why can't your sister do that as well?"

"Well, that's where we differ in life. I'm more about building lives, she's into destroying them." I held my hand up. "Before you judge her, you need to understand...you worked there. You know the incredible amount of pain she was put through to become what she is...I can understand her desire to crush them. I just can't be a participant in it right now."

"Because of your students?"

I nodded slightly. "Tricia, my mentor is dying. I'm no longer a full-time reporter. I have students with powers I don't fully understand. I've managed to lose two women in six months, and I'm having a tough time staying centered."

Rising, she stood in front of me and took my hands. "You are only off-balance if you let yourself be. You're so much stronger than this, Charlie. You survived all those foster homes, all those different schools, and all those rejections. You can *do* this. Your mentor obviously believes in you. You owe it to her to believe in yourself."

A slow grin spread across my face.

"What?"

I squeezed her hands. "I came here because I needed something, and I got it."

"Oh? And what was that?"

"Good advice from my mother."

※※※※

"Buckled up?" Sal asked on her way to the cockpit of Danica's new toy, a white jet with paint job on the nose that looked like claw marks that peeled back the metal.

"I'm strapped in, Captain," I said, saluting.

Sal grinned and disappeared into the cockpit, leaving me alone with my thoughts.

Yesterday, I was in Santa Cruz visiting my mother. This morning, I had received a summons from the Others to come to a conference. You don't say "no" to the Others when they send a personal summons. Danica refers to them as Mount Olympus. It never ceased to get a chuckle out of me. Anyway, they had sent a messenger to Marin that they wished to see me. This surprised me, not because they *were* Mount Olympus, but because the last time we had spoken, we had words...well...I had had words. I had disagreed with the way they wanted us to ease slowly into the real world. While I didn't think we should come busting out of the closet, I *did* think they needed to be more progressive in their approach. My ideas hadn't gone over very well, and they'd pretty much shot me down, so I had gone home without finishing my mentor training.

I had regretted that decision more than once.

So, here I was.

Summoned and responded, I was taking my first ride in Danica's jet, which she'd aptly named after herself: *The Boss*.

"Flight time under two hours, Echo," came Sal's disembodied voice. "Sit back and relax. We've got clear skies until Northern Oregon."

Staring out the window, I was surprised at how calm I felt. My visit with Tricia had settled me more than I'd expected. She'd said all the right things at all the right times. Like...well...like a mom. I felt so much better after seeing her. I needed balance and to get centered and Tricia had managed to offer that for me—so much so, that when I finally closed my eyes, I fell fast asleep...and that hadn't happened in weeks.

"Thank God. I've been trying to reach you for days."

I stared at Jacob Marley, my friend from the bayou who had died not too long ago. He visited my dreams on occasion, usually offering up some sage advice. I wondered what he was doing here now.

"*Jacob!*" Throwing my arms around his neck, I hugged him to me. *"It's been too long."*

Pulling away, he smiled into my eyes with eyes of melted chocolate. Jacob had been my best friend on the river and had taught me everything I knew about the river, about necromancy, and about life. Mine had never been the same since he'd died, and I missed him terribly.

"I can't reach you when you are off-kilter, and boy have you been outta whack."

"I know. I'm working on it." We sat across from each other on the bed in my dream. "It feels like everything I'm doing is over my head."

"Don't be ridiculous. You are so ready for all of this." He smiled, his white teeth bright against his black skin. God, how I missed that smile. "You have to trust that Mel knew what she was doing by choosing you. You may second guess yourself, but you've never done that to her, so don't start now."

"Do you think I can teach those kids?"

"Without a doubt. You're perfect for the job. When did you lose your confidence, girl? What happened to your sense of self?"

Looking away, tears came to my eyes before looking back up at him. My heart would never heal from this loss. "When I let you die."

"Oh, Echo. You didn't let me die. It's what needed to happen. I was going crazy hearing all those dead people always coming at me. I fought the good fight, but they were slowly eating my sanity."

Jacob Marley had been a necromancer—one who can talk to the dead. Problem was, they were always trying to talk to *him*, and it slowly drove him crazy. Before he lost it completely, he was killed...and his exit from this planet cut a gaping chasm through my heart that would never fully heal. He'd been such a wonderful part of my childhood that his absence was felt every day of my adult life. Every single day.

"I know that, Jacob. Up here." I pointed to my

head. "But my heart will never recover. I miss you so much."

"I know you do. I miss you, too. You're doing wonderful things with those kids, Echo. They need you. They need you like Cinder needed you. Dani's given you everything you need to make a difference. Go out and make that difference, Echo. Believe that you can, because everyone else does."

My eyes filled with tears. I hadn't realized how much I had needed to hear that.

"So I need you to suck it up, sister. I know you miss me. I know you miss Finn. I know you miss Melika, but life goes on...well...not for me...but for you, yes. Things change and the successful rise with those changes. It's time for you to rise, my friend." Reaching out, he wiped the tears from my face. "Always believe. No matter how bad the odds appear, if you believe, you'll get through it."

"Oh, Jacob, you always believed in me more than I believed in myself."

"And that needs to change right now. These kids need you to believe in yourself, in them, and in your common cause. Remember Mel used to say when you are least sure of yourself is when you need the most faith."

"I'm trying, Jacob. I really am."

"Echo?"

Opening my eyes, I stared at Sal. "Man, girl, you were sleeping hard. We're here."

Here was the San Juan Islands. The Others lived on an island exclusive to them for safety.

When I came down the steps of the plane, I went straight into the arms of Bishop, Melika's aged mother.

"There she is." Bishop hugged me tightly. "You look beautiful, my dear. Let me look at you." She stepped back and let her eyes roam up and down my body. "Not eating enough. Working too hard. Not enough lovin'. That about sum it up?"

Before her retirement, Bishop had been one of the greatest fortunetellers in New Orleans. What made her great were her powers. Bishop was a seer—a clairvoyant—with a high success factor in her readings. Then Hurricane Katrina came along and displaced a lot of people. Bishop was one of them.

"No one can fill Melika's shoes, Bishop, and no matter how hard I try—"

"You will wear your *own* shoes, Echo, my dear, and you will wear them better than anyone else." Taking my hand, she pulled me to the waiting Town Car. "And right now, everyone is waiting to see them."

Scooting in next to her, I couldn't help but smile from ear to ear. Bishop had taken such good care of us when we were in the bayou. She'd been a wonderful role model and I adored her.

"What's this about?"

"The summons? I can't say. Everyone's been talking about what happened in Alaska. You were pretty incredible from what I hear." She shook her head. "Used to be I could have seen it before it happened. No matter what anyone tells you, getting old is not any fun."

"I'll remember that."

When we arrived at the compound where the Others lived, I reflected back to the only other time I had been here. I had come here for training, to learn how to work with young supers, but I had left after the first day, pissed off and not wanting anything to do with my trainer or anyone else. I wasn't ready.

Now I'd been summoned and I had no idea why,

because I still wasn't ready. I was ready to teach, yes, but ready to take orders from a blind dickweed? Uh uh.

"*You are about to find out, Echo, if that is true.*"

My car door opened and there stood a telepath.

"Miss Bishop, we will see to it that Echo gets back to your place when she's finished."

"Thank you, Reinhart. Be careful with her. She's my charge and I won't have you old goats berating her or hassling her in any way. You hear me?"

He was tall and stooped over, as if the world's weight had been bearing down on him, his white hair like cotton. "Yes, ma'am." Reinhart helped me from the Town Car and walked with me into the conference center where a seven-member panel awaited me. I took the hot seat in the front clearly meant for me.

"Echo Branson. So good to see you again." The woman addressing me was the head of the Other Council, Ramona, a precog, telepath, and empath—a triple threat who had led the council for the last six years.

"Nice seeing you again, Ramona." I turned and nodded to the others. "Council, I am surprised at the summons. As you know—"

"Yes, yes, we know about your school," said a white-haired gentleman named Erik. I'd met him once before and didn't like him. He was a stuffed shirt. "As well as all that transpired in Alaska. What *you* probably aren't aware of is that Tiponi Redhawk should not have been in Russia in the first place."

The moment Tip's name rolled off his tongue, I was back on my feet. "I'll not sit idly by while you, or any of you for that matter, second-guess what me or my people are doing to help these kids."

"Miss Branson, please—"

"No." I shook my head. "I came here because I thought *maybe* you were willing to revisit our last conversation, but you have seriously underestimated my loyalty if you think I'll sit here quietly while you play the Monday morning quarterback from the safety of the islands." I turned to leave when Reinhart stepped in front of me.

"I'm afraid we've offended you, Miss Echo," he said softly. Reinhart appeared far too young to be a member of the Others. "Please, have a seat and Ramona will explain everything." His eyes shot darts at Erik. Reluctantly, I turned around and sat back down. Leaning forward, hands clasped in front of her, Ramona smiled. "We appreciate you coming, Echo. Really we do. We did not summon you to discuss Tiponi's extraction of the triplets. I apologize."

I said nothing.

"How are they, anyway?"

My eyes roamed from one face to another. "Getting better every day."

"Have you determined the limits of their powers yet?"

I wasn't going to give them any more than I had to. Even though they were on our side, I wasn't feeling like handing out free information. "Getting there."

"And the girl, Nika?"

I shook my head. "Unsure."

Erik made a sound of disgust.

"They are acclimating quite well to their new environment. They are happy, healthy, and growing stronger every day. That's about all you're going to get from me."

"Good. Good. That is wonderful to hear. And how about Cinder?"

I bristled. I did not like anyone asking questions about her in particular. "She's fine."

Ramona silenced Erik with a look I didn't miss.

"Cinder is a happy kid. She is learning how to control her powers, and she is off-limits to you and anyone else who thinks she's up for grabs. I'll fight to the death for that kid, no matter who thinks she is better off without me."

"What do *you* know about fire starting, Miss Branson? The girl needs a real teacher." Again from Erik.

"Erik—"

"I'm just stating the truth, Ramona."

I rose again and approached the table. "Cinder stays with me, Erik. Unless and until she chooses to leave. And if you or anyone even *thinks* about coming for her, my people will blow you to pieces."

Erik rose and we stood eye-to-eye, the air thick with tension.

"Both of you, please sit down," Ramona said firmly.

I stepped away from the table, my eyes still locked on Erik's, willing him to bring it so I could smash him against the wall. I so wanted to hurt him.

He slowly sat down.

I turned to Ramona. "If this is about Cinder, this meeting is over. I will destroy anyone foolish enough to mess with my family."

Ramona held her hand up. "No need for such harshness, Echo. This meeting isn't about Cinder, and I apologize for Erik's behavior. We're all concerned the girl be properly trained, of course, but—"

"And she will get that training *from me* and in the manner I see fit." I said this with more conviction than I'd ever felt. "So if this isn't about her, why am I here?"

Ramona consulted a piece of paper. "As you know, Jasmine Barnes made a few...miscalculations in judgment down in Vegas a while back. We've had her on a short leash since then, and we've put her to work keeping us abreast of everything that is going on in Vegas."

I shook my head. "Quite frankly, Ramona, I couldn't care less about what's going on in Vegas. My plate is already pretty full, and helping Jasmine out of a bind doesn't interest me. I know what she did to Bailey, and, quite frankly, want nothing to do with her."

"If you will give me five more minutes of your time, I'll explain what is going on and how it relates to our last conversation. Can you give me that much?"

Nodding, I sat back down.

"In the last few years, there have been some issues with supers who refer to themselves as "Indies," or independents. Indies are not affiliated with any of us...not mentors, not organizations like the Group, nothing. They prefer to live by their own set of rules—often at the endangerment of the rest of us—because they will use their powers to make money and gain fame."

I nodded. "I knew there were those of us flying solo, but a group?"

"Precisely. These Indies used to be scattered, but someone has pulled many of them together and they have chosen two cities in the United States to live, Vegas and —"

"Atlantic City." I blew a breath out. "Where there's free money to be had if you possess the right powers."

"Yes. Jasmine has reported that a second group of Indies from the Midwest has settled in Vegas and there's now tension between the two groups. It doesn't bode well for us to have warring factions."

"Especially when there's no one to clean up after them. They make messes we'd rather not deal with." This came from an older gentleman sitting next to Ramona.

I held my hand up. "Ramona, I have absolutely no desire to investigate a pissing contest between two groups of supers. My time is far more valuable than that."

She looked over at Reinhart, who nodded. "We thought you'd say as much, so we are willing to pay you for your services."

I stared at her now. "Pay me? You can't be serious. I don't need your money and you insult me by off—"

"We're not offering it *to you* and we are not offering money." Ramona leaned forward even more. "All we want is for you to mediate between the two—see if you can't get each side to concede a little. The way they are going now, it is only a matter of time before something blows up in all our faces, and we don't need that right now."

"Mediate. That's it?"

"That's it. Do this for us and we will arrange for an experienced pyro to help Cinder gain control over her powers."

She said the one thing that would convince me to do this. She knew I'd do just about anything to help that kid.

Closing my eyes, I tried to reach Tip once more before opening them. She still wasn't answering. Well,

I had to hand it to them, they knew just the right card to play. "Who?"

"Sonja Satre."

I shook my head. "I've been trying to—" then it dawned on me. If Sonja went to the highest bidder, The Others must have offered her something she couldn't refuse. "What button did you push to get Sonja to agree to do this?"

Ramona barely grinned. "Up until Alaska, we allowed Sonja to do as she pleased so long as no one got hurt. She made an error we are not willing to forgive."

I stared. "An...*error*? The woman attacked us in the middle of the street, and then she came back later to finish the job. That's a little more significant than an *error*. She tried to kill us, and would have if Cinder hadn't..." and then I laughed, much to the surprise of everyone in the room.

"Something amusing about that?" Ramona asked, frost dripping off every word.

"Actually, there is. All this time I've been thinking that Cinder needed tutoring, and yet, she kicked Sonja's ass. Hard. Maybe Cinder is fine without the Sonjas of the world." I rose again. I wasn't interested in anything they were selling. "I have to thank you, though, for setting me straight. All this time, I thought I wasn't good enough to teach Cinder, when the fact of the matter is, she doesn't really need any of us."

Erik cleared his throat. "Sonja has a child, a child she has kept a secret for three years. She thought that by taking her to Alaska, no one would find out. She was wrong."

Now *that* was a surprise. "Wait. She has a *kid*?"

They all nodded.

I thought about this a moment. This news

changed things. "Okay, so she has a kid. You're telling me you're using a child to barter—"

"Not at all." Ramona glared at Erik. I wondered why the rest were so silent. "We have offered your services when the child is of age, of course. If Sonja will train Cinder, you will do the same for her daughter."

I shook my head. Three years ago, I would have taken her, but I was a different person now. "Send her somewhere else. Sonja and I are not exactly friends and I have no desire to deal with her as a mother, friend, super, or anything else. It was presumptuous of you to offer my services for *anything*."

The seven members exchanged glances. Clearly, they had no idea what to do about me. I suspected they thought because I was so young, I would be malleable. They didn't know me very well. I was raised by Tiponi Redhawk, who was pushed around by no one.

"Echo, you wish Cinder to be trained. We need a mediator. Sonja wants her daughter to be able to go to school where she's not a freak. Be reasonable. We can all get what we need here, Echo."

"Be reasonable? She's a whore going to the highest bidder. She proved that in Alaska. Why would I want someone like that around my kids?"

"That was before we told her we knew about her daughter. The money she's been earning the last three years was hush money for the father, who thought blackmailing her was a good way to make a living. We have since...taken care of that situation."

I said nothing.

"Echo, we understand why you would be upset, but there were extenuating circumstances that have now been cleaned up. Perhaps a little forgiveness is in order."

I still said nothing.

Then the door opened and Bishop stuck her head in. "Excuse me, but if I may?" Bishop didn't wait for a reply and entered the room unbidden. "Echo, if it helps, I think Melika would forgive Sonja. Doing something to protect one's child is...well pardonable. Think of what you'd be willing to do to protect any of *your* charges."

I nodded and Bishop flashed me the okay sign before going back out.

She was right, of course. I mean, Cinder wasn't my child, but I'd stop at nothing to protect her. Sitting back down, I addressed Ramona. "So I go down to Vegas to mediate between these two groups of idiotic supers and you loan me Sonja for a couple of weeks?"

"That's the deal on the table, yes."

I thought for a moment. "You do realize that Cinder has a very special relationship with my best friend, right?"

"We've heard the stories, yes."

"I can't really make any decisions about Cinder or the school until I consult my people."

"Your...people. Naturals?" Erik said the last word with disdain. "You must be joking."

Ramona held her hand up. "Erik, please. Echo, I applaud you consulting with...your team. We would wish you to not penalize the girl for her mother's actions."

I nodded. "I understand, and I'll keep that in mind. You realize if Sonja so much as looks cross-eyed at me or Cinder, Danica has both the will and the means to blow her head off her shoulders. So don't offer up someone who has any issues with us, because she won't last very long."

Erik made a grunting sound under his breath.

"We are very clear about Miss Johnson's role in your life, Echo, and we do not see Sonja as a problem. There is much she could teach young Cinder. Sonja is an amazing PK. One of the few who could show Cinder so very much about her powers. Please just consider this. We would never suggest it if we thought she was a danger to you and yours."

I started for the door, and with my hand on the knob, turned and said, "For us to allow a stranger who tried to do us in into our home is going to have to be discussed." With that, I walked outside to find Bishop waiting in the Town Car.

"You knew," I said, reaching for her hand. It was thin and cold.

"Oh, dear child, I see things all the time, but I never quite know what to believe."

"How can I believe she wouldn't try to fry me or the others the first chance she got?"

As Reinhart closed my door, she said, "I expect you to do what is best for your family. That's what my daughter would have done. It is how *you* should always comport yourself in the world. If you take care of your family, it will take care of you."

Nodding, I thought about Cinder and how much she struggled with control over her powers, how much she wanted to be able to master the thin red line. And yet, even with all that, I was reduced to pettiness. "I don't like Sonja."

Bishop chuckled. "You don't have to like her. As a matter of fact, I'd be disappointed in you if you did, but she has something you need, something Cinder needs. This isn't about you."

Staring out the window at the gray day, I felt the

same gray seeping into my soul. "You think I should do it."

Bishop turned to face me fully. She looked better than the last time I'd seen her. She'd taken a hard hit to the head during Hurricane Katrina and we thought we'd lost her, but today, she was vibrant and rosy-cheeked. "To be honest with you, dear girl, I should think you would want to do something in Vegas, with or without Sonja and this silly deal."

"What do you mean?"

"I know my daughter taught you better than this, Echo. You can't hide behind the walls of the vineyard. You can't pretend those Indies and their actions won't affect you. You know the domino effect of our actions. I should think you would feel compelled to go to Vegas whether or not there was anything in it for you. It is what we do."

Thoroughly shamed, I bowed my head as two large tears formed.

"No, no, dear girl, I am not chastising you. I'm only saying—"

"That Melika would have stepped up without hesitation."

She shrugged. "Yes, but then, she has a Tip. And you do not."

I opened my mouth to reply, but thought better of it. No, I didn't have a Tip, but I did have a Bailey and a Danica. I *did* have a team of strong women. And yes, I knew only too well how the domino effect worked. We were all at risk if the Indies got themselves some notoriety. Melika would have sent Tip to straighten everything out, but Melika was sick and she needed Tip with her. The Others had chosen to send me because there was no one else.

Leaning over to her, I hugged her frail neck. "Thank you."

"Oh, Echo, don't you know how proud Melika is of you?" She pulled away and wiped my cheeks. "A day doesn't go by that she doesn't count you among her many blessings. She knows you'll do the right thing. So do I."

The right thing, as I would discover later, was often difficult to discern in a basketful of wrong things, but for now, I knew there was only one right thing to do.

Make Melika proud.

※※※※

It took Danica, Bailey, and me less than ten minutes to come to a consensus: Cinder's training was of paramount importance, and we needed to go to Vegas to see if we could make some headway in a supernatural turf war. It didn't surprise me how quickly they agreed to go to Vegas. Their love of Cinder was so evident, I was slightly ashamed I had let my personal feelings about Sonja get in the way of Cinder's tutelage.

The only person with a real issue was Danica. On one hand, she wanted Cinder to have more control, and on the other, she hated the idea it would be from a woman who had not only tried to kill us, but had taken a keen interest in doing so to a child...*our* child.

It didn't take long to convince her. All I had to say was that she had *carte blanche* to drop her like a stone if she ever got out of line. Girls from the 'hood operate on a different set of principles than the rest of us. They understood the *get them before they get you* mentality. It's why it had been so easy for Danica to pull the trigger before.

"Yo, Boss?"

Looking up from my iPad calendar, I saw Sal. "Yes?"

"We have a visitor."

I looked at my watch. "Who is it?" Getting up, I looked at the large screen T.V. coming down from the ceiling. The chateau had some of the best security around.

"Bob, please show cameras one and three."

Bob was the name of the computer which ran every major electronic device in the chateau. Roger, one of Danica's think tank members, developed it. Bob stood for Bot on Board, and was a project Savvy had been working on for several years. Bob did everything... including washing the windows.

"Shit."

"I can have her escorted away from the gate."

"That's not necessary. I'll go meet her out front. Would you please tell her I am on the way?"

On the way was but a short golf cart ride, also powered by Bob.

Pulling up to the large wrought iron gate, I got out and spoke into the intercom. "You can open her up, Sal." As the gates slowly opened, I found myself standing four feet from Officer Marist Finn, my most recent ex-girlfriend. She was wearing worn jeans, a brown bomber jacket, and an interesting smirk on her face.

"Impressive," she said, not moving. "With all this security, one would think you have something to hide." Her brown eyes scanned back and forth so typical of someone in her profession, as if she was expecting a perp to jump out at her.

"Maybe I do."

She chuffed and shook her head. "Must be exhausting, Echo, keeping all those skeletons from poking their heads out of your closet. Exhausting, frustrating, and such a drag."

I wasn't going to do this with her. "What brings you to Marin, Finn?"

"Well, you won't return my calls. I even went to Luigi's. I think I deserve better than to be treated like I'm invisible." Hurt dripped off of every word. "So here I am."

"I moved."

Her eyes narrowed. She wasn't amused. "I could tell. You can imagine my surprise at seeing you had moved...moved without so much as a forwarding address. That's harsh, Echo."

Before I could ask my next question, she answered for me. "And no, Delta wouldn't cop to it. None of them would. It was like I'd been frozen out. It was bad enough that I lost you, but you seemed to have hijacked my social group as well. Thanks for that."

"What would you have me do? Fire them?" I was having an out-of-body experience watching myself be a bitch. She did deserve better from me, but I was so afraid if I was soft, she would see it as an opening, and I couldn't afford to give her one.

"You've frozen me out of my *own* life, Echo."

"What do you want me to say, Finn? You... well...I guess you sort of are, but it's not something I made happen. I didn't intend to hijack your social group."

She looked so hurt. "One can't be *sort of* frozen out. I either am or I'm not."

I shrugged. "Then you are."

She nodded, looking past my shoulder. Why was it cops always seemed to be searching for trouble? "I appreciate your honesty," she said. "So you're running a vineyard? You barely know a Cabernet from a Merlot."

"Finn, is there a reason besides busting my chops that you've come here?" The very question alone made my heart ache. Marist Finn was one of the good guys...but I wouldn't...*couldn't* rekindle our romance no matter how much I missed her. And though I understood her anger, this was neither the time nor the place to rehash it. This could only go south if we kept this up.

"Wow," she said, finally looking in my eyes. "When you get over someone, you get over."

Inhaling a deep breath, I moved closer. "Don't make assumptions, Finn. Our relationship ended because there was no place else for it to go. Surely you understand that by now."

Running her hand through her brown wavy hair, she shook her head. Finn was a good-looking woman, towering near six feet, with broad shoulders that tapered to a flat waist. In her uniform, I just wanted to eat her like a chocolate bunny.

"Frankly, I don't understand anything. Something happened when you went to New Orleans after Katrina. I think it happened when I was there, because you've never been the same since."

What "happened" was that Finn had seen a group of us using our powers. We knocked her out, but not before she saw too much. While she vaguely recalls what she thinks she saw, she can't wrap her mind around it, so she did what most people do when they don't understand: She stuffed it deep inside her and chalked it up to a movie or a dream. Well, stuffed issues fester over time and, if that wasn't bad enough, I knew I could no longer pretend to be something I wasn't, nor was I prepared to tell her who and what I truly was.

So, I had broken it off.

That had been our biggest problem: There was so much I couldn't tell her and so much she didn't tell me. What kind of a relationship was that?

"A lot happened there, Finn." Shaking my head, I continued. "This just isn't our time. I need you to accept that."

She looked down at me, her eyes switching between pain and sadness to fiery anger. "Just like that? *It's not our time?* You know, I could handle it if it were someone else. I really could. But to be dumped for nothing? That cuts to the marrow, Echo. The least you could do is let me escape with *some* dignity intact."

Walking to her, I laid my palm on her cheek. I so wanted to tell her that my wish was for her to escape with her *life* intact. "Then yes, there *is* someone else. We are not yet romantically involved, but, well, we're taking it slow." My gut rumbled with that sick feeling you get when you're doing the wrong thing.

"You met someone in New Orleans, huh?" Her eyes were damp, the fire sizzling slowly out.

"I did."

Nodding, she jammed her hand into her pocket and pulled out her car keys. "I just have one last question and then I'll be on my way."

I felt like vomiting, but if believing there was someone else made this easier on her, then that's how I was going to play it. I didn't need to hurt her any more. "Okay."

Stepping closer, she got right down into my face. "You still love me, don't you?"

I blinked, my tongue heavy in my mouth. I recovered as quickly as I could. "I'll always care about you, Finn."

Her eyes changed in that moment as a slight grin of hope twitched on her face. "Uh huh." Kissing my forehead, she turned and started back for her car. When she opened the door, she turned back to me. "A lesser woman would believe you and walk away with her pride delicately taped together. A lesser woman would let you walk away, steeped in your own mystery. A lesser woman wouldn't be able to read how much you still love me. And you do, Echo Branson. I know you do. So this isn't the end of this conversation. I can't blow away like a wisp of smoke. I believe in fighting the good fight. So consider it brought." With that, she got into her Mustang and headed back to the city.

"Dog with a bone," came Sal's voice through the camera speakers. "Good luck with that one, E."

Watching Finn's tail-lights fade in the distance, I knew it would take more than luck to shake my feelings for Marist Finn.

⁂

Cinder, Shila, and I sat by the river after a productive morning of focusing techniques. Ever since Shila had arrived, Cinder was a different person, happier, calmer. She was certainly in love with that ball of fur, and the feelings were mutual…well… that's what Bailey said.

"We need to talk," I said, lying back on the grass only to have my face engulfed in puppy breath.

Cinder picked Shila up and snuggled her before lying down next to me. *"Am I in trouble?"*

"Not at all. I was wondering how you would feel about being trained by a high level pyro."

"Really?" She sat up. *"I'd love that!"*

Smiling, I sat up, too. "By Sonja Satre."

The smile slid off her face. *"Uh uh. No way."*

"Hear me out."

"She played on the wrong side and you want to let her in here? Forget it. I'd rather be stupid."

I petted Shila's big belly. "You're not stupid and you're not going to be stupid." I told her about the deal with the Others. When I finished, Cinder frowned in thought. "She could teach you so much."

"Do you trust her?"

Opening the new and improved Vidbook Danica was pitting against the iPhone, I typed the word *now*. Fifteen seconds later, Danica and Bailey came through the vineyard. I placed a hand on Cinder's leg to keep her from prematurely firing a ball of flame.

"The cavalry's here," Danica said, winking at Cinder, who jumped to her feet and hugged Danica. "Hey, Firefly."

Shila made a beeline to Bailey, who scooped her up and nuzzled her face. I'd never seen animals so warm and friendly as they were to Bailey.

"Thank you for coming," I said to both of them.

Danica knelt down on one knee and Bailey held Shila until she settled into a coma. Bailey could tame a Tasmanian Devil.

"I wasn't too keen on Sonja coming here either, Firefly. She's not in my good graces."

Cinder shook her head and made a face like she'd just eaten raw oysters.

"We came by today to let you know that Sonja coming here is entirely up to you. If you decide you want to learn from her, then you have our word that we'll make sure she understands what the consequences are should she even *think* about betraying our trust."

Bailey nodded. "She would be monitored constantly if you didn't feel like you wanted to be left alone with her."

"In short, we will do everything in our power to make you feel safe."

Reaching behind her, Danica withdrew her Glock from her waistband. She never left home without it. "Sonja may be a lot of things, Firefly, but she's still a human."

Cinder barely smiled and said something telepathically to Danica.

"I believe as long as we have her daughter for leverage, we'll all be safe. We would never put any of us in danger, Firefly, you know that."

"But it's up to you," I said. "You think about it, and we'll discuss it in the morning, okay?"

Cinder looked at each one of us, nodding as we each made eye contact with her.

"Take your baby, and go tell Tack I want to see him."

We watched her take Shila and head back to the chateau.

"Thanks, guys."

"What do you think? Think she'll be okay with it?" Bailey asked.

Danica nodded. "She's a smart kid. She knows Sonja is powerful and could teach her a great deal. The kid is ready to bust a move. She needs this."

Bailey nodded. "One wrong move, Echo, and

Sonja's gonna be grapevine fertilizer. As long as she is aware of the rules and consequences, I say bring her on."

I nodded. "It's not like we won't be watching her every second of the day, and we'll have her kid."

"Taylor," Bailey said.

We looked at her.

"Put Taylor on her. She's sneaky enough to be able to keep track of Sonja without her ever knowing that. With Vidbook in hand and Taylor in stealth mode, Sonja will be covered twenty-four/seven."

"Would she—"

"Absolutely. She's become rather fond of the Matchstick. If we know Taylor has her in her sights during the evening, and we have her during the day, then it's all good."

"Then let's do it. If Cinder agrees, then I'll call Bishop and have them set it all up."

We stood there for a moment before Danica put her hand out. Bailey and I put our hands on top of hers.

"Firefly deserves the best training money can buy. If that's Sonja, then I say we go for it."

The decision made, I watched Danica and Bailey make their way back to the chateau, grateful they were a part of Team Echo.

Inhaling deeply, I looked out over the river Danica had created for me, suddenly wishing Tip was here with me. I hadn't felt that deepest chasm of loneliness until this moment. For the first time in a long, long time, I missed Tip's presence to the depth of my soul and wished I could just lay my head in her lap and sleep. We had been good together long ago…I wished…oh hell…it was over, and I needed to move on. We were not the same people we'd been back then.

Suddenly, Tack came walking out of the vineyard. "How were your lessons this morning?" I asked.

Tack grinned at me with a smile that would charm the skin off a snake. He was adorable in his nearly teenage boyhood, with deep dimples and a lopsided grin he wasn't aware made all the young girls swoon. I really liked him. "Very good. I am learning how electricity works."

Tack was a technopath—an artificially created supernatural created by Genesys. His power, as I was slowly learning, was like heightened static electricity he used to control electrical impulses. By focusing on certain electronic parts, he was capable of manipulating those impulses in order to get a certain reaction from a device.

For example, since most cars now have some sort of computer chip system, if he scrambled the impulses going to and from it, he could essentially shut the car down. He just had little control over it because he'd not been trained before he had escaped from Genesys' lab. Prior to his added ability, he had been a level two mover.

"You like Roger, huh?"

He nodded. Tack had big brown eyes with long lashes women would die for. He was slightly taller than Cinder, but still a good four inches shorter than me. "It is hard not telling him who I am or what we all can do. He could teach me more if he knew."

And right there was the crux of the problem between me and the Others. I felt it necessary to share with trustworthy people. They did not. Roger was as loyal as Shila would eventually grow up to be. I made a mental note to sit down with Roger and explain exactly what Tack was, because without Roger's help, Tack would be flailing around with all this energy, much like Cinder was.

"Tell you what, Champ, I'll think about it, okay?"

Smiling widely, he nodded.

"You're happy here, aren't you?"

"What's not to love? Miss Johnson made it all. It's a cool place to live, Echo. Thanks."

I studied Tack a moment. He was so eager to learn, so willing to work hard and try new things. He deserved better than to learn how electricity worked.

Two hours later, Tack had shown me that he truly was learning how to build his shields, so I let him play on the rope swing for another forty-five minutes before we walked down to the barn to check out the harvested grapes.

"Tell you what. You help William for the rest of the day. I'm going to go talk to Roger before he leaves."

Tack took off, yelling thank you as he ran. Kids and barns. What's the attraction?

I called Danica to have her meet me at the chateau. She was only a few minutes away.

When I got back to the chateau, Roger and Sal had their heads together over a bunch of computer guts laying on a table.

"Roger, can I see you a minute?"

He looked up from his trance and nodded, following me out of the room. Cinder was being tutored in math, so I borrowed her for a moment and took them into the media room.

"Did I do something wrong?" Roger said, pushing his glasses back against his face.

"Not at all."

The door swung open and there stood Danica, dressed to the teeth. "You didn't start without me, did you?"

I looked at her hard. She was gorgeous in her teal silk Donna Karan outfit with silver earrings and chunky peace sign necklace. "Where've you been?"

"Breakfast meeting."

I crossed my arms over my chest. "You know better than to lie to me."

She fought and lost to the grin spreading on her face. "It was a breakfast meeting with a guy who wants better security."

I waited, knowing she would cave.

"A casino owner."

"Oh God. Are you still playing with Nick Harper?"

"He was in town. We had brunch. No big deal. Am I here to talk about me or was there something important you called me for?"

Nick Harper, like ninety-nine percent of men, fell for her immediately. This was not the first time he'd flown to the city to see her. I knew it wasn't serious because Dani didn't do serious, which was good, since he was high-level mobster who scared the crap out of me.

"We can discuss that later. Right now, I've decided it's time for Roger to know."

Danica looked from Roger to me and back again. "Okay."

"That's it? Okay?"

"He's here all the time and he's the best teacher for Tack. You know I trust the boys with my business and my life. I think we should have told them a long time ago."

"Geez," Roger said. "Tell me already. The suspense is killing me."

Stepping back, Danica nodded for me to go ahead.

Inhaling a deep breath, I began. "I'm sure you've figured out by now, Roger, that this isn't a regular place and me and my charges aren't either."

He nodded. "They're smarter, that's for sure."

I smiled. Danica took over. "Rog, you know I believed in you guys and gave you a home when no one else did, right?"

"Right, and we've come through for you, boss. None of us has ever looked for another job. Ever."

She shook her head. "This isn't about your job. This is about loyalty. I need that loyalty now. I need one hundred percent heart and soul loyalty."

Roger nodded. "You've always had that." He looked at me. "And so does Princess."

I'd always been Princess to Danica's Queen Bee.

I put my arm around Cinder's shoulder. "And that is why we're sharing our most important secret with you. A secret that cannot go out of this room or this chateau. It is so huge that you telling even your closest friend could ruin or, at the very least, drastically change our lives."

He blinked and nodded again. "I understand. Whatever it is, it will never pass my lips. Your secret is safe with me. You have my word."

Cinder looked at me and I nodded. "A small one. We're indoors."

Nodding, she held her tiny hand out as if holding a bug in her palm. Danica put her hand on Roger's shoulder and whispered. "This is no trick and you're not being punked. Do you know why I call her Firefly?"

Roger shook his head.

When Cinder opened her hand, a small ball of

flame the size of a golf ball burned in her palm.

"Oh shit." Roger's eyes were wide. "That's… that's not—"

"Possible? Sure it is." I nodded to Cinder, who made the flame ball grow before tossing it up and down in her hand like it was a baseball.

"We're supernaturals, Roger. Each of us has our own unique powers. The kids are here to learn how to better control their abilities. That's my job now. That's why Danica built this place—so that me and the kids would be safe."

Roger couldn't take his eyes off the ball of flame. "I'd read…but never…wow…it's like I am working with super heroes. Man…this…this is huge."

"We thought you should know, since you're working with Tack."

"He's one, too?"

We all nodded. I told Cinder to extinguish the flame. She did. "Tack is a technopath; a being capable of manipulating electricity. I need you to know why you're working with him, Rog. Tack needs help in understanding how his abilities influence electronics and technology. To do that, he needs to know how it all works first."

Roger ran his hand over his face and nodded. "If he doesn't understand how everything works, using his powers could be disastrous."

We all nodded once more.

"Exactly. You know more about electronics and technology than anyone I know. We need you to help him as best you can."

Roger blinked again. It was all pretty heady stuff. The natural mind has a hard time processing it all. "I can do that." His eyes traveled over to Danica.

"Oh hell no, muffin head. While I am definitely extraordinary, I am *not* like them."

Cinder had flames flickering on all five fingers.

"Jesus. I've read about pyros in comic books. I've even played one in various online games, but to see it in person is...well...I am flabbergasted."

"She's a special one." Danica put her arm around Cinder's shoulders. "Very, very special. So, you can see the need for total secrecy."

"Oh hell yes."

"Good. I've always trusted you, Roger. Always."

"And it's well-placed, Boss. You know that."

Danica left Cinder's side and joined me at the door. "Indeed I do."

"So, what now?"

"Now," I answered, "You are better prepared to teach him what he needs to know."

As I started for the handle, Roger asked, "You're their leader, Princess?"

"Mentor. I'm just the one who trains them so they can live in the world as normally as possible."

"Are you...are you one of them?"

I stopped and smiled. He had always had a huge crush on me. "Yes, Roger, I am."

"Can you...show me?"

Danica was shaking her head when I pushed an energy shield against him, shoving him against the wall and pinning him there.

"Whoa! Awesome!"

"It's not nearly as awesome as other powers, but it'll do in a pinch. Give me your word, Roger. Not even the other boys should know."

"You have my word, Princess. Mum's the word."

Releasing him, I nodded. "Thank you, Roger.

Welcome to Team Echo."

※※※※

One Day Ago

Just as I hung up the phone, Bailey walked in. "That was Jasmine. Looks like we're joining the party in the nick of time."

"What party?"

"There's been a murder of one of the Vegas supers."

Opening the Vidbook, I sent a voice text to Danica to let her know we needed to get down to Vegas sooner than we realized. She said she'd be on her way.

"Oh shit." Bailey sat down on the couch with a flump. "They couldn't wait until we got down there?"

"Well, looks like it's go time."

"Good. I've been going stir crazy here."

"You're going to have to stay crazy a little longer. You're staying here."

"Noooo. Come on, E! I need some action!"

"It's Vegas, Bailey, and I don't need you dealing with all that Jasmine baggage. Uh uh. Your talents are best kept here with the kids.

"Oh, I get it. Send me to the jungles and the frozen tundra, where I can summon wolves and wild bears, but a cool gig like Vegas and now I'm chopped liver? I'm over it, E. Jasmine is a bitch with head issues and I've moved on. You need me."

"You have a point. Fine. You can come, but you back off from her. We need to know what she knows."

She smiled. "Awesome. So, who else is going?"

"Danica and you."

Danica came in. "Guns and muscles. Smart. So, what magician got whacked?"

"Max Rhodes is an illusionist, not a magician, and it was his assistant who was murdered."

"Clark, you're giving me a headache. So, the magician lost an assistant to a homicide?"

"I don't know any details yet."

Nodding, Danica said, "Bob, please get Delta Stevens on the Vidbook."

Bailey and I looked at her.

"What?" Danica asked. "Who else do we have who can investigate a murder in a nano? That woman has mad skills in this area. She'll come."

Before I could answer, Delta Stevens' face appeared on the big screen. "Hey kids. What's going on?"

"You free for a trip to Vegas? There's a possible murder we need investigated."

Her left eyebrow rose in question above emerald green eyes. Delta Stevens was an ex-cop, and current private investigator I'd met when dating Finn. She was also part of Team Echo now, an invaluable resource, and a great friend. "You want me to investigate a murder?"

"We need to make sure a murder has occurred. We don't trust the source."

"Are Vegas cops on it?"

"Umm, no. No confirmation yet."

The dawn of understanding hit her yes. "I see. This is an under-the-table investigation, isn't it?"

I nodded. "We just need confirmation before we go down with guns blazing."

"Give me the details. I'll leave first thing in the morning."

"Sal will have the plane ready at eight," Danica said. "You can hop a ride with us. Connie going with?"

"No. Dakota's got a temperature. I'll be flying solo."

"No you won't. Danica, Bailey, and I will be flying down with you."

"The big guns, huh?"

Danica exchanged looks with Bailey. "Why does everyone say that?"

"Gee, Rambo, I have no idea."

Delta interrupted us. "Is there something I need to know, Echo? Vegas may have mellowed a lot, but the gangsters are still around."

Danica opened her mouth to defend Nick, but I shot her a look.

"None of them involved as far as we know."

"Cool. Then I'll see you all at eight." Delta hung up and Bob returned the screen back to the console.

"What are we going to do while she investigates?"

"We need to pay Jasmine a visit first and get her take on the whole thing. Once we have an idea of the players involved, we'll pay them a visit and see if we can't sort things out. We sure as hell can't have supers killing supers."

"No shit."

"And Bishop said the poachers are beginning to win big. This means people are going to start noticing them, and that's the last thing we need."

Danica looked over at me. "I'll get us a place to stay and a car."

Bailey nodded.

"Well then, ladies, I suggest we all get packed for Sin City. I'll see you in the morning."

As I started for the door, Bailey put a hand on

my shoulder. "It's the desert," she said softly.

"Excuse me?" Had I missed the first part of the sentence?

"Vegas is a black hole. It's the desert. Bad vibes in desert. We'll need to be very careful, Echo. The desert swallows people whole. Watch your step."

With that, she went back to work, leaving me with a feeling of dread settling in my stomach.

Void of life? Vegas?

I would soon find out.

Present Day

I was finding out at this moment as Bailey wove in and out of traffic. There was plenty of life *and* death here and we'd only been here a couple hours.

Delta said she would wait at the shop, and the Others told me a crew would be there within thirty minutes to clean up the mess left by those three women. Someone knew we were coming and wanted us dead.

When I told Delta my people were coming to take care of the body, she replied, "All I need is to take a look at it and get some pics. After that, put her some place safe."

Some place safe? I would have thought that a freezer in a florist's would have been pretty damn safe.

"You can slow down, Bailey," Max said softly. "They aren't following."

Bailey barely slowed. Danica lightly touched her shoulder. "Don't need the cops after us, Bails. Slow the fuck down."

Blinking, she did. "Who the hell were *they*? Those fucking bitches blew out the damn windows!"

"Associates of Townsend Briggs," Max replied. "His people." Max explained to Bailey what the rest of us had just found out.

When he finished, I leaned over and whispered to Danica, who was returning the Glock to her purse, "What did they want?"

She motioned her chin to Max. "My guess is him. They wanted *him* and weren't going to stop until they got him."

"Got? You don't mean—"

"Kill!" Jazz said, a little hysterically. "Those fuckin' Indies came to kill Max Rhodes and anyone in their way!"

It became very quiet in the car.

"Well, sister," Danica said, breaking the silence, "We're not about to let that happen, are we, Clark?"

Looking from Danica to Max and back again, I shook my head. "No Dani, we sure as hell aren't."

༄༄༄༄

As much as I hated to admit it, the safest place to leave Jasmine and Max was at Nick Harper's gangster abode. I have to say, I expected gauche. I expected palatial. I expected over-the-top, Tony Soprano-type expenses. What I got was a gorgeous Tuscan villa, modest in size, a light salmon color, surrounded by a ten-foot tall wrought iron gate and circular driveway. From the outside, the home was quite classy and could have been the home of an accountant or librarian. Its elegant simplicity impressed me.

Two Guido types came out dressed to the nines and escorted Jasmine and Max to the guest quarters behind the house before offering to take us back to the florist's. Mario then dropped Danica, Bailey, and me off a few blocks from the shop and told us he'd wait.

"Nice of Nick to help us out," I said.

"I told you he was a good guy. You just never gave him a chance."

"He's a *gangster*, Dani. He kills people. He launders money. He sounds like he's from the Jersey Shore."

Danica laughed. "Cops are crooked, politicians take bribes, no one is what they seem, Clark. You of all people should know that. Open your teeny tiny mind up. I'll be sure to thank him for you."

Bailey leaned over, hands on knees. "Jesus, E, what the fuck have we gotten ourselves into here?"

Danica nodded. "Kinda feels like we walked into the middle of a play and we don't have the script."

We walked those next couple of blocks in silence, until we came to the street just before the flower shop. My eyes were scanning left and right, the hackles on the back of my neck standing up. I knew they were nearby…I just didn't know how near.

Danica barely looked at me before putting her hand in her purse. She knew me well enough to know I was feeling something.

"Dani, I'm thinking you need Shooters Anonymous," I said, waiting for the light to turn green. The weather was cooling slightly, but I was still sweating.

"Why? Because I can pop off a round before you can say *Dani's got her Glock on*? Come on, Clark. Who knows what else those Barbies had in mind for us? I'm sure it wouldn't have been pleasant."

"To go after a Nensha is bad business," Bailey said softly.

Danica and I both stopped walking and turned to her. "What do you know about them?"

"I know that Nenshas have the capability of projecting their thoughts into other people's brains. There were guys in the sixties or seventies who claimed they could project their thoughts onto blank film. It was a hoax for one of them, and the other was truly one of us, but everyone thought his tricks were a hoax as well. Tip taught me about Nenshas when we were preparing to collect one."

"And did you?"

"No. She...killed herself before we could reach her."

My Vidbook vibrated. It was Delta.

"What did you find out?" I asked.

Her emerald eyes were intense, and she ran her hand over her face. "Seventeen stab wounds that I could find, all front entry, not all from the same knife. Defense marks on her hands and forearms where she tried to protect herself. This was a brutal killing." Delta looked away.

I cocked my head. "What?"

Looking back at the camera, Delta shook her head. "When I was a cop, Connie and I would place bets on what sort of knife made the wounds of our victims. We got pretty good at it. Anyway, there were at least three different sized blades stuck in that poor girl."

Bailey, Danica, and I looked at each other. "What does that mean, Delta?"

"Could mean any number of things. Could be

more than one killer. Killer could have used whatever was at hand. Killer might be trying to throw us off. I'm not sure…yet."

"The most likely scenario?"

She tapped her chin while she thought. "More than one killer. Stabbing is personal, unless the knife is grabbed spur of the moment. Grabbing one knife is one thing. You'd grab it and plunge it in seventeen times out of passion or anger. You wouldn't leave it in and then grab a couple new ones. That's message-sending. This feels like a warning."

I nodded. "So you think more than one person used three knives to kill that poor girl?"

"I do. I took photos and sent them to Connie. She'll give me her views as soon as she takes a closer look at them."

"Perfect. Thank you."

Delta consulted her notes. "There's more. No reports were filed. There's nothing on the books. This hasn't been reported…so you're clear there. Won't be any police investigation"

I nodded, glad to know we could keep this under wraps. "Good. Thank you so much. I'll call Sal and have her come—"

"My job's not done here, Echo. There are throwing daggers and knives missing from the backstage area where she was killed. There's more work for me to do, and I need to dig a little deeper before I go. I'll stay out of your way, but there's a lot more we need to find out before we clear this case. We need to make sure no one else is at risk. There's a killer on the loose, that much we do know. You must keep that in the forefront of your mind while you're down here. I'll touch base every odd hour."

This didn't surprise me. Delta Stevens was nothing if not thorough. She wouldn't rest until she had more info. Besides, she was right. The killer was still loose out there. "Be careful, Del. This appears to be a part of a turf war for stage time."

"Should we be expecting more bodies?"

Truth was, I didn't know. She'd be staring at a couple more bodies had Dani and I not been there. "It's on."

She nodded. "Gotcha. You guys need anything from me? Weapons, game plan?"

"We're good for now."

"Be careful out there, Echo. Vegas isn't a Sinner's Sandbox as much as it is a litter box."

I thanked her and hung up. "The different knives piece is weird."

Et tu, Brute?" Danica asked.

I looked at her.

Danica rolled her eyes. "Caesar's last words to Brutus after the members of the senate each stabbed him. That lessened the burden of guilt, made it easier for each man to plunge a knife into him. Maybe that's what it was about: Lessening the burden of guilt."

"Or sending a more ominous message?" Bailey offered.

She shrugged. "That, too. Seventeen, though? That's definitely a crime of passion like Storm said. The overkill is too…"

"Over?"

"Definitely."

As we neared the shop, I lowered my shields to see if I could pick up any supers nearby. No one was near. To Danica, I said, "I need you to take the Navigator to Nick's and see what more you can get out of Max. If Delta is free, maybe she can dig into him. I'm not saying he's hiding anything, but he might have information even he doesn't know he has."

"What are we looking for that you didn't find out?"

"Fill in the backstory. What was Hannah to him and/or anyone else? Get names and numbers of his other assistants so we can see what all they know. I want a list of all supers working for him, around him, near him, or who are just his friends."

"And where are *you* going?"

"Back to the hotel. I need to make a bunch of calls. We need to know where the Cleaners took Hannah, and I want to know their thoughts on what they saw."

Danica shuddered. "Those people creep me out. They're like ghosts."

"They're supposed to be. Come on. You can drop me off at the Bellagio."

"Why there?"

"I want to see the water show."

Danica stared at me. She knew me too well.

"Those three young women had dark auras, Dani. Not quite evil, but definitely malevolent. The energy from the water acts like a psychic shower for me—to cleanse that grungy energy off me."

Danica threw her arm across my shoulder as she always did as a way of letting me know she understood and had my back. "Been a long time since you read auras, Clark, so those must have been pretty fucking dark. Be careful."

I didn't pick up any psychic energy from the shop as we neared. I was really glad, too, since my pistol packin' pal had an itchy trigger finger. Danica was fearless. It was one of her character traits I loved most. "I will. A little sightseeing will do me good."

When Mario dropped me off in front of the Bellagio fountains, Danica leaned across the back seat as I stood on the sidewalk. "I'm just going to do my schtick and meet you back at the Pentagon, okay?"

"Are you worried?"

She chuffed. "More than you can imagine."

"We've faced stronger and meaner."

Bailey rolled the passenger window down. "I'll call the chateau to make sure everything is going well. Be careful."

When she drove off, I walked to an opening in the crowd and watched in awe as the enormous water fountain danced to music and lights as if it were alive. With every burst of water in the air, I felt the darkness of that energy wash away from me until, at last, the show ended and I was clean.

It was a beautiful afternoon to walk back to the Pentagon. I meandered along the way, looking at shops and seeing what shows were playing where, just letting the evil slough off my psyche. Vegas, like New York, has a certain vibe about it. There's an energy in the air that fills you like a narcotic. You want to be a part of something fun and exciting, and I—

Suddenly, a hand clamped over my mouth and I was being dragged into an alley I didn't even know was there. I tried to use my shield, but the surprise grab cost me focus and time.

The hand on my mouth was preternaturally warm, so I lowered my shields to gauge the threat level. I was in for quite a shock.

"Don't panic, Charlie," came words right into my ear. "And don't you dare bite me. It's me."

The hand released my mouth and I whirled around to come face-to-face with my sister.

"Kristy, what in the hell are you doing?"

She pulled me a little deeper into the alley before releasing me. "Good to see you again, too." Kristy wore her long blonde hair in a ponytail, dark glasses and, for the first time since I'd known her, was actually wearing normal clothes—jeans, biker boots, and a black leather jacket I was pretty sure was hiding her work clothes underneath.

"Work" meant locating younger, untrained supers for a group called S.T.O.P or Save The Other Paranormals. Her work clothes were specially designed to withstand the heat and lightning she could often exude.

"I knew you would be coming down here," she said, pulling me deeper into the alley. Dark alleys couldn't scare the likes of my sister. She was a scion after all, and could shoot lightning bolts from her fingertips. Literally.

"What do you mean you *knew*?"

"Something fucked up is going on down here, Charlie. I was hoping you'd just stay at your place and leave it alone, but I should have known better, huh?"

"There's been a murder. I'm just here to make sure I can contain it before it goes viral."

Kristy shook her head. "There's more to it, I think. Those old farts of yours sent you down here, didn't they?"

I'd only recently met my older sister, and when we first met, we were playing on opposite teams, so it was strange to be standing in an alley discussing the supernatural goings on in Vegas with her.

"Maybe."

She shook her head. "Damn them. When are they going to stop sending you into the danger zones and hot spots?"

"I'm a big girl, Kristy. They count on me to help quell the uprisings of our kind."

"Oh I'm sure. *We* came for Max Rhodes once. He has a rare gift—"

"Nensha, I know. I've seen it in action. Mind boggling, really."

"We thought so, too. He would make an excellent asset to the Group." They had originally collected supers who were lost or had no place to go. Their purpose now was to destroy Genesys. To do so, they sought out the most talented and powerful of us.

"I take it he declined."

"It wasn't that he declined, Charlie. Lots of supers do. It was what he said after we offered. He said he had plans. Big plans. We've been keeping an eye on him ever since in case those plans fall through, because we figured those 'plans' would blow up in his face."

My eyebrows rose. "Oh?" Kristy nodded. "Indies are trouble, Charlie. They refuse to follow any sort of rules. They have no governing body or principles. Their powers are not sharp, their secrecy shoddy, and they are socially irresponsible about using them in public. The list goes on."

"But yet, here you are."

Kristy paused and listened before returning her attention to me. "If Max is in some sort of trouble, we can offer him sanctuary. We can show him how to hone his powers so they are even sharper than they are now. We have a great deal to offer him." She paused. "Are you planning on fighting me for him? Because if you are—"

"I'm not here as a collector, Kristy. He's all yours."

She stood back. "No shit? I have to say, I'm a little blown away by that."

"Look. I don't need the headache. You have my word that we're not here collecting. I just need to sort through this mess so we don't have supers killing each other and exposing the rest of us."

"Ah. I get it now. They sent you here to separate the little warring factions of losers."

"I would have come regardless. Their conduct, Indie or not, is unbecoming and dangerous to the rest of us."

"Sorry to be the one to tell you, love, but you have no power down here. These fucked up Indies would just as soon drop you like a hot rock than hear you out. I don't know what all the geriatrics told you about these kids, but they're half in the bag, mentally. They are messed up in the headbone, and they are loyal to the almighty greenback."

This *was* news. "Whattayamean?"

"Charlie, most of the supers down here have never had any sort of formal training. They've never learned to construct shields. No shields equals brain defects on some level. I'm not saying all of them, but a good number of them are whack jobs."

"Not Max?"

She shook her head. "His power is about projecting, not injecting. There's a lot he could learn, but he's not interested. What I think he prefers is being the King of Fools, and trust me—there are plenty of those down here."

"Then why are you here, exactly?" I have to admit, it freaked me out to think she'd been following me.

Averting her eyes, she shrugged. "I knew you were coming the moment we heard the Atlantic City group was on its way. I didn't know about the murder until I got here."

I looked behind her. "You alone?"

She shrugged. "Never really alone, Charlie, you know better than that."

For an awkward moment, we both stood there, embraced by the paper-thin connection of sisterhood.

"I'm touched that you're looking out for me, Kristy. I'll be sure to let our mother know that you really do care." I shot her a smile to tell her know I was busting her chops.

"Well, we think this might be a good opportunity to ask Max if he'd like to rethink our initial offer." Kristy's eyes softened as she looked at me. "Just be careful down here, Charlie. It's one thing to face a powerful super like Malecon, but a whole different ballgame when there is a pack mentality. These Indies stick together and they have a compunction about firing on anyone threatening them. Keep that crazy ass friend of yours close by."

Nodding, I picked up a vibration I was certain she wouldn't have wanted me to feel. There was no love lost between Danica and Kristy. Bad blood was an understatement. "You came here to *warn me*?"

Jamming her hands in her leather jacket, a slight blush rose to her cheeks. "I been doing this a lot longer than you have. I just…yeah…" She shrugged her emotions away. "Maybe."

I lowered my voice to a whisper. "Would you do something for me?"

"That depends." Her voice immediately became

icy again.

"Do you think you and I could sit down for dinner...like two normal people? Like sisters? So far, every contact we've ever had has been work-related. We've not ever had time to just sit down and just talk."

"When?"

"How about tonight? Eight o'clock?"

She thought a moment. I felt her hesitation. "Sure. Why not?"

I smiled. Not in my wildest dreams had I ever imagined Kristy and I being cordial enough to actually have dinner together. For a kid who spent her childhood being passed around from one foster home to the next, the thought of bonding with my only sibling thrilled me. "There's an Italian place across from The Pentagon. Amici's."

She nodded. "Just you, though, right?"

"Of course."

"Good. Fine. Then eight o'clock it is."

I felt her trepidation like church bells. "Don't be so worried. I brought back up and as soon as we deal with these amateurs, I'm out of here."

She nodded. "Be careful, Charlie. This is going to get worse before it gets better."

"Why do you say that?"

"Townsend Briggs is a nut job."

☙☙❧❧

We all sat around the big glass table in our spacious penthouse, waiting for Delta to finish her report of her findings, which wasn't much more than she'd already reported.

"The knives used were all the ones used in Max's

show. No surprise there. There were no witnesses, the place was cleaned up, but not cop clean. I need an autopsy done. Is that possible?"

I nodded. "I'll make some calls and see what we can do." I made eye contact with Bailey, who jumped up and went into the other room to make that call.

I turned to Nick. "I also need to see the videos from that night. See who came and went. Do you know anyone at the casino that could do that for us?"

Nick nodded. "I should be able to swing that. It's good to have people indebted to you."

Delta raised an eyebrow. I knew working with a gangster element was making her butt itch, but we needed Nick Harper. "I'll be sure to keep that in mind."

Nick stared at her and, thankfully, opted to keep his rebuttal to himself.

I continued on. "I'm going to need to speak with this Townsend and his people for a more thorough investigation. Can that be arranged?"

"Why?" Danica asked. "We know he did it."

"Actually, we don't," Delta said. "He may have had a part in it, but we can't call him guilty until we know for sure. Besides, the working theory is that it was more than one person."

"Then what?" Danica asked. "We find him and....kill him?"

Delta locked eyes with me. It was my call. "To be honest, I haven't thought that far down the road."

"You need to start," Nick said. Did he ever take those shades off? "Because this is a small town and there are eyes and ears everywhere. Trust me on that. My guys will dig something up, but you need to know what the endgame is here."

I nodded, suddenly feeling the pressure of the

hunt. "Fine. Until then, we can't run around accusing people. Has anyone heard from Townsend? Seen him?"

Nick put his phone to his ear. "I'll get his twenty within the hour. If I can't, then I'm firing a butt load of people."

"Moving on," Danica said, winking at Nick. "Here's what we got from Max and Jasmine." Danica slid a piece of paper across the table. "I have the boys doing background on all the names."

I perused the piece of paper and nodded. It was just basic stats so far. "Good job. So, what do we know about Hannah?"

"No love connection with Max. She was strictly his assistant, but she *did* come from Atlantic City. She'd worked with Townsend prior to coming to Vegas, also as an assistant. Apparently, he was pretty verbally abusive to his staff. Max says she didn't say much about him, just that he was an asshole."

"Were she and Townsend lovers?"

"Max didn't think so."

"But he wasn't sure?"

"Not at all. He offered up an opinion that maybe she'd made the move and was rejected, but he had nothing positive."

"What about the rest?"

Danica patted her closed Vidbook lying on the table. "Once the boys track down some info, I'll let you know."

"Now, what about this Briggs guy?" Nick asked. "What do we know about him?"

"Max repeated the same story he told you, Clark. Townsend Briggs came here for a piece of Max's action. He wanted a grander stage and bigger audience than what he had in Atlantic City. Max rejected the offer and now…well…now there's trouble."

"These guys from Atlantic City," Nick started, "Are they…card counters?"

Danica and I exchanged glances. Card counting was the least of their worries where this crowd was concerned. "Not that we know of. Why?"

Rising, Nick motioned to his driver. "I'm gonna run to a couple casinos and see who's having any issues with your band of merry gamblers." When Nick got to the door, he turned. "Almost forgot. I have great seats at *Cirque du Soleil's* water show for all of you. Take a moment, will you, to enjoy some hospitality? It's a great show. Late seating. Your tickets are at will-call under Danica's name."

When he left, Delta was shaking her head. "Dani, have you lost your mind getting involved with a gangster? What were you thinking?"

Danica held her hand up in that ghetto girl way. "We're not really involved, Storm. We hang out. We do dinner. We talk. I'm eye candy with a brain in a town full of brainless eye candy. No worries. Besides, we need Nick's connections, and I've always wanted to go to Cirque."

"It's not wise to be indebted to crooks, Dani. When they say there's no honor among thieves, with the exception of Taylor, that's true."

"Nick's not like that."

"Of course he is! He's a gangster, for God's sake! He didn't get what he has by being a nice guy. He's gonna want payback for all the man hours his people are putting in."

I could see Danica's dander rising, so I stepped in. "Del, I have a pretty good gut about these things, and Nick's on the up and up. He's just being a friend to Dani."

She chucked. "Oh really? Got a lot of faith in your gut, do you?"

I nodded. "I do. I'm…seldom wrong about people." Delta knew we were special, but she had never asked for specifics and we'd never offered them up, though we had talked about doing so sooner than later.

"And you think he's on the up and up with us?"

"I do."

Delta shook her head. "Bad business being in bed with the mob, but I guess if he can get us what we need, and you guys trust him, so be it."

I studied Delta a moment. I'd met her through Finn, and she had turned out to be one of the greatest women I'd ever met, like a supernatural in so many ways. She and her people were every bit as tenacious and special as me and my people. She was a welcome addition to our little group.

"Well I, for one, want to go to the show," Danica said, pushing away from the table. "Can we take a breather from all this later and go to the show?"

They looked at me.

What could I say? No? "I'll meet you guys there. I'm having dinner with…umm."

Danica cocked her head. "With…umm…who?"

"Kristy."

All three of them stared at me.

"That bitch is here?" Danica asked, not bothering to hide her disdain.

I nodded. "I ran into her this afternoon."

"Ran into? She here for Max?"

I thought about my answer for a minute. "You know, I think she's here for me."

"Oh bullshit, Clark. I'm sorry. I know you

desperately want to believe that, but Kristy is..." She shook her head. "She's after whatever it is she really came here for."

"I don't think so. And even if she is, I'm okay with that. The fact that she even agreed to have dinner is enough for me."

Danica cut her eyes over at Delta, who raised her hands in the air. "I'm out. You have dinner with your sister and we'll meet you at will-call." Delta shoved her aging 357-magnum into her shoulder holster. "Dani?"

Danica was fairly glaring at me by now. She truly hated Kristy. The first time they'd met, Dani had held her Glock up to Kristy's face and would have blown her head off if I'd let her. I was pretty sure Kristy felt the same way. You just don't get over something like that.

"Dani, it's okay, really. She's my sister. I have so many questions. So much I need to say to her. Someone had to extend the olive branch. Who cares which of us it is?"

"She's a nut job, Clark. You remember that, okay?"

An hour later, I met that *nut job* for dinner.

☙❧

We didn't hug. Kristy was wearing the same clothes she had been wearing when she pulled me into the alley.

"You're surprised," I said.

"You didn't read me?"

I smiled as I slid into the sparkly red booth. "Of course not, but am I wrong? You're surprised."

She looked around the corner. "I figured Butch

would try to talk you out of it. I'm not her favorite person."

"Can we put that on the table right now?"

"Put what on the table? Your best friend the Pit Bull? Sure." Kristy waved the waiter over.

"I'd like to explain Danica before we do anything else. She is easily misunderstood, but she's been my best friend for more than half my life. She's not just pulled that gun on people...she's used it more than once to save my life. In a world where you can trust fewer and fewer people, I'm fortunate to have a friend who has my back regardless of the monsters we might face."

"Okay, okay, Jesus. If I didn't know better, I'd think you were in love with her."

I didn't skip a beat. "I am. With who she is. She is the most amazing woman I have ever met. She loves me and knows me well enough to realize I would meet you regardless of what she thinks of you. She made no effort to talk me out of coming."

"But?"

"But I am not in love with her, nor is she in love with me. We are...two pieces of the same puzzle."

Kristy nodded. "Fine. You want me to lay off her, I will, but I won't ever turn my back to her."

The waiter came by, offering menus and specials. We both ordered iced tea at the same time and laughed about it.

"I don't drink," she said matter of factly.

I nodded in understanding. "Neither do I."

"The last time I was drunk, I set a barn on fire," she explained. Her laughter was light, her words were not. "There was a time when I had no idea what all I could or couldn't do. I was like a live wire in water."

"Pretty incredible powers you have, though."

Unfolding the napkin, she laid it across her lap. That was when I realized she had hands exactly like our mother. "Can't say I sat around as a little girl dreaming about the day I could shoot lightning from my fingertips, but I suppose it could have been worse." She opened the menu. "It was worse for a lot of those kids, though. In retrospect, I got off easier than some of those kids who never made it out."

"I can't even imagine."

She shook her head. "No, you can't. What they did to us...what they do, is nothing short of horrific." She looked away. "How's mom?"

I swallowed hard. Kristy's anger at the world was justified. My father had taken her all around the world to escape a fate he eventually succumbed to. For nine years, my mother remained in hiding in a psychiatric ward so Genesys couldn't reach her, and so she could be near me. Our father took Kristy out of the country and never brought her back. The last time Kristy had seen our mother was when she was three.

"She's very happy. Lives on the beach with a really nice man. I don't know if you remember Jig, our grandmother, but she's a fiery old thing."

"Powers?" She lowered the menu. Her pupils were pinpricks and the color was almost a lavender.

I shrugged. "No idea. It never really came up. Why?"

"Well, unless we are adopted, one of them had to have powers."

I'd never given it much thought, and this surprised me. Surely Tricia would have told me if she had powers. "I didn't pick anything up." Suddenly, I stared at her. She was tall, blonde, statuesque, while I was not as tall and quite brunette. We looked nothing alike. It made me wonder.

She nodded and pushed the menu across the table. "Next time you see her, ask. You'll know the truth before it leaves her lips anyway."

"I never...it didn't—"

She leaned over on her menu. "You were *erased*, Charlie. That bastard took all of your memories. Of course it wouldn't dawn on you. Fragments of your childhood can't make a complete picture of the truth."

She had no idea what it was like to have her memory completely erased. I had not one memory from my childhood. Not even a fragment. He had erased it for fear of Genesys locating me and reading my mind. So instead of having memories of my childhood, I had a blank slate.

Completely blank.

"It wasn't until I met you that my own childhood picture started filling in. How our bastard of a father handled you. How Hayward so easily turned me over to the source of all our woes and never once looked back. All those years, I could never connect the dots... until I met you." She waited while the waiter brought our iced tea.

I wasn't ready to order yet, the words swimming before my face. How had I missed this?

Unexpectedly, Kristy laid her hand on my forearm. Like Cinder's hands always were, they were warmer than a natural's. "I've been wrestling with saying anything to you, Charlie, because I'm sure that finding our mother made you really happy. And who knows? I could be wrong." She shrugged. "Maybe it skipped a generation."

Looking up, I locked eyes with hers. "Well,

there's one way to find out. Do you want the answer?"

She shook her head. "Nope. I don't really care about my past or whoever's DNA I carry. It's really not important to me anymore. There was a time I wanted to know, but no longer."

The possibility that we had been adopted by Hayward had never occurred to me. How could it? I had no memories of anything.

The waiter came back and I ordered lobster ravioli and she ordered a Caesar salad.

"What *is* important to you, Kristy? What makes you happy?" The questions came out of my mouth before I even knew they were there.

She looked down at her hand still on me and lifted it off. "To be honest, Charlie, I can't remember what happy feels like. I left that emotion behind when Genesys tortured me with those gruesome experiments. Happy became a thing of the past. Maybe I'll find happy again once they're totally destroyed, but there are more important things in my life than my happiness."

"And then what? What will you do once your vengeance is sated?"

"I haven't a clue. I don't look back and I seldom look ahead. I live in the moment. I learned as a guinea pig that that was all I had...this moment." She looked away. "Prolonged torture will do that to a person." Bitterness oozed from every syllable.

We couldn't have been any more different than at *this* moment. I could not fathom the torture she'd experienced at the hands of Genesys and had a hard time realizing that her childhood was actually worse than mine. I was just unloved. She was tortured. I didn't know what to say.

Kristy leaned back. "So, how's your school? I

hear you took over for Melika."

I grinned slightly. She was a master at changing the subject. "Been keeping tabs on me?"

She chuckled. "You're hard to miss, Charlie. The supernatural world is all abuzz about your Alaskan experience and the way you guys sank that ship. Your name is spoken with a great deal of respect in our world."

Her sense of pride was so strong I felt it through my shields.

"Well, being a mentor is a helluva lot of work and more responsibility than I ever thought I'd have, but…well…they're my family and it's what I do now."

"Between being a mentor and doing this shit down here, how do you find time for a relationship? Is there anybody special in your life, or are you all work and no play?"

I remembered Danica's admonition not to trust her, but I couldn't bring myself to shut down or shut her out. "There isn't at the moment, no. My life is too crazy right now to drag another woman into it."

Kristy tilted her head at me and I knew what she was going to say before she said it. "You're gay?"

I laughed. "I am."

A genuine smile broke across her face as she picked up her tea. "Man, you had a buncha closets to break out of, huh?"

We both laughed, and I realized that beneath her hardened exterior, there was a woman…my sister… yearning to be loved.

"I'd heard a rumor that you and Tiponi Redhawk were lovers, but I chalked it up to a wicked rumor."

"Past tense. Tip and I go way back, but there's no present and no future there. I'm single and by my recent past record, will probably be that way for some time."

"You and that big Indian, eh? You don't look like you belong together."

I swirled the ice around in my tea as I thought about the appropriate reply. "We don't. What about you?"

She shook her head. "Not interested. Men bore women. Women are too needy. I prefer my own company most of the time. If I need a release, there's always some man willing to help me out." She laughed. "Relationships are more trouble than they're worth."

When she excused herself to go wash up, I pulled out my Vidbook. "Just checking in," I said to Danica, who answered in half a ring.

"I appreciate that. Spoke with Sal, and everything is fine at the chateau. Apparently, Shila the Wonder Dog is learning tricks that involve fire."

"Go figure."

"Cinder's changed since you gave her that puppy."

"*I* didn't."

She smiled. "No, but you let her keep it, and it was the best no call you ever made. We're seeing a whole new side of that kid."

I nodded. "How are the triplets?"

"Sal said they are eager students and she's enjoying them. Alexei is her favorite. Cutting sense of humor. Everything is fine at home, Clark. Are you okay?"

"I'm good. It's…just so strange to be sitting here with my sister having a nice conversation. I'm more used to her attacking me with lightning bolts."

"Yeah, weird. If you need to make a getaway,

give me a call."

"I don't think that will be necessary, but thank you. Okay, my food is here. I'll see you at will-call."

"Don't be late."

Just as I hung up, I felt it. Powerful supernatural energy that made me turn my head and glance out the large plate glass window I sat fifteen feet from.

There were Townsend's girls. Three of them, and they were staring right at me. The moment I locked eyes with the tall brunette, everything slowed down.

Everything.

It was as if I was caught in a time warp, and as the large window imploded, huge shards of glass sliced through the air toward my face. End over end they came, and I knew this was going to hurt. Even as I raised my hands for a shield, I knew there wasn't enough time. The entire window came at me like glass bullets, slowly cutting through time and space.

I was screwed.

And then, out of the corner of my eye, came Kristy. Like a ghost or mirage, she shimmered as she moved, faster than my eye could follow, electricity crackling all around her. She was something non-human at that moment...more like a bundle of energy moving faster than the naked eye could follow.

Leaping in front of me and I heard myself scream, "No!" in a voice that sounded detached from my body.

As she sailed in front of me, the glass shards melted into marbles and beads before hitting her and bouncing on the floor like marbles. The heat from her body was so intense, the wine menu melted along with the plastic flowers in the vase.

As the glass fell harmlessly around us, Kristy landed with a loud thump on the floor, completely winding her.

The warm desert air quickly entered through the open window, but that was all that came through the opening, as the three women stood there gawking at their epic failure.

Recovering my senses, I jumped in front of Kristy, arms up, hands pushed forward, and sent a wave of energy out the window at our attackers, who toppled back into the street, narrowly missing being run over by a taxi that swerved and a tour bus that slammed on its brakes.

Running to the window, I considered going after them, but they took off. Instead, I returned to my sister, who was on her hands and knees.

As I helped Kristy to her feet, blood ran down her forehead. "You've been hit." Holding her head in my hands, I surveyed the damage.

At that moment, something happened between us. It was as if everything that had ever happened, or not happened, didn't matter anymore. Wounds healed, scars lessened, and hearts repaired. I had fallen into her *in the moment* attitude about life—and at *this* moment, *we* needed to kick someone's ass. You don't come after my sister and think I'm going to let you walk away.

As Danica would say, "Oh hail no."

"I say we hit back," she said, pulling the shard of glass from her forehead. "You up for it, or do you have to check with the nearly dead first?"

"Lead the way, sis."

We both looked down at the bloody shard of glass before she said, "Last one to land a punch is a rotten egg." Then she leapt through the now open window with me right behind her, hands at the ready. We would not be snuck up on again.

Whatever Genesys had done to my sister had given her abilities far beyond our different genetic makeup. I thought her lightning bolt was impressive, but that woman could move like greased lightning. I was barely out the window and onto the sidewalk when I saw her turn a corner, expletives flying along with her blonde hair.

Not to be outdone, I kicked it into fifth gear and realized there was another way out of the street they ran onto. "I'll head them off," I huffed, cutting away from the chase to run parallel through a parking lot. As I rounded the corner, all three saw me and stopped. Two turned when they realized doing so meant running into Kristy. Whirling back to me, I see could that, in *their* eyes, I was the lesser of the two evils.

"You owe us dinner," I said, raising my hands and lowering my shields. There were two movers and a...I couldn't make out the third one, so I raised my shields.

"Fuck you," came a snotty reply from one of the movers. These girls were young—early twenties, maybe. When she lifted her hand, I gave her another dose of my shield. That knocked them both back into trashcans, leaving me facing the third.

"Is that all you've got, bitch?" She fairly sneered. Her short pixie hair was platinum white with blue tips, and she had these ice blue eyes filled with hatred.

"No, sweet pea, that's where you're wrong. That's not all she's got. She's got *me*." Kristy rounded the corner, and with a flick of her wrist shot what looked like a forked lightning bolt from her fingertips.

Pixie's response told me what she was, and though I'd never seen one before, I'd heard how lethal they could be and immediately threw a force field around myself.

As the air around us dropped forty degrees, Pixie created a shield out of...ice? Water? I had no idea. All I knew was she had stopped Kristy's bolts with an ice shield, and when one of the movers rose, she threw the shield at Kristy, who could not completely get out of the way.

"Kristy!"

Too late, the block of ice crashed into her, sending her against a brick wall. A loud whooshing sound escaped her lips as she crumpled to the ground.

Pixie returned her attention to me. "Your turn, old lady."

Old lady? I was only six or seven years older than they were. Oh, how I wished I'd brought Cinder with me.

As Pixie once again lowered the temperature on her way to another ice sculpture, the other two were getting to their feet. I knew by Kristy's energy that she was hurt, but not fatally, a condition I would share with her if I didn't figure a way out of this.

"Why are you doing this?" I asked, watching the two movers approach Pixie. I just needed two more steps and—

BAM!

Using what little telekinetic power I possess, I managed to pull one of those metal emergency ladders down on top of one of the movers, who crumpled like a soda can beneath a car tire. I was pretty sure I'd just killed her. I felt no emotions from her at all.

Two against one. The odds were getting better.

That was when I remembered Dani's gun. Reaching into my purse, the handle felt cool in my hand. When I whipped that little baby out, the look on

Pixie's face was priceless.

"Now ladies. Hands down."

Neither moved.

"Put your goddamned hands down."

Pixie lowered hers. The mover followed suit.

"Now. What in the hell is this about? Why are you so hell bent on picking on two people who could drop you like a fucking stone?"

Pixie stared at me. "A gun? Really?" She shook her head with disgust. "If you could *drop us like a stone*, you wouldn't *need* a fucking gun."

I looked at it before pointing it at her. "Really."

"Why bother having powers if you're going to act like a natural? How pathetically boring." Pixie's shirt fell away from her neck and I could see she was covered with tattoos. "You're just as weak as they are." She turned to the mover and motioned with her head. "She doesn't have the guts."

Throwing her hands up toward me, the mover tried to knock the gun out of my hands, but only managed to knock my arm away. It gave Pixie just enough time to bridge the distance between us and wrap her arms around me, pinning the gun to my thigh.

"Nighty night, Echo."

As I struggled to get free, she turned into a human popsicle. It was like a giant ice cube had wrapped itself around me. My body began to get very, very cold. The gun, useless at my side, felt frozen in my hand and fell from my grip, clattering to the dirty street. I tried to muster up an offensive shield, but was too cold to concentrate.

Then I saw Kristy struggling to get to her feet. The mover saw my gaze and followed it, a sardonic smile on her lips as she turned towards my sister to deliver the deathblow.

As her hands rose, I reached deep inside me for a part of myself I had only seen on the rarest of occasions: that part of me that was all super and no natural. It was the most mammalian aspect of my being, and what separated me from the rest of the world, and I tapped into the feral aspect of myself so raw and so gritty, it frightened even me. I think of it as "The Beast."

And we needed that Beast right now.

Feeling the buildup of raw energy, I knew this would be the only chance I would have to save my sister. From the core of my supremely created genetic makeup, I let her rip, and the power I threw out dislodged Pixie's arms from around me and hurled her so high and so hard, it was like she'd been shot out of a cannon.

As all three pairs of eyes watched her whomp hard to the ground, the mover wheeled toward me, hands at the ready. She could throw anything at me that was within her reach.

And I had nothing left.

The Beast taps every ounce of my psychic energy. All I could do was make a play for the gun, which skittered as if kicked, fifteen feet away, compliments of the mover.

Slowly turning to face her, I steeled myself for the worst. Images flew past my mind's eye like playing cards being flipped at the corner. I saw the bayou. Melika. Tip sharing my bed. Jacob Marley showing me how to bow energy.

Bow. As in rainbow or bow and arrow. To *bow your energy* means to create an arc so that energy being directed at you travels up in the arc and boomerangs back to the source. We had worked on it a few times when I was a kid, but it wasn't anything I had ever mastered. I didn't even know if I had enough energy to create a bow, and I wasn't sure it would even be strong enough to do what was needed.

Then I remembered who I was and who *they* were.

They were not *me*.

I reached down deeper.

The mover threw energy at me. It wasn't her strongest, nor was it well-directed. Lack of training. Poor focus. Unaware. Whatever the reason, she was out of her league, and when her energy hit my bow and rolled over the top, it returned to hit her smack in the middle of her chest, knocking her back against a bunch of trashcans that clattered all around as she flailed for balance.

"Fucking bitch!"

Using two trashcans to help herself up, she glared so hard at me, she didn't see Kristy raise up to her knees and fire a bolt of something into the metal trash can the mover's hand rested on. Whatever that bolt was, it electrocuted the mover to such a degree, she could not remove her hand from the can, which was the perfect conductor for Kristy's energy.

"Kristy—"

She did not look at me. Instead, she kept shooting this intense white energy at the trashcans. The mover was vibrating and smoking, and the smell of burnt hair filled the air.

"Kristy—"

She was now on her feet walking toward the mover, her face a mask of red hot anger. The bolt of lightning increased its intensity until the woman fell to the ground, smoking and dead. The stench of burning hair permeated the air as the body smoldered.

As Kristy stood over her, she retracted the bolt and glowered down at the mover. "You should have killed me when you had the chance."

I joined Kristy at the feet of the dead mover. The stench of scorched flesh and death filled my nostrils. "You killed her," I said, without emotion.

"Yep." Turning, Kristy walked over to Pixie and grabbed the front of her shirt, pulling her to her feet. "Now we can get some answers." Kristy pushed Pixie against a wall. Pixie's knees went weak, but Kristy held her up there with one hand. "Stand up, asswipe."

Pixie's eyes rolled up, but Kristy shook her and then slapped her hard, the sound bouncing off the buildings.

Now, *I* was out of her league.

"Who the hell sent you and why?"

Pixie blinked and tried to focus on Kristy's face. "Eat me."

Kristy grabbed Pixie's face in one hand and squeezed it, her hand glowing slightly as her power centered only on her hand. Pixie's eyes opened wide.

As Pixie lifted her right hand, I pinned it to the wall with the last energy I had left. "Answer the question," I said. I cast a quick glance at Kristy. Her forehead cut had left her bleeding pretty badly. She looked very scary with her angry eyes and bloody face.

"Here's the thing," Kristy said conversationally, releasing Pixie's face. "You tell us what we need to know and you can walk away to live your life. You take up anymore of our time and I'll burn you so bad, you'll wish I'd have killed you. Are we clear? You've got five seconds to tell us everything we need to know."

Pixie looked at me. She was finally afraid. So was

I. Kristy wasn't bluffing and I didn't want to see what Kristy would do to her.

"Townsend Briggs ordered it." She looked at me. "You," she said, motioning with her chin to me. "Not you."

"Not me? What am I, collateral damage?" Kristy asked.

She nodded. "He wants *her* killed. We've failed twice. There won't be a third chance."

"I don't die very easily," I said.

"No shit."

Kristy heated her hand up once more and I wondered what they had to have done to her in the labs to give her such power. "Why? Why is he gunning for Echo? Doesn't he know who she is? Doesn't he know what a shit storm he's starting by doing this?"

"Knows and doesn't care. She stands in his way."

"When *his* people start dying, will he care?"

She shrugged. "Probably not. He's not the caring type."

"Why does he want her dead?"

Pixie glared at Kristy, then the venom seemed to evaporate from her. "He set up a really good gig here. He's got movers winning at craps and roulette, thinkers winning at poker and twenty-one, and he's smart enough to make sure we don't win so big that people notice. We've made a small fortune skipping from one casino to the next. It's been very profitable. He's not willing to give that up or to let her mess with this gig."

"With the exception of his magic show, right? He can't seem to make that happen for himself, can he?"

She tried to shrug. "Not too much longer.

Townsend is superior to that wiener, Max. Su-peer-e-or."

Kristy rolled her eyes at me. "Okay, look, Fantasy Fay, your boss/boyfriend/—"

"Leader. He's our leader."

"Your *leader* has made a gross error in judgment by coming after my sister. Gross. Error. I'm gonna give you one chance to tell me where he is. And you might want to be very careful about what comes out of your mouth or I will melt it shut. *Comprende?*"

Her eyes grew wide and she looked over at me.

I shrugged. "She'll do it. Look at what she did your buddy over there. And if you lie, she will come after you. She has the means and the power to do so. So consider your next words very carefully."

Kristy nodded. "If you don't want to spend the rest of your life as a burn victim looking over your shoulder, I suggest you tell us where we can find him."

"He left town to pick someone up in Palm Springs. He...he won't be back until late tomorrow night."

"And by back, you mean..."

"Back in town. No one knows where he stays."

"What else do we need to know, Buttercup? How many of you are there from Atlantic City?"

"Thirteen. No. Twelve. Wait."

"What do you know about the girl who was murdered?"

She blinked and swallowed hard. "Wasn't my job."

"Not what I asked, Tinkerbell."

"I...I don't know. I swear. He gave us all a job to do. M...mine...ours was to eliminate Echo. We didn't—"

Kristy tightened her grip. "Eliminate? You mean *kill*, right? Your job was to kill my sister?" Kristy's aura was turning from grey to black. This was going to go south in a heartbeat. So I reached out and touched Kristy's shoulder.

"She's told the truth. All of it. Let her go."

Kristy was still glaring at Pixie, her aura changing to charcoal. "You tell your *leader*, if anything happens to my sister, *anything at all*, I will hunt each and every one of you down and one-by-one slowly fry you from the inside out until your eyes burst and your tongue swells so big you suffocate on it. I will make sure that your remaining days on this planet are filled with horror. Any questions?"

She shook her head. "None."

Kristy backed off. "Raise your hands and lose your life. Now, get the fuck out of here."

Pixie glanced down at the woman conked by the fire escape. "Are they both—"

"Dead," I replied. "You see we don't mess around, either. So you tell Townsend to get his ass back in town and meet me at the fountain in front of the Bellagio at six p.m. tomorrow. If he fails to show up, and makes us come after him, that shit storm my sister mentioned will land right in his lap. Now get the hell out of here before she decides to cook you like a slice of bacon."

Pixie took off running.

Kristy looked at me. "Slice of bacon?"

I shrugged. "I'm hungry. We never got dinner."

She chuckled. "We need to get the hell out ourselves."

Nodding, I looked at the two women lying on the ground.

"Don't give it a second thought, Charlie. They

would have cut you to ribbons with glass shards. We were the better team today." Kristy started walking briskly away. "I've got cleaners if you want me to send for them."

I looked back over my shoulder. "Screw it. It's Vegas."

She nodded. "Sure is."

I caught up to her long strides. "You saved me at the restaurant. Thank you for that."

She kept walking, her hand in the air. "You did the same for me. We're even."

"Kristy?"

She turned. "You're welcome."

"No. Thank you for meeting me for dinner."

"Ditto. Sorry we were interrupted."

"I'm just glad you were there. I can't believe Briggs is so threatened by me that he sent goons after me."

"Pay attention to that, Charlie. They won't stop just because they failed twice. You don't seem to understand how important you've become. I'm not just talking about mentoring, either. You've made a name for yourself and now that your mentor is…retiring, people are going to come gunning for you."

"Why? Nobody came after Melika."

"That you know of. Why do you think she chose the bayou? It's too hard for anyone to sneak up on you there." She leveled her gaze. "You never realized that, huh?"

I shook my head. "I figured there were many reasons."

Kristy nodded. "It's safer there. As a matter of fact, I wish you still lived there."

I nodded. "Sometimes, so do I. Where were you

off to?"

"Well, I need to head on out to Los Angeles, but I can stay if you need me to."

It wasn't so much that I needed her to stay as it was I wanted her to stay, but even that selfish part of me was malnourished. Shaking my head, I joined her and we walked out of the alley and onto the side road running parallel to the main drag. "You don't have to do that. My people are here with me."

She looked down at me a moment before reaching out to touch my ear, the ear she had bitten when we were little.

"I never apologized for biting you." Her voice was softer than I'd ever heard it.

"It's okay. I never apologized for taking your doll."

"You sure you're going to be okay here?" She reached up and wiped some of the blood off her eyebrow.

"I'll be fine, really. Once I get this all straightened out, I'll be heading straight for home. I'm trying to settle in to the new place."

She tilted her head as she studied me. "You miss Louisiana, don't you?"

I nodded. "The bayou. I miss the river."

"What else?"

How could she know? "Jacob Marley. I really miss him."

She nodded. "What else?"

"Nothing."

She shook her head. "I can hear it in your voice. It's a woman, isn't it? Is it that cop?"

Funny thing was, I did, but hers wasn't the name on the tip of my tongue…pun intended. "Not her."

"Oh my god, please don't tell me you were in love with Redhawk. That Indian pisses everyone off."

"I'm not. I just miss her."

"But you were together, right?"

I nodded. "A long time ago." When we came to the corner, I said, "You need to get that head sewn up."

"Will do"

"Thank you. For everything."

"No problem. We need to split up here, Charlie. They could be sending others after us. Go on now. Be careful. Stay safe. Those kids need you."

I wanted to hug her, but neither of us made the move. As she walked away, my Vidbook buzzed. It was Danica.

"Where in the hell are you?"

Watching my sister walk away, I felt the sting of tears in my eyes. "You'll never believe it."

※※※※

I had Mario and Danica swing by to pick me up outside of the Harley store on the main drag. It is hard to miss the giant Harley busting out of the storefront, so meeting them there was a sure bet.

While I waited, I went over all the things Pixie had said. Yes, she'd told the truth, but that didn't explain why Townsend would be foolish enough to start a war with *me*. It was a stupid thing for him to do. It was one thing to go after Max's people; I could even understand some of that twisted logic. But me? Something wasn't right. Townsend had sent his girl goons after us at Jasmine's shop, and at first, I'd thought they were out to get Max. When they showed up here, I realized I'd been wrong about that.

They'd come for me. Why?

The numbers weren't adding up.

Sirens in the distance told me someone had found the two dead girls in the alley. Their deaths would be listed as crushed by a falling ladder and electrocution. I didn't really care. They did not completed their task. I wondered if *they* knew why I'd become Townsend Briggs's target?

"Going my way?" Danica asked, opening the door of the Navigator.

When I got in and she saw me, her face fell, and she leaned forward to ask Mario to raise the clear partition between the seats.

I hadn't really assessed how I looked after being battered about.

"What. The. Fuck. Happened. To. You?" Turning around, she looked to see if we were being followed. "Are you okay? Where is your sister? What the hell is going on?"

"Dani, I'm fine. Kristy saved my life, and apparently it's a life Townsend Briggs has tried twice to snuff out." I told her about Pixie and the restaurant and how Kristy had leapt in the way of the shards of glass.

Danica simply stared.

"It was dicey for a moment there. Had Kristy not come to—" I shook my head. My hands were shaking. "She was incredible, Dani."

"You're sure she didn't have anything to do with it?"

"Absolutely. She took a really hard hit, and if she'd wanted me dead, she would have let those shards turn me into human Swiss cheese. No, my sister kept me from lacerations that, if not deadly, would have scarred my face for life if not killed me."

"But why you? We haven't really begun our investigation. You've never even met that asshole before. We've certainly not threatened anyone. Yet. That's gonna change first chance I get."

"Uh uh. We're not here to play their little battle games, Dani. We need to find out who killed Hannah, and—"

"Isn't it obvious?"

"It wasn't Townsend," I said. "That much I know. He gets others to do his dirty work. He's the man behind the curtain. That's why he sent the girls. He's a coward."

"And you both let this Pixie just *walk* away?" She shook her head. "You should have let the lightning rod render her into pieces."

"We don't want or need supers killing each other, Dani. Once she was neutralized, it was time to get answers and then let her go. Killing is their way, not ours."

"And you're sure you're okay. You don't look okay."

What could I say? That they'd scared the crap out of me? That Kristy scared the crap out of me? Her powers were beyond anything I had seen, with maybe the exception of Cinder. I was shaken, rattled and rolled, but I knew if Danica knew that, she'd start looking for Townsend right at this moment.

"I'm fine."

"Okay. What do we know about these bitches?"

"You can tell they are feral. They don't know how to use an eighth of their powers."

"Maybe not, but it sounds like they use them enough to get by. Nick said he was certain something was going down with two of them at a poker championship tomorrow at the Luxor. He's sending his best men to watch this kid to see how he does it. I didn't have the heart to tell him he wouldn't be able to find out."

"Name?"

"Vince Thomas. According to Nick, the kid never loses. Building quite a reputation."

I nodded. "See? They're stupid. They don't even know how to fly under the radar. Who's the other?"

"Female by the name of Joy. No last name, she just goes by Joy. She's a spinner."

"So she'll be there? How can Nick be so sure?"

"It's a tournament. They've signed up. He got his hands on the list of players."

I looked at Dani, realizing my body was beginning to stiffen up. "Wait. They *signed* up?"

"Yeah. Pretty ballsy, if you ask me."

"That could mean they are at the end of their run. If Townsend is as smart as he appears, it's possible he is rotating his people in and out of the casinos and is looking for a big score before going to ground."

"Well, he can't rotate them out of a tournament." Danica pinched the bridge of her nose. "A telepath could have free reign financially down here. As long as the dealer sees his cards, a halfway decent thinker would know everyone's hand."

"Oh, he'll win, all right. There's no doubt about that. They may not have trained their powers, but they sure as shit know about gambling, counting cards, and keeping track of everyone else's hands." I shuddered at the thought.

"You planning on stopping them?"

"Not yet. We need to get to the bottom of Hannah's death first. Max is going to have to go back on stage. We need to smoke Townsend Briggs out into the open." I stared out at the lights of the city and wondered what their enormous electricity bills must be like.

"Then what?" Danica asked.

"We need Townsend to see that Max isn't afraid, nor is he alone. If Max goes back on stage—"

"Townsend will send more goons after him. You're seriously going to use him as bait, Clark?"

Turning from the window, I explained my plan. "These Indies are untrained, right? They've spent more time learning how to beat Vegas than learning about, oh, I don't know, shield-building. If Nick can get another player into that tournament, we can try using him to read the players. This might give us a shot at finding out where Townsend Briggs is hiding out."

"I have no idea if Nick can do that. These tournaments are probably pretty regulated, but Nick can do just about anything here," Danica said softly. "Consider it done. Still…to do this well—"

"We need to be players."

Danica and I exchanged glances. "I think I see where you're going with this, Clark. Just who did you have in mind? And if you say who I think you're going to say—"

"She's the best there is. We can fly her down just for the night and then send her back to Melika."

Danica shook her head slowly. "Bad idea. The more time you two spend apart, the better. Besides, isn't she still pouting? What a flippin' head case."

"This isn't about my love life, Dani. This is—"

"An excuse to see her?" Her left eyebrow rose in question. "Is that what this is about?"

"Not even!"

She made a chuffing sound that sounded like "chyeah", and folded her arms across her chest. "Whatever. Just know that you aren't fooling me one bit. One night, Clark. She comes, does what she can, and then we ship her back. Deal?"

I nodded. "Deal."

As she turned from the conversation, I could have sworn I heard her mutter something about getting my own private jet.

∂∂℔℔

The Cirque water show was off-the-hook amazing, and we had the best dry seats in the house. I had to hand it to Nick Harper: That man could turn on the charm, and literally everyone knew him. I mean everyone. He looked like the dapper gangster he was, wearing a navy sports jacket, khaki slacks, black tasseled loafers, and slicked back hair. Everyone from waitresses to pit bosses waved or shook his hand along the way to the theater. He was obviously well-liked and in his element.

As much as I wanted to dislike him, that was becoming harder and harder to do.

While the show was a visual feast of colors and diving from moving platforms, I missed the first twenty minutes as I explained to Tip via Vidbook what I needed from her. To be honest, I was surprised she even answered.

"Can't you get someone else? Surely there are plenty of other telepaths who would love to come help the mighty Echo Branson."

I stared at her on the monitor. Her voice was icy cold, the antithesis of her smoldering eyes. She looked exhausted. Gaunt. I could tell the ordeal with Melika was getting to her. I needed to forgive her shortness and anger. What she was going through would make anyone else just as edgy and impatient. "You know that no one else is as good as you, Tip, and I need better than good for this. I need great. I'm afraid more people will die if we don't get to the bottom of this quickly."

Running her hand over her face, Tip blew out a big breath. "Honestly, Echo, I couldn't give two shits if the whole fucking paranormal community went up in flames. My one and only concern is Melika right now. One. And. Only. *Capisce?*"

As much as I didn't want to, I let it go. Because I finally had her in person, I was at least going to get some questions answered. "*Capisce.* How's Mel?"

Reluctantly, she told me Mel was in good spirits and that Malecon had been a godsend. He hovered, he read articles, quizzed doctors, and had generally taken over the care of our mentor. He was so attentive, Tip had finally warmed up to the idea that he was in Melika's life and would remain so until…until he wasn't any more. They were twins, after all, and nothing could break that bond.

"We're getting by. One fucked up day at a time, so you'll forgive me if I don't find your little drama worth listening to."

"You look exhausted," I said softly. "Are you taking enough time out for yours—"

"I'm fine."

There was that frosty, monosyllabic response again.

"It doesn't look that way, but whatever." I waited. When she did not ask about me, I offered it up any way. "I'm good. Thanks for asking. I can't seem to get a break from all the—"

"Not my concern, and frankly, I'd rather not hear it. You're exactly where you want to be, as usual. Stop whining about it. Is there anything else?"

My mouth was agape. She had never, ever spoken to me like that. "Anything else? Not from you." I snapped the Vidbook closed and returned to my seat.

"How did it go?" Danica asked.

I shook my head. "She said no."

Bailey and Danica both stared at me. "What the fuck? What's the matter with her?"

I shrugged.

"Did you tell her those bitches attacked you?"

Shaking my head, I pointed to the stage. "We can discuss it later. Right now, I'd really just like to enjoy the show."

And enjoy the show I did. It was as if every performer was one of us, they were that good.

"That was awesome," Bailey whispered to me. Threading her arm through mine, she giggled like a schoolgirl as the amazing acrobatics came to a close.

It was at this moment I realized how close Bailey and I had become, and how much I leaned on her. She'd really stepped up when I took over for Melika. I had needed a second in command, and she had more than risen to the occasion. So far, she'd been a rock... my rock, or at least a very strong member of Team Echo, and right now, our team needed a telepath.

☙☙☙☙

After the show, we went out to a nice, trendy club, had a drink, and then piled back in the car to head back to the Pentagon.

I'd explained my conversation with Tip to them. Danica muttered and cursed under her breath and stomped away. Bailey reached for my hand.

"I know that had to hurt, E. You have to know Tip's just in a really bad place. She's watching Melika slip through her fingers and there's nothing she can do. The helplessness for a woman who's always so in control must be devastating."

Devastating wasn't even close. My heart was torn in two. It seemed I wasn't able to console or help *anyone* at the moment.

But that was about to change.

Delta was meeting with a contact who knew something about the night of the murder. She had kicked solidly into cop mode and was a force of energy that made us all stand back in appreciation of her investigative skills.

"I should have gone with her," Danica said as we pulled in front of a fortuneteller's shop. "I don't like the idea of any of us roaming around alone. It's clearly not safe."

"She didn't want to scare off the contact, and, well Dani, you're not the subtlest of people."

She opened her mouth to reply, but couldn't fight the truth. "Shit. You know I hate it when you are right."

"Which is most of the time."

Bailey turned to Jasmine, who had been very quiet most of the night. "So Jasmine, you say this clairvoyant saw these events unfold and came to you about them?"

Jasmine shook her head. "No, I said she *saw* something big was going to go down. She has a good grasp of the Indie population because Townsend Briggs first sought her counsel when he arrived in Vegas. She stopped reading for him when she realized what he was up to."

"Is she afraid of him?"

Jasmine shrugged. "Not afraid…wary. There's a difference."

We all filed out except Jasmine.

"I'd like to check on Max, if you guys don't mind. I need to do everything I can to help him find the courage to go back on stage."

I nodded. "Good idea. We won't be long." Leaning into the driver's window, I asked Mario to drop her off and come right back for us.

As the SUV drove away, Danica and I started for the shop, but Bailey remained standing there watching the car drive off. "I still don't trust her, E."

"Join the club."

Bailey shook her head. "No, I don't mean in general. I mean with *this*. All of this. The hackles on my neck stand straight up whenever she's near. Can't you get a read on her? There's something…I don't know. Read her again, E. More carefully."

Danica laid her arm across Bailey's shoulders. "That girl would have to be plumb brain dead to try to cross Echo while we're here. And to be honest, anyone who messes twice with you deserves to be left in the desert for dead."

Bailey wasn't buying it. "It's more than that. It feels like she's keeping an eye on Max more than being concerned about him. I say we keep her out of the loop from here on out. Give her just enough intel to sate her."

I studied Bailey's eyes. They were wild, like a cougar's, sharp, intense, focused. I had to agree with Danica. Messing with us was a dead man's decision while these two were around.

"We can do that. Or, I can tell her to drop all her shields and do a deeper read of her. If she's not being straight up with us—"

Bailey shook her head. "No. Don't make it obvious. If she is playing both ends against the middle, it's best to keep her near. Maybe she'll lead us to where we want to go."

I looked at Danica, who nodded. "The vultures in the desert will have a nice dinner," Danica answered.

Bailey nodded. "I think that's a good idea, E. She's ringing all of my bells in a big way. I know my opinion doesn't count as much because of our... checkered history, but I'd rest easier if we kept her out of the inner circle."

"I understand," I said. "Better safe, eh?"

The three of us walked into the darkened chamber of Madame Lucille's Palm Reading and Tarot Card Shop. Like nearly every other clairvoyant I knew, the shop sold New Age beads, Celtic design jewelry, Native American do-dads, and an assortment of themed tarot cards. Behind the shop, through a purple and silver beaded curtain, we found Madame Lucille waiting for us.

"Come in, come in," she said, rising. I think she rose. It was hard to tell. She was a little person, about four feet tall at most with two eyes looking in opposite directions. "I'm Madame Lucille. I've been expecting you."

Madame Lucille was off my grid as well. Not independent and not trained, she'd spent the first half of her life as a carny, assisting the world-renowned Lady Sophia. It wasn't until Lady Sophia died that Madame Lucille stepped into her shoes with abilities far beyond that of her predecessor, a mere carny performer. In 1979, when the carnival came to Vegas, Lucille had stayed and opened her own shop. According to my notes, she was either dead on, or way off. Again, an untrained mind lacks the focus needed to utilize its inherent powers fully.

After the introductions, Madame Lucille climbed back in her chair and started shuffling a tattered deck of tarot cards with purple designs on the back. "I understand you want information pertaining to the murder of Max's assistant, Hannah."

We all nodded. I waited for her to lay down the cards, but she merely kept shuffling them.

"First off. Let me tell you straight away that we who live here are no fans of the Indies. They are a danger to everyone, the way they flaunt their powers." Her face reminded me of an apple-face doll with wrinkles upon wrinkles. Her hands, those of dwarfism, were gnarled from arthritis, and I wasn't sure which eye was looking at me. "And that Townsend Briggs is the worst of 'em all."

"Why is that?"

"I can understand those young kids pursuing easy money in the casinos. God knows casinos can afford it. But Briggs? That man is after fame, and that's a danger to us all unless that fame comes to one who understands and values the importance of our remaining underground."

"And you don't think Townsend Briggs values that?"

"He values fame. Covets it, really. He is a hazard, and his reckless pursuit of it has already left one dead, perhaps more."

"What can you tell us about that night?"

"I saw lots of shadows, deception, subterfuge. People coming and going, lots of confusion." She closed her eyes and thought for a moment before tapping her finger on her chin and opening her eyes. Then she flipped over a single card. It was Justice.

Danica cut her eyes to me. I had no clue.

"The upright Justice card means a favorable resolution to a conflict or legal action. Contracts, settlements, or divorce will be in their favor. Clarity, fairness, and most of all...judgment." She looked up at me.

"What?"

"The judgment is surrounding *you*."

"Me?"

Danica sat up straighter and looked out the beaded curtain, suddenly on high alert. Her hand reached into her Coach bag and stayed there.

Madame Lucille said, "Yes, you. I drew this card for you. Someone is sitting in judgment *of you*."

"I'm sure that's all well and good, but we need help with Hannah's murder, not the people in my life who disagree with my way of doing things."

Lucille looked up from the card. "I'm sorry. I must have lost you along the way. This *is* about that poor girl's murder."

The three of us looked at each other in confusion.

"It's tied to *you* in some way."

"Jasmine," Bailey muttered under her breath. "It has to be her. Goddamn it."

I held my hands up. "Whoa. We're not jumping to conclusions based on a tarot card." To Lucille, I said, "What do you know about the Indies? About Briggs? I'm looking for facts here."

She plucked up the Justice card and stuffed it

in the middle of the deck. "Briggs wants Max's show. Everyone knows that. He sent his minions to inquire about it. Max told him 'no way'. They sent missives back and forth until Max finally told him to shove off. Well, Townsend shoved back. The night Hannah was killed, I believe there were three people with her."

"Three?"

She nodded. "Two of them attacked her. The third did not. Like I said, they were only shadows to me. I wish I had more...a face, a detail, something, but my powers did not reveal those to me."

"So no male, female, race, nothing?"

Lucille shook her head and resumed shuffling the deck.

"Nothing like that, but I *can* tell you this much: Hannah was, indeed, the intended target."

"She was the warning salvo."

Lucille nodded slowly. "More or less."

"Seventeen stab wounds seems like overkill to me, even for a warning," Bailey said softly.

"That's 'cause you're not from the cement jungle, Bailey. A drive-by aimed at one person sprays dozens of bullets at the intended victim. It's symbolic in nature, read: We will cut down everything in our way if you don't do what we want."

Bailey visibly shuddered. "How barbaric."

Danica shrugged. "It is what it is. Survival of the fittest."

Madame Lucille started laying all the cards out face down. I didn't want a tarot reading from a never trained fortuneteller. "The message was sent via Townsend's people as a loud and clear message that Max and his entourage are vulnerable. I would remove Max's girlfriend from the show for starters. If you are planning on putting him back on stage, the less you endanger anyone else, the better." She pointed to a few of the cards and nodded. "I see your plan. Using Max as bait is a dangerous game, indeed."

I nodded.

Danica looked at me and I knew exactly what she was thinking. We needed to replace Max's assistants, lure Townsend's thugs out once more. Only this time, we'd be ready. This time, we'd fight back.

"I really appreciate your time, Lucille. We're going to do everything we can to get this mess cleaned up in a hurry."

She nodded and pushed away the hundred dollar bill Danica had set on the table. "Supers killing supers is a bad thing, but supers who don't know enough about concealing their powers? That's trouble for us all."

As the three of us stood up, Madame Lucille grabbed my wrist in her tiny claw. "One last thing, if you'll humor an old woman. Choose any card on the table."

I looked down at the complete deck spread out on the table. When I was fourteen, Bishop had explained to me how she used the tarot cards as props to deliver what she inherently knew from having the sight. She said the cards weren't really saying anything, but were the conduit through which a medium spoke. Bishop had trained her powers. Lucille had not.

"Just one."

Reaching down, my hand hovered over all the cards until I finally flipped one over.

It was Justice again.

Lucille nodded as she gathered up the cards. "No coincidences, Echo. Remember that always."

When we got out to the street, Mario wasn't there, so we started walking back to our hotel.

"That card is jacked up," Danica grumbled. "And if Mario worked for me, he'd be unemployed." She was wearing four-inch pumps and a Donna Karan favorite. The pumps must have been killing her feet.

"Call her," Bailey said.

Danica and I both looked at her. "Who?"

"Jasmine. Call her and tell her to meet us at the hotel. We need to tear her open and see what falls out."

"Come on, Bailey, you're not seriously weirded out by that tarot card thing, are you?" Danica threaded her arms through both of ours. "Are *you?*" This was directed at me.

"Other than indicating there were three people there at the time of the murder, Lucille had little to offer us. She's an untrained clairvoyant. I'm not even sure we should believe the three people story."

"We're still going to flush them out by bringing Max back, right?"

I thought for a moment before nodding. "In Vegas, you're only as good as your last show. He needs to resume or they could cut him loose. He needs to resume so Townsend stays in town and in the game."

A familiar vibration echoed from all three of us. We all reached for our Vidbooks and flipped them open. On all three of our screens was Delta's painful expression and battered face. Blood dripped from her nose and a large gash above her left eye was just starting to coagulate.

"Holy shit," Danica gasped, punching buttons on her keyboard. As usual, Danica kicked into high gear faster than I did and had Delta's position in a nano. "GPS has you in our sights, Delta. We're only a few blocks away."

Delta's eyes slowly closed. "Hurry."

Danica kicked off her pumps and started running. "No time for a cab. Come on!"

Bailey and I fell in behind her, each of us still clutching our Vidbooks. My legs had to pump double time to keep up with their long strides.

With her eyes on the GPS, Danica maneuvered through groups of people untouched, never slowing down or hesitating, thanks to the energy I threw out in front of her. When she came to the back service entrance of a restaurant, she stopped, put her Vidbook in her purse, and retrieved her Glock from the side pocket. "Clark?"

Lowering my shields, I could only feel Delta's pained emotions. "No one else there. Well, no naturals. Just Delta." Glancing over at Bailey, I nodded. She called Nine-One-One while Danica and I ran through the dark alley to find Delta laying crumpled on the filthy ground next to a disgusting dumpster.

"Oh shit. Shit!" Danica looked all around us, Glock held firmly in both hands. She checked the fire ladders, the window ledges, everywhere while I tended to Delta.

Kneeling down next to Delta, I could feel she was alive…in pain, unconscious, but alive. I could also sense Danica at my back, gun at the ready. Nerves of steel, that woman has.

Brushing Delta's bloody hair aside, I winced at the laceration running perpendicular to her left eyebrow. It was still bleeding profusely, as the face is wont to do. She had other abrasions on her chin and cheek. Whoever did this to her nailed had her but good. "Hang in there, Storm. We got you covered."

The sirens of the ambulance announced its arrival, and the three of us stood back as Delta was loaded into the back of it.

"Mario's out front," Bailey said, lightly touching my bloody hand. "We'll follow."

When the ambulance doors closed, two things happened to me; I felt this incredible sadness wash over me one moment, followed and pushed out by an intense vengeance-filled anger that lit me on fire.

Come after *me* and *my* friends, will you? Oh hail no.

"Clark? Come on." Danica pulled me through the alley.

When we got in the Navigator, Bailey sat up front and told Mario to follow the ambulance.

"Should I report to the Boss that one-a-ya's got jumped?"

Danica looked to me. I shook my head. "Not yet. We don't need a bunch of...*them* storming around down here, including Connie and Megan. I don't want them to know just yet."

Danica's eyes grew wide and Bailey jerked her head around. "Oh no, E. Bad, bad plan. You *have* to tell them. Connie will kick all our asses if you keep this from her."

"We will tell them. Let's see how she is first. Until then, no calls to anyone." Sitting back in the seat, I swallowed the lump in my throat at a decision I wished I hadn't had to make. I wouldn't worry Connie unnecessarily, nor would I jump the gun and start scaring the crap out of everyone. We just needed to gather some facts first, and that was exactly what I was going to do.

"Clark's right, Bailey. One call to Megan and we'll have our hands full of the whole crew down here. Let's see what we can before opening up *that* can of worms."

Danica and Bailey both waited for me to answer. "She'll kill you if—"

"That's a chance I'm willing to take. We have enough going on down here. We can't afford to have Delta's crew kicking ass and taking names, and that's exactly what they'll do. You both know that."

Danica nodded. "I have to agree with Clark on this one. Let's just wait and see how Delta is."

How Delta was was beaten up pretty badly, but no permanent damage. She regained consciousness on the way to the hospital. We were waiting to be allowed in to see her.

Stretching her long legs in front of her, Danica laid her head on my shoulder. "I'm thinking this game just got down and dirty."

Bailey paced back and forth. "Delta Stevens isn't someone who *gets* beaten up in dark alleys. What the fuck happened out there?"

"You're the ladies waiting for Delta Stevens?" a tall, balding doctor asked. He reminded me of a praying mantis.

Danica and I were on our feet next to Bailey. "Can we see her?"

"You can. She's suffered some bruises and contusions, but she'll be able to go home once we get that eyebrow stitched up."

"Thank you."

We found Delta behind a blue curtain, her head into the pillow. She looked awful. A bruise was developing under her left eye; she had an enormous egg-shaped bump on her forehead opposite a cut that had three butterfly bandages on it. Her eyes were closed. I felt her energy was low and subdued. She was in pain and confused.

I'd never felt that emotion from her or any of her people.

Danica shook her head at me and started backing away.

"I could smell your perfume anywhere, Danica," Delta said as she peeked out her one good eye.

"Delta, I am so sorry."

She held up a hand. "Uh uh. You don't get to be sorry for something I volunteered to do. That's not how we roll."

"Do you feel up to telling me what happened?"

Delta reached for a cup of ice that Bailey quickly handed to her. "I'd left my card around town at all the places I'd investigated. I got a call to meet someone who knew something about Hannah's murder." Crunching the ice, she set the cup down and reached up to touch the egg on her head lightly. She winced the moment her fingertips grazed it.

"You met someone in a dark alley?"

"Of course not. He was working in a kitchen. I met him there, but it was so busy, we stepped out back." She gently fingered the butterfly bandage and winced. "And then..." She shook her head slowly and looked hard at me. "Up until today, I've been willing to let you guys keep your secrets about whatever it is you are. But Echo, tonight I got my ass kicked by a guy *who never laid a hand on me.*"

I glanced over at Bailey, who shrugged. I was on my own with our truth. It was why I was their leader. "You're right. You deserve to know the truth. Just not here."

Delta closed her eyes and nodded. "Let's get me patched up and then you can explain it all to me."

The doctor came back and started shooing us out.

"Echo?" Delta asked just as we started out the door. "Please tell me you didn't call Connie or Megan."

"Hell no."

She sighed with relief. "Smart girl. That's the last thing we need right now. You don't want to see her whirling and twirling down here. Don't go far, I'll be out of here in no time."

And she was.

Once Mario dropped us off at our hotel, we got Delta to her room some time after two in the morning.

"You get some rest," I said, pulling the covers around her shoulders.

"Not until you tell me what that was. I never got closer than ten feet to that kid and he tossed me around like a rag doll. If it hadn't happened to me, I wouldn't have believed it." She patted the bed on both sides, and Bailey and I sat down. Danica remained leaning against the door. "That's what Genesys was all about, huh? Those people in the chopper...your sister...all of them—all of you are—"

"Are paranormals. Supernaturals. Yes. We are... gifted."

"And that kid tonight? What was *he*?"

"By the sound of it, a telekinetic, or TK. He used energy to beat you up."

She nodded slowly, her bruise turning a deep purple. "I see. And you guys?"

I nodded. "We are as well. We are supernaturals with slightly different genetic makeup that enables us to use and manipulate energy. You knew we were different...just not how different."

"I'm not," Danica added. "Unless you consider my superhuman intellect, in which case, I totally am."

Delta grinned slightly. "You both have... paranormal powers." She jutted her chin out to me and Bailey.

We nodded.

She rubbed her eyes. "It's all starting to come together for me now. Genesys, the chateau, how you guys are always talking in code. All of the pieces are finally coming together. You're their leader, aren't you?"

"I prefer mentor, and yes, I am. My job is to help young supers learn how to control their powers. These people down here were never trained. They're here to win big at the casinos using their powers. Something went down between two illusionists, and Hannah was killed. Probably as a warning to Max, but we're not sure. I'm here trying to shut this down before it becomes news. We are, as of yet, still just a myth to the American public. My superiors would like it to remain that way."

"Your superiors? So let me get this straight. We're caught up in a turf skirmish between supernaturals?"

"That pretty much sums it up."

She smirked. "So you're here to clean up a mess."

I spent the next ten minutes explaining to Delta what would happen if our existence became less urban legend and more fact. By the time I finished, she understood completely, but wasn't too thrilled at one of us having jacked her up.

"So we need to catch the killers, put them all on a bus, and ship them back to Atlantic City, right?"

I rose. "Right. But there is no longer a we. For now, though, you need to get some rest. I'll answer more questions I am certain are coming in the morning." As I rose, I gently touched her leg. "Just so you know, you're on the bench."

She tried to sit up, but I used my power to hold her to the bed.

"What the fuck?"

"Part of my powers. You're done here, Delta. This isn't your fight and that's not up for debate. " I released my hold on her and headed for the door.

We were almost to the door when Delta said, "That kid was a TK. I get that. He flung me around like a ragdoll. What are you two?"

"Rest, Storm. We'll talk in the morning."

After closing her door, I felt a little sick to my stomach. I'd left a wonderful woman because I couldn't tell her the truth about me and here I was now, confiding in yet another friend.

"You can't second guess yourself on this one, E. This is the second time Delta's put her neck on the line for us knowing she only had half the pieces to the puzzle. It was time she knew."

Danica was nodding. "We've trusted them in everything but that, Clark. What more do they need to do to prove themselves? These are women of integrity. They're loyal to a fault. I say it's about time."

"It goes against what Mel and the Others believe is best."

"Yeah? Well, I don't see them out here trying to fix this. We're in the trenches doing all the heavy lifting. They don't get to play Monday morning quarterback from atop Mount. Olympus."

"D is right. These women are part of our family now, E. *Our* family has naturals in it. So what? Who fucking cares? We're gay, straight, black, white, super, and natural. It's a sign of the times. Diversity is the new…rainbow."

I smiled at Bailey. She was right. They both were. This was not the first time a super had punched Delta. She deserved to know the whole truth.

"If you tell Delta, you're gonna have to tell Connie."

"What about Megan and Sal?"

I rubbed the back of my neck. "Sal probably already knows. She monitors the chateau with eyes of an eagle, and Megan is…well…if Delta trusts her so, so must we." I looked over at Danica and cocked my head. "Dani? What's the matter?"

She hesitated before answering. "Connie already suspects there's something different about you, so it will be nice to not have to lie about it anymore."

"Then we agree. The four of them will know."

Bailey and Danica both nodded.

"Okay then," I said. "I, for one, am sick of Townsend's buddies getting the jump on us. Tomorrow, we turn this thing around, but first, we get Delta, get some rest, and then figure out how to put this thing to bed."

After we got Delta home and tucked in bed, the three of us went into our respective rooms. I showered and climbed into bed, and was almost asleep when Danica came in.

"Clark?" She whispered, poking her head in the room.

"What's up?"

Danica sat on the edge of the bed. She was wearing a UNLV T-shirt and shorts. "I know it hurts your heart that you told Delta when you never had it in you to tell Finn. It was written all over your face. I wondered if you wanted to talk about it."

"Delta and Company are in a need-to-know situation. I can't keep putting them in harm's way not armed with all the facts." I shrugged. "They deserved to know."

"And Finn didn't?"

"That was...different. We've been through things with Delta. They've melded seamlessly with our family, don't you think?"

"I do. I just wanted you to consider telling Finn, if that would make you happier. If you want to have her back in your life, it's still possible. I think you'd be happier."

I tilted my head. "I *am* happy, Dani."

"No you're not. You're busy. That's not the same thing. Actually, that's *nothing* like the same thing. You've been lonely ever since you guys broke up. I know you really dug Officer Yummy and that not being able to tell her bummed you big. Maybe now—"

I held my hand up to stop her. "I'm not going to run back to Tip, Dani, if that's what you're worried about."

"Well, you *do* have a pattern."

"Not this time. I appreciate your concern, but I really am happy. Busy, yes, but also happy. I love having the kids. I love mentoring. We've made a good life there. Love will come when it comes."

"Well, for your sake, I hope it comes soon." Danica took my hand in hers. "You did the right thing tonight. Don't you doubt it."

"Thanks." When she left, I thought about my heartbreaking decision to break up with Finn. Yes, I'd wanted to tell her, and yes, she deserved to know…but one thing I just was never sure of: I wasn't sure if she was the one. Closing my eyes, I tried to call Tip, but there was no answer. I hadn't really expected any, but it was worth a try. It was just as well, because in less than a minute, I was sound asleep.

∞∞∞∞

"She's gone!" Bailey was pacing like a woman possessed.

I sat up in bed to face an agitated Bailey. "Who?"

"That bitch, Jasmine! I just got a call from Nick. She's gone. She left his compound. Bolted like the fucking coward she is. Goddamnit, I knew she was behind this."

Danica came in behind her. "Took her shit and left on foot. A truck came to—"

"Whoa. Slow down. What time is it?" I looked at my clock. It was just after seven a.m. "I don't understand what the problem is. Jasmine is gone?"

"She snuck out. Didn't say goodbye. Didn't even use the front door."

"Nick's security caught her wa—"

"Wait." I rubbed my eyes. "Jasmine has a life to lead here as well. I wasn't expecting her to babysit Max or to stop living because the Indies are here. She's probably at the shop."

"Then let's go see." Danica looked at Bailey, who nodded.

My gaze traveled back and forth between them. "Just what is it you think she's done?"

Bailey sat on the edge of the bed. "You're kidding, right?"

"Besides that."

"Clark, Bailey tattooed her face. Her *face*. You don't think she's seriously pissed off? You don't think she doesn't see this as her opportunity for retribution? You don't think—"

"We need you to read her," Bailey interrupted. "Until you do, she can't—"

I held my hands up in surrender. "Whoa. Let's get our priorities straight first. I understand you think Jasmine leaving is a sign of guilt, but first, how's Delta?"

"Sleeping. Hard."

Tossing the covers back, I got out of bed and headed for the coffeepot. "Both of you back up a little. I need some coffee."

They followed right behind me. "How 'bout you get ready while we go collect Miss Jasmine?"

Pouring the dark brew, I thought about the two attacks on me. Where had Jasmine been the first time? She was with us in the back. Why would she have played a victim to that first attack? Was she just a dicey decoy or was she as bad as these two thought her to be? I had read her, yes, but not deeply. Was it possible she had managed to fool me? Had I inadvertently read one of her little ghosts, or was she just an innocent bystander?

It wasn't appearing that way.

"She knew we were on to her."

Stirring creamer into my coffee, I shook my head. "You guys, she's a necromancer, not a telepath. You're giving her way too much credit."

Danica shook her head. "She knew *something*, Clark. She knew Delta was being set up—knew we'd figure it out eventually. She's on the run from us because she knows she's toast."

"Yeah, E, she beat a hasty retreat under some rock, and we need to start turning over some stones."

I shook my head. "Other than a revenge motive, do you guys have any proof of this theory? Because it seems to me—"

"Oh come on, E! Tell us you've at least considered that Jasmine is playing both sides!"

Setting my coffee down, I lowered my voice. "Of course I have. We've already discussed this, but right now, Jasmine's play in all of this is the least of our worries. Would it be easier if we had her under lock and key? Absolutely. Well, right now we have a murder, two failed attempts on my life, one assault and battery on Delta, a magician who needs to get back to the stage, and a bunch of arrogant Indies who need to be taught a lesson. You really want to put Jasmine and her antics at the top of that list?"

Just as I finished, Delta stood in the doorway of her bedroom, propping herself up using the doorframe. "Does that pretty much sum up our mission?"

"What are you doing up?" Bailey took one of Delta's arms, but Delta didn't budge. "I'm fine. Sore as shit, but my mind works fine."

Danica shook her head. "You do know we can stuff you right back into bed, right?"

Delta held her hands up in surrender. "I'm stiff as hell and need to walk it off, but I'll be fine."

"Coffee?" I asked, as Bailey and Danica helped her to the small table.

"Please. Feels like six elephants smacked me around with their trunks, but I can't lie down anymore. I'm getting stiffer with every hour. So, Jasmine's taken off and we've got a whole bunch of loose ends to tie up."

"Oh hell no," Bailey said. "Remember, there's no *we*, honey. You need to give yourself a little time."

"Doesn't sound like we have time. Echo?"

I looked at her bump. It had gone down a little but was very discolored. The bruise on her cheek was a deep purple. She'd taken six stitches to close the cut on her eyebrow, but her emerald green eyes were dialed in. Saying no to Delta Stevens wasn't going to be easy.

Turning from her, I looked at Bailey and jerked my head towards Delta. Bailey stood, eye-to-eye with Delta, and placed her hands gently on either side of Delta's face. Closing her eyes, she breathed in and out slowly.

Delta looked over at me, her eyebrows framing a silent question.

"She's a shaman. A healer. Trust her."

Bailey opened her eyes and lowered her hands. "Not today, Delta. You need more rest. Your body is using its reserves to heal."

"I can handle—"

"It's not an option," Bailey replied staunchly. "You can stay here and rest or we call Connie and Megan and then—"

"Okay, okay. I'll stay in for the day, but keep me abreast of what's going down. Tomorrow, we're going to find the little asshole who beat the crap out of me and see if he can't lead us to the killer."

Everyone grabbed a cup of coffee and sat on the couches in the sunken living room area. Delta gingerly settled down on the couch. She looked pretty pale, and I knew Bailey was right about her healing herself.

"Okay, as much as we'd all like to start thumping on some noggins, we need more information before we can progress any further. We need to see if there is another telepath down here we can get to the poker tables. I'll be at the fountain at six. Until then, I want to see Max back on stage and I want to pay a visit to as many of the Indies here as possible."

"To what end?" Danica asked.

"They need to know there's a new sheriff in town and she's not real thrilled with their actions. I hate to ask this, Dani, but we might need some of Nick's... muscle. Just for show right now. You know, to let them know we know."

"I'm on it."

"The casinos have far too much energy for me to get a read on where they are, so I'm thinking we ought to pay another visit to Madame Lucille."

Both Bailey and Danica groaned. "Come on, E. That woman is a crack pot."

"Maybe. But we need to pay a few visits and we can't do that if we don't know where they are." I turned to Delta. My heart hurt for her battered face. "I owe you an apology."

"No you don't. Before you guys came along, I was scared shitless that my high adrenalin days of old were just a memory—that I'd been reduced to busting philanderers and health fraud artists. You've breathed breath back into my life, Echo, so don't ever be sorry for that. We're grateful."

"You got assaulted, Delta. You could have been killed."

She smiled. "If I had a dollar...the point is, what fun is a life without risk? Without adventure? What fun is it to live a predictable existence? I've seen a helluva lot in my career, but nothing like you guys. Last night, I laid in bed putting all of the pieces together, and suddenly, it all made sense. Your sister, your students, the security. All of it. I *get* why you need to keep a lid on this thing, Echo. The world is always looking for the next target to hang its intolerance hat on. It's not ready for the likes of you and your people. So, if there is anything me and *my* people can do to insure your safety, we want in. We've devoted our lives to protecting the disenfranchised, Echo. Right here, with sore ribs and a battered face, is exactly where I want to be."

Laying my hand on top of hers, I noticed, for the first time, her scraped knuckles. "Did you actually land a punch?" I lifted my hand from hers and looked at the red knuckles.

"A punch? No. Several. What did you think? That I let some kid whip up on me without getting some licks in?" She chuckled. "Then you don't know Storm as well as I thought."

"Exactly what happened?" Danica asked.

"Well, when I realized someone was throwing something at me, I figured he couldn't split his attention and do two things at once, so I chucked my boot knife at him and followed it. Sure enough, he batted the knife to the ground but couldn't recover fast enough to keep me from hitting him. I got three solid punches to his face before he blew me back against the wall and the next thing I knew, shit was flying at me. Trashcan lids, bottles. I think I took a beer bottle to my forehead. I hit my head pretty hard and was trying to stay conscious when I saw him standing over me with my boot knife in his hand. That's when I thought it was over."

"Why wasn't it?"

"Someone started out the back door, so he

slammed it shut on them and took off running." Delta tossed the knife on the table. "He dropped it when he took off."

I looked at Bailey, who rose and grabbed the knife. "He held the knife?"

Delta nodded. "Yeah."

Bailey cocked her head. "He was planning on killing you with a *knife?*"

Delta shrugged. "That's how it appeared. I let go of my consciousness as soon as he took off."

Bailey looked at me. "Odd that a TK would even consider using a knife when he could have crushed her skull with anything lying around, don't you think?"

I nodded. "Good point. Danica, you go get Max and bring him here. He's going on tonight or he's leaving Vegas. Those are his only options."

Dani nodded and looked hard at me. "And what about you? Where are you going?"

"I'll meet you both at Madame Lucille's at ten. Today, we are paying a not-so-friendly visit to our Indies."

⁕⁕⁕⁕⁕

Madame Lucille stared at the boot knife from the alley.

"I know a scryer back home who could read that for me," I said. "I'm bettin' you can as well." I cut my eyes over at Bailey, who stood with her arms crossed.

Lucille looked across the table at me. "I don't know."

"Sure you do. We only need to know the male who held this recently. That's it. Give us a name. That's all I need."

She blinked, never taking her eyes off the blade. "Just a name? You know that's not how it works. Once I touch it, I'll see everything. I don't want to see everything."

"And I don't want to be attacked anymore. Give me a name and we won't be back. I know you don't want to be involved and I don't blame you, but it's my job to get a lid on this thing right away. I need your help to do that."

Slowly, she took the knife in both hands and held it in front of her as she closed her eyes. We waited while she did her thing.

When Lucille opened her eyes, she set the knife down. "Ricky Ryan handled this blade."

Pushing away from the table, she shook her head. "He's a nasty character, Echo, whoever he is. Strong powers but unpredictable. He's made a mess of things in the past. Be careful."

"Anything else?"

"Nothing. That's it. And please...don't come back. I don't want any problems."

I tilted my head at her. I didn't need to lower my shields to know how scared she was. "Are you that afraid of them?"

"Every day, they get bolder and bolder."

We all stood up. "Don't worry, Lucille. Things will settle down in a couple of days."

"I hope so. They're pretty brazen, and young folk without fear are the most dangerous folk on the planet."

"I know. Thank you for this."

When we walked out, I opened the Vidbook and called the boys. "Ricky Ryan here in Vegas, maybe from AC. I need anything you can find."

Bailey turned to me. "We're going after that little

puke, right?"

I nodded. "As soon as the boys find us an address or something to go on, yes."

"And what about Jasmine? When are we going after her?"

Staring at her, I knew the time had come for me to put this whole thing with Jasmine to bed. "As soon as we locate her. I promise."

Bailey studied me. "How can you stand it? How come you're not seething?"

I tilted my head at her. "Who says I'm not?"

"You should have let Nick take care of her, gangsta style."

"The jury is still out, Bailey. We don't *know* anything yet. Not for sure."

We got back and found Danica and Max sitting at the table.

Danica held the Vidbook out, a look of triumph on her face. "Three nineteen Kalamazoo Place. That's where we'll find Mr. Ryan. He's a student at UNLV, transferred from a community college in Atlantic City. You guys may be powerful, but nobody trumps that think tank of mine."

Delta agreed to "keep Max company" while we went after Ricky.

"Let's go."

Twenty minutes later, Danica stood on the porch of Ricky Ryan's house. It looked like this was our first jackpot in Vegas. There were four other supers in the house.

When the door opened, a young girl stood barefoot in a stained Ozzie Osborn tee shirt, Daisy Duke shorts, and bare feet that screamed for a pedicure.

"Yeah?" She chewed gum like a cow, and was a

low-level thinker, who didn't even bother scanning Danica.

Big mistake.

Bailey and I waited around the corner by the garage. I could see Danica from where we stood and the moment the door opened, I threw a shield in front of her. Ozzie Osborn didn't even notice, that's how untrained she was.

"I'm here for Ricky Ryan. Is he around?"

Ozzie eyed Danica with suspicion. As Danica reached in her waistband for her Glock, I released the shield and joined her as she barged her way in, shoving Ozzie aside.

"Sit the fuck down," Danica ordered, holding the Glock gangster-style.

Ozzie quickly sat on the couch next to a boy so engrossed in his X-Box he didn't bother looking up.

When Bailey entered, a rough-looking dog of questionable heritage accompanied her. It must have been all she could scare up in Sin City.

The dog's presence made the boy turn. His eyes grew large when he saw us, fixing his gaze first on the gun then on the dog.

"Come on, boy," Bailey said. She brought the dog into the family room, where it sat staring at Ozzie.

"Sit down in that chair," Bailey ordered.

"Who the fuck are—"

The dog growled and the boy jumped into the beat up leather recliner that had seen better days. "Sit on your hands," Bailey ordered.

Danica was making her way down the hall, gun poised. "Clark?"

"Only two more. One is Ricky Ryan, so be careful." I was right behind her. "The one on the left is an empath," I whispered. "Ricky Ryan is on the right."

"This room?"

I nodded.

Danica swung the bedroom door open. The kid lying on the bed with headphones on didn't move. In two long steps, Danica was at the side of the bed, the gun pressed to his forehead. He opened his eyes and started to throw his hands up, but I had my heaviest shield across his chest. He was pinned there with a Glock pressed to his face.

Ripping the headphones off his head, Danica said, "It would be ill advised for you to attempt to free your hands. You do, and I will drill you with one well-placed bullet. Do you understand, nutsack?"

He nodded, his eyes crossing as he stared at the muzzle of the gun.

Walking up to the bed, I looked down at this kid. He was about twenty, dark hair and eyes, with a deep bruise on his left cheek, compliments of Delta Stevens. "She's not kidding, Ricky. Now, you're going to sit up, hands under your ass, and you're going to answer all my questions honestly. I'm a very high-level empath the likes of which you have never seen. I'll know the moment you're even thinking about lying. You do, and you've listened to your last song. Do you understand?"

"Wha…what do you want?"

"She asked you a question, buttmunch. Do. You. Understand?"

He nodded and I watched as urine saturated the front of his jeans.

Danica pressed the muzzle into his bruise. "You made a huge mistake attacking our friend, asshole, and now, you're going to answer all our questions about that stupid decision. Now sit up."

Ricky slowly sat up and slid his hands under his butt. He was scared to death, and rightfully so. Danica wasn't bluffing.

"Remember, boy-o, my buddy over there will know the nano you lie, so do yourself a favor and just tell us what we want to know the *first* time. You attacked our friend. Who are you working for?"

He looked at Danica before locking eyes with me. "I didn't attack—"

"Who are you working for?

Townsend Briggs, but—"

"Did he send you?"

"Yes."

"Why?"

"You know why."

Danica clipped him in the head with the muzzle of her gun. It made this horrible cracking sound.

"Ow!"

"Answer the goddamned question. Got it?"

He nodded.

"What were your orders?"

"They weren't my orders. I was only the—"

"What. Were. Your. Orders?"

"We were supposed to hospitalize her. Send a message that you're sticking your nose in where it doesn't belong. Attack the natural but don't kill her. Killing her would have been easy, you know?"

I felt Danica's anger match my own. "And you'd be pushing up daisies right next to her."

"He...he just wanted to get you out of Vegas."

"Oh, really? And why is that? Because we're going to shut down his get rich quick scheme?"

He barked a laugh. "You're kidding, right? You came down here with naturals and you think you have the cannons to stop him? Townsend will have you for lunch."

I stepped closer. "Is that so? Well, where is your master while you're out abusing your powers?"

"He's not my—"

Danica smacked him again and he swore.

"Did you kill Hannah?"

"What? No. My job is roulette and muscle. I don't know who did that to her."

All were the truth.

"Where is he?"

"I don't know. We haven't heard from him in a couple of days."

I leaned forward. "And you aren't going to, either. Pack your bags. You're all going back to Atlantic City today. Within the hour."

He looked at Danica, who nodded. "We'll just come back to Vegas when you're gone."

I smiled as I took my Vidbook out and snapped a photo. "And the men who actually run this town will ship your pieces home in a body bag."

The camera had caught his attention. "What are you gonna do with that?"

I hit the send button and sent it to the Bat Cave. "Every casino owner in the United States will have your photo in less than ten minutes. The gangsters in this town will have it in five. All will know that you are a card-counting, magnet wearing cheater. Step into a casino at your own risk. Your days of using your powers for personal gain via gambling are over."

"Gangsters?"

"The Mob, dickweed," Danica replied. "Or are you too young and stupid never to have watched Scarface or the Sopranos? You want to see the damage *those* mere mortals can wreak? Then by all means, come back."

"You're bluffing."

"Get a fucking job." Danica pushed the gun deeper into his skin. "Go get the rest of their pics, Clark, and check on Bailey. I got this punk." She bent closer to him and whispered, "And in case you're thinking about doing something foolish, I've killed before and will do so again if you ever lay your powers on anyone I care about."

I left him in Danica's scary hands as I snapped and sent photos of everyone in the house. Bailey and her dog were watching over the two in the family room, and the empath was apparently sleeping off a drunk.

When I came back, Ricky Ryan had his eyes closed and Danica had the Glock pressed between his eyes. She was whispering something to him that I was pretty sure were threats.

"She's got it covered. Okay. Here's what's going down. You four need to pack and get in our car. Our driver will take you to the airport. You are to leave town and not come back. If you do not, there's a hole in the desert with your name on it. And that's no idle threat. Do you know who I am?"

He shook his head.

"My name is Echo Branson. You might want to remember it in the event we meet again."

He swallowed hard and nodded.

"Good. Don't even think about returning. Our driver is connected, well connected. Don't mess with him. Don't mess with any of my people because there's no place on this planet you can hide that we won't find you."

On cue, Bailey's mangy mutt jumped on the

bed, teeth bared, front paws on Ricky Ryan's chest so quickly, the kid didn't have time to move his hands.

"That's for emphasis, kid," Danica said, lowering the gun. "We're not fucking around."

"Now, get your shit and get out of town. When you get home, get a job. A real job. Your uneducated powers have no place in this world. If you go to Atlantic City and do the exact same thing, I'll just come there and have this conversation with you all over again. Are we clear?"

Staring at the big-headed dog, he nodded.

"Keep your hands behind your back, Ricky. You so much as twitch those hands, my friend here will bury a bullet in both knee caps. Fat lotta good your powers will do you from a wheelchair. *Capisce?*"

"Y—Yes, ma'am."

Good. "Bailey, get all their phones. I don't want them calling anyone."

It took less than five minutes to get them packed and into the SUV. As I closed the door, the youngest of them, Shasta, handed me a note. I discreetly took it from her as I finished giving my orders to Mario, and stuck it in my pocket.

When the Navigator pulled away, the three of us looked at each other.

"Umm, Clark?"

"Yeah?"

"You're beginning to scare the shit out of me. You've become one tough mamma-jamma. *Do you know who I am?* Jesus Christ, I almost wet myself."

"Ditto," Bailey said from behind me. "E, I'm pretty sure that odor I smell is from someone shitting their pants."

We walked to the Starbucks down the street,

ordered coffee, and then sat on a comfortable sofa to regroup.

"All I know is, there is a lot more to taking over Mel's position than just teaching the kids. It's about being the law some days, a judge others. We're going to clear the supers out of here so when Briggs gets back to Vegas, his mindless army is seriously depleted. Let's even our odds up a little, right?"

"You don't think any of those kids were the killer?"

"Uh uh. I read each one."

"How?"

"They've only learned how to construct rudimentary shields, if they have any at all. I read their aura. A murderer, or someone who has killed someone recently, has a tar-like residue on the aura, and none of them did. They're just babies doing what daddy tells them to."

"What about Jasmine?" Bailey asked as we sat at the dining table. "What if she's a string puller in this madness?"

"Bailey, I know she burned you when you were younger, and your retribution of that was just, but you have to stop fixating on her. The Others wouldn't have sent us to her if they thought she was a bad seed."

Bailey shrugged and looked away. "They don't always see things with crystal clarity, E, but I'm trying to let it go. I just...can't."

Danica poured three packets of brown sugar in her coffee. "I'm with Bails on this one, Clark. The Others are old and decrepit. When is the last time they even *saw* Jasmine? And where in the hell did she go?"

"To hell, I hope. What did that little empath hand you?" Bailey asked.

"Oh. Right." Digging into my pocket, I pulled out a meticulously folded note about the size of a matchbook. "Well, I'll be damned." Holding it up to both of them to see, we all chuckled at our good fortune.

Taking the note from me, Danica opened her Vidbook. When Roger's face appeared, she read off the numbers for him.

"You make the call, boss, and we'll triangulate where that little piece of info is sitting."

Smiling, Danica turned to me. "Well, Clark? I think it's about time we knew where Townsend Briggs was holing up."

And, just like that, we had him in our sights.

It was early afternoon by the time we got back to the Pentagon. Roger had pinpointed Townsend's whereabouts just outside of Vegas in a small desert town called Indio. When Danica called, his voicemail picked up. It was all Roger needed to be able to get the GPS software to zero in on him. You gotta love technology.

"I wish we'd just fucking nab him, E. Go all Rambo on his ass and see if he cracks."

I shook my head. "Sorry, Rambo, but we'd never get close enough before he bolts. We can't afford to have him on the run."

"Taking their phones was smart, Clark, but they can always call him from the airport."

"Look. He knows we're here," I said, pulling up Jasmine's and Townsend's driver's license photos, courtesy of Roger. "We're not hiding. We're just not walking into a trap. Townsend is going to have to come to us. He'll be off-balance with his people bailing. Even if he runs, where is he going to go? I'll have every spotter in a thousand-mile radius looking for him, but that could take days or even weeks if he goes to ground. We need to find him and diffuse the situation down here."

Danica stared hard at me. "Is there something you're not telling us? I...I've never seen you so... determined. When I said you were scaring me, it wasn't a hyperbole. You're actually starting to look and act like a superhero."

Sitting around our table with four Vidbooks in front of us, I shook my head. "Just stepping up is all. Attacking us was a huge mistake. Coming after me or my people is a transgression I cannot allow to go unpunished. I have been pushed into a corner for the last time, so if I seem a little...determined, it's because I have some really tough decisions coming down the chute. We're no longer looking for just a killer. We're looking for someone who has no compunction about killing other supers. I can't allow that kind of lunacy to spread."

"What can you do, E? Killing him seems hypocritical in light of what you just said."

"I know. I've put a call in to the Others. They are willing to send cleaners to pick up whoever is leading this parade. They'll deal with them in their own way."

They both stared at me. "What the fuck?" Danica said. "You don't think Townsend Briggs is behind all this?"

I looked over at Delta, who had a little more color to her cheeks than she had this morning. "Go for it, Storm."

Delta folded her hands on the table. Her knuckles were beginning to scab over. "I've been in the bad guy game long enough to know a front when I see one. Townsend Briggs is *not* the man with the plan. He might be a player, even a major player, but I believe he is a red herring. From what I learned from Max this morning, Briggs isn't really that powerful."

I nodded. "He is, for all intents and purposes, just one rung higher than those kids we sent packing."

"How can you be so sure?"

"Anyone who can really lead doesn't do so from afar. It's an act of a coward, not a leader. He may want what he wants, but he's not really here trying to get it, is he? No, whoever is in charge of covering all of this up is in Vegas. I wouldn't be surprised if Briggs wasn't a decoy…someone for you…us, to focus our energy on while someone else moves around behind the scenes." Delta paused. "Whoever set those two tourney players up is the same person who orchestrated Hannah's murder."

"And you're sure it's not Briggs?"

Delta shook her head. "Not sure, no, but years of experience tells me this thing isn't what it looks like. Believe me, I've had enough things slide sideways on me to know. Look at what we know about this guy, then do the math." She started ticking off her finger. "One, he's incapable of getting his own gig, so he kills an assistant? Why the assistant and not Max? Wouldn't *that* have been a bolder move? A step closer? Killing the assistant as a threat is a risky move. He should have just killed Max, but he didn't."

Danica and Bailey both nodded.

"Two, he's not even in town. He knows these kids are losers, yet he puts them in charge of rattling your cages? He must know you are well-trained. Why toss garbage at diamonds?"

Danica smiled. "I love that analogy."

"Three, Jasmine is sketchy at best. At first I thought she might be just another distraction for you guys, but the closer I look at this thing, the more I have to agree with Bailey and Danica. The string puller is here in Vegas, and the person with the greatest motive to go after you, Echo, is Jasmine."

"Oh hell no," Danica groused, pushing away from the table and pacing across the floor. "Bailey was right, all along. It *was* that bitch Jasmine!"

Delta stared at her hands. "That would be jumping to conclusions, Dani. There's just no positive proof of her involvement other than her disappearance. Not yet. There could be any number of reasons why she left Nick's place. Any number of reasons why she wasn't at the flower shop when you cruised by. After all, this *is* Vegas." Delta glanced down at her notes. "It isn't that she left that's odd. It's that she hasn't communicated with you. That raises all sorts of red flags. Could be she's hiding. Could be she's dead, but at this point in the game, I have to go with Jasmine as the puppeteer and Briggs as just another puppet."

Bailey pushed her lemon slice down into her ice cubes. "Then what do you suggest?"

Delta turned the floor back over to me, and at that moment I understood why she and Connie had been so successful as cops. She understood and valued teamwork.

"I have a low-level telepath coming within the hour. I'll brief her and she'll go down to the tournament to get a read on the super player. Now, one of three things will happen. The player, Vince, will panic and make a run for it, and I'll track him if he does. Our telepath will stay in the game a few more hands, before losing and coming to interrogate him. Or, he will play a far-too-confident hand and actually stay in the game."

"And the third possibility?"

"Someone will run interference. That scenario can only be played out if there is a higher level super capable of blocking our telepath. If I'd been able to secure a stronger telepath, this would be much easier but—"

"Tip was smart enough to stay away," Danica muttered.

I ignored her. "That's where I come in."

Delta nodded. "While you three deal with the poker player, Nick and I will be watching the roulette cameras. Nick, of course, has no idea what's going on—just that his place has lost too much money at roulette, which totally favors the house."

"Bailey, you'll be watching that tournament and doing everything you can to offset Joy's energy."

Bailey ran her hand through her hair. "My TK powers are weak at best, E."

"You aren't trying to control the wheel or the ball, Bailey. You're just going to disrupt them enough so Joy isn't completely controlling either."

"And it's okay if she wins," Delta added. "She's not our primary target."

"Nick's men are all on high alert. No one's getting out of that casino unless they can become invisible." Delta looked at me, the question in her eyes.

"No. We can't do that."

"Not yet," Bailey mumbled.

"Okay. Then it's all up to our telepath. Once she gets the info, we move, and we'll have to move fast. It's clear everyone knows we're here."

Danica stopped pacing. "Right. Everyone knows you're here. These piss ant Indie motherfuckers have been one step ahead of us every day. There's a leak and we all know who it is. I don't know why we don't just track her ass down and end her sorry life."

Holding my hands up, I shook my head. "Insufficient data, but I *do* hear you both. I want to do what we can with the Indies. Personally, I think you guys give her too much credit. Her only motivation is revenge and let's face it, there are a million other ways to go about that without dragging me into it. Why all the machinations and killing an innocent assistant? Doesn't make sense."

Delta nodded and rose gingerly. "Echo's right. We need to focus on what we know, not what we speculate. If those two players can give us more intel, we'll at least have a better idea of where to go next. We'd better get going. I'm meeting Nick to go over the cameras and general security. He's beefing up security and has asked his fellow owners to do so as well. Sending those photos was brilliant." Delta winced at the pain in her ribs as she made her way to the sofa.

"Did you," I hesitated. "Did you tell Megan or Co—"

"Are you crazy? Uh uh. I told her my Vidbook monitor was acting up." She laughed. "Slid that one by Megan, but not Connie. She knows me too well. I told her I'd been in a scuffle, but was fine." She smiled. "And no, she didn't buy that either, but she's not on her way down."

"Okay," I said. "Delta's going to check out the video. Bailey, you're going to stake out the roulette area. Danica is going to check on Max, who is going back on stage tonight, and I'm going to wait by the fountain and see if Townsend shows up. I doubt he will, but if he does, Mario will be waiting next to me. Townsend surely won't try anything in broad daylight."

"If he shows."

"The tournament starts at eight p.m.," Delta said, lying on the couch. "Just make sure you're all in place before then."

When her eyes closed, I looked at Bailey and Danica. "Okay, fine. If nothing comes of this tonight, we'll go after Jasmine."

"Yes!" Bailey and Dani high-fived.

"But for tonight, can we concentrate on Vince and Joy?"

"Yes."

Bailey rubbed her hands together. "Game on."

❦❦❦❦

"Why are we at the airport?" I asked Danica when Mario pulled up curbside. It was a little after two and we had just left to pick up the telepath when Danica told Mario to swing by the airport.

"Sometimes, I let my big, fat mouth get in the way of things. Sometimes, I use it for good. Now I know you might be pissed off that I went behind your back on this one, Jane, but that's a chance I am willing to take."

I groaned. "What have you done now?"

Danica pointed to the door opening to the baggage claim.

When Tip stepped through the open glass doors, I'd never been happier to see her. It had been months since we'd been in the same room, and though I knew she was still angry with me, just the fact that she came meant the world to me.

"You called Tip?" I was flabbergasted.

Danica nodded. "Bailey did. She knew if Tip was made aware that you'd been attacked *twice*, she'd put her anger at you on the back burner and come help. As usual, Bails was right. The Big Indian said she'd be on the first plane." Her eyes sparkled as they always did when she was in love with her master plan.

I jumped out of the Navigator, only slightly surprised that my heart was banging in my chest. The last time we'd seen each other, it hadn't been pleasant. "You came."

"Hey," she said, wrapping her long arms around me in hug that was far too brief. "You should have told me the real shit that's been going on down here." She pulled away and looked at me. Anger no longer fueled her eyes. "You should have told me everything."

"When? You've been so angry with me. How was I supposed to slide in, *and oh by the way, a bunch of Indies are trying to kill me?*"

She shrugged. "I still am, but even then, that sure as hell doesn't mean someone gets to take pot shots at you. Not without losing a limb or two." She smiled. She actually smiled at me.

I think my heart melted beneath her grin.

"God, it's good to see that smile."

"I'd have been her sooner, you know? You should have told me all of it. Thank God Bailey has the sense God gave a goose."

"Um, it's not like you've been approachable. Ever since Alaska—"

"Leave that be, Echo. Please. You know, I'd never

step on your toes. I know you're trying to find your own way with this mentor role. I'm trying to respect that, but I have a lot on my plate with Mel and all."

Looking into her chocolate brown eyes, I stepped back, wishing her arms around me hadn't felt so good. "And I appreciate that, Tip. I really do. How is she?"

"She's dying, right in front of me and there's nothing I can do to stop it. It's breaking my heart." Tip's eyes watered. "Mel thought getting away was a really good idea. Malecon called his pilot and, well, here I am."

Suddenly, I wondered if the anger I'd been seeing in her eyes was even directed towards me. Maybe she was just angry at life in general. "I wish you'd let me help."

She shrugged, more anger and frustration oozing from her. "Nothing you can do. Besides, your job is to train those kids. That's what Mel wants you to be doing. She thinks it's bullshit the Others sent you to deal with this shit, and I agree."

"You do?"

"Hell yeah. This is petty ass bullshit, and, quite frankly, a waste of your time and talents."

"They offered up Sonja to teach Cinder."

Tip bowed her head—something she did when she was about to lose her self-control. "I see. Someone ought to have a little chat about the appropriateness of fucking blackmail."

"Blackmail? It's a deal that I—"

"Want for Cinder. I get that, love, I really do, but—" She shook her head. "They're out of line once again."

We walked back to the car in silence before I couldn't let well enough alone.

"Tip...I'm so sorry I didn't—"

"Let it go, Echo, please. We have a job to do here. Let's do it so I can get back to Mel."

I nodded and walked her back to the Navigator. "This whole thing has slid sideways on us...gotten convoluted in ways I never could have imagined."

She studied my face for a long time, her eyes softening. "There's something you're not telling me. What is it?"

"Let's get back to the hotel. I'll tell you everything on the way."

And so I did. I told her everything. I couched it all as if it was a movie I'd seen. She listened quietly, which was unusual for Tip. Her silence alone was enough for me to see how much she had changed. Then, as I told her about the battles and skirmishes, the small vein in her temple began throbbing. Tip isn't one to sit on her hands when those she loves are being attacked. She's a doer. She acts. She wanted to act now, and her self-restraint was admirable under the circumstances, considering one woman she loved was dying and the other was in danger.

And she did love me. She would always love me. That much I was certain of. She may choose not to show it, but it was there.

When I finished getting her up to speed, Mario pulled into the Pentagon and dropped us off. Danica excused herself to tend to Delta.

"Hungry? There are a ton of places to eat."

"Actually, I'd like a drink."

I tilted my head, realizing how tired she looked. Tip seldom drank. "You okay? I can't remember the last time I saw you drink."

She nodded, but I knew better and waited until

we were seated in the hotel restaurant. By drink, Tip had meant iced tea.

We sat in silence as I waited her out.

"Mel gets weaker every day," she said so softly I almost didn't hear her. "When I was packing, she pulled me aside and gave me this." Pulling an envelope out, she slid it over to me. "To be read when…when she passes."

My stomach dropped at the turn of phrase. I could not, for the life of me, picture this world without her in it, yet it was becoming clear I would have to sooner than later.

I wasn't ready.

Picking up the envelope, I smelled it and smiled as tears filled my eyes. It smelled just like Mel. "This must be so hard on you. I don't know how you do it."

"I don't have time to think about me. It's all Malecon and I can do to keep her spirits up. I think she fears losing it before she goes. She has such a fear of the tumor making her have dementia or something. She doesn't want to appear pathetic."

Nodding, I slid the envelop into my backpack. "Like she could ever be that."

"I don't question her fears. What I do question is why you are still dilly-dallying with the Others. They bring you nothing but headaches."

"They asked for help. I answered. It's what we do, right?"

Tip's eyes locked onto mine, holding the same tears mine had. "Since when did you become so diplomatic?"

"Since I was put in charge." A slow smile crept across my face as I reached for her other hand. She still wore the silver band I'd given her for Christmas years ago, only now, on her right hand. "Thank you so much for coming."

Pulling her hand away, she wiped her eyes before the tears could fall. "Okay, tell me what you need me to do."

So I did.

And the more I talked to her, the happier I was that she was here...with me now, helping me through all of this. With her near me, I felt stronger—more in control. I had the confidence that we really were going to get to the bottom of all this.

All of this.

Her question about the Others caught me by surprise. Did I need to separate myself and my charges from them after this? Did I owe them anything? What were my choices once Mel was gone?

"Okay, you've caught me up to speed. I have a pretty good idea what you want me to do at the poker tables, but I want the extraneous stuff as well. No detail is too small."

For thirty minutes, I gave her the low down on Jasmine, Nick, and what had happened so far. When I got to Delta, she held her hand up.

"You brought one of your naturals into this?"

"You say it as if she's a pet."

Her eyebrows rose. "Well?"

"Oh stop. Trust me. Once you meet her, you'll know why. She's not like any natural I've ever met. She's almost like one of us."

"Whoa, that's high praise."

"She's earned it. Besides, she's an ex-cop and I needed discreet investigative skills."

The waitress came over and we ordered two iced teas and chicken wings.

"Does she know?"

I nodded. "She got her ass kicked by a TK. There was no hiding it from her anymore. It was wrong to hide it from her in the first place."

Tip cocked her head at me. "So you told your natural *friend* but not Finn, who was your lover?" She made a sound of disgust.

I looked away. "Different circumstances entirely. Stay focused here."

She laughed. "So your merry band of naturals all know? I'm sure that thrills the Others."

"Look. It was easy for Melika to keep us a secret out on the bayou, but things have changed. We live in the real world now. I can't do it alone, and my *merry band of naturals* might as well be supers. That's how good they are."

"But you're not alone on the coast. You have Bailey and Danica—"

"And my naturals, which, if you could see what all they can do, you'd wonder if they weren't an entirely new breed of human."

She held up her hand. "Okay. I get it. No wonder the word out has been that you are hard to work with. You're totally bucking the Others."

"Not bucking. I'm here, aren't I?"

"Yeah, I get that, but why? What have they ever done to help you?"

"They saved our asses in New Orleans, Tip."

She nodded. "Just remember…they don't do anything unless there's something in it for the community. They aren't always altruistic, and, to be honest, they can be very manipulative."

"I know. I'll keep that in mind."

She leaned forward. "Don't you miss the bayou at all?"

Her question caught me off guard...as if she'd thinking about it since she landed.

I missed it more than I could articulate. I missed her, but I would never admit that to myself or anyone else. "Of course I do, but Tip, kids today can't live out there. It's too primitive. To try to send them back into the technological world after living on the bayou—" I shook my head. "Is a recipe for failure."

"I disagree, but then, what else is new? You also think you need to be wrapped up with the Others, and I totally disagree with that. No, we can't have supers killing each other over something as mundane as fame or fortune, but they could have sent any number of other supers to handle this. Why you?"

I'd been wondering that myself. "I am not at all sure I know why."

"Well, I spoke with Bishop about the Indies before I came down, and she said we needed to be very careful. Don't underestimate them."

"We've been attacked three times. Careful fell out the window two attacks ago."

"Their danger lies in their gang mentality. Because they've had no training, they use their powers like thugs. Every time they get away with something, they get bolder, less afraid, and far less cautious about being seen. This leads them to carry out brazen acts like killing the assistant and attacking you."

"Twice."

She nodded. "Twice. That's serious business. To attack a mentor—" she paused and shook her head. "What would have happened if someone, besides Malecon, attacked Melika?"

"We would have hunted them to the ends of the earth." The words came out before I could think them.

"Oh."

She smiled. "Right. And we would have squashed anyone who tried."

Nodding, I thanked the waitress when she brought our iced tea over.

"We need to do more than squash these punks, Echo. We need to crush them. Hard. Painfully so. We need to send a really loud message that *you* are off limits."

"I won't kill anyone as a warning, Tip. That's not how I operate."

Pouring sugar in her tea, she nodded. "I knew you'd say that, but I won't promise it won't happen. Thugs, Echo, with thug mentality. Whoever it was who attacked Delta could have killed her instantly, but he didn't. He toyed with her. He enjoyed the moment of complete control. Thugs, darlin', and you're a fool if you think you can reason with them. They understand nothing but brutish behavior. Sometimes, to communicate with thugs, you have to speak their language."

"I didn't say don't hurt them. I just said don't kill them."

She grinned again. Oh how I had missed that lopsided smile. "I'll do the best I can. Now, help me eat these wings, because I have a feeling it's going to be a long night."

༄༄༄༄

When Tip and I arrived at our suite, everyone was waiting for us. Bailey and Danica were sitting at the table, pouring over a map of the strip and Delta was digging something out of one of her black bags.

"Tip, this is Delta Stevens. Delta, Tiponi Redhawk."

Delta stuck her hand out first and she and Tip shook hands, their gazes equally appraising.

"Have we met before?" Tip asked. "You look awfully familiar."

Delta grinned and her one dimple creased. "I get that a lot." Releasing Tip's hand, Delta reached into her bag and pulled out a six-inch case. "You people may be able to read each other's minds and auras and palms and what not, but we need some good old technology to keep us all on the same page." When she opened the box, there were eight tiny plastic pieces; four were flesh-colored, two were black, and two were brown. "The Rockwell earpiece," she said. "Best in the business. CIA and FBI use them. Mic built in. Almost imperceptible because it goes deep inside the ear. Just talk as you would if we were standing next to each other. The mic will pick up your voices."

We all reached in and took one.

"I'm touched that your earpieces are an equal opportunity device," Danica said, plucking the darker earpiece out of the case and placing it in her ear.

"Now, we're all on the same channel, so if one person is talking, no one else can talk, so keep that in mind."

"Breaker, breaker, one nine," Bailey said, placing hers in her ear.

"Smart," Tip said, putting the reddish one in her ear. "Sometimes we forget that what we do doesn't always translate in group work, especially if that group work includes naturals."

"I'm all about teamwork, Tiponi," Delta said.

Tip studied her through dark eyes. "I understand your team is now working with Echo."

"We are. It's been a nice match with her people and mine. We needed to get back into action. Retired life was killing us softly."

I could tell right away that Tip liked her. Tiponi Redhawk always did appreciate stronger women, and I was certain Storm was the strongest natural woman I'd ever met. "I don't think I could ever retire."

Delta caught Tip's hazel eyes and something close to kinship flickered there. "No? What is it *you* do?"

Without batting an eye, Tip replied, "I bail out damsels in distress."

Delta tossed her head back and laughed. "Oh, I like this one!"

Danica looked at me like WTF is *that* about?

I didn't have the heart or the balls to say 'boys will be boys'.

Once everyone had their positions set and we'd gone over everything one more time, everyone but Tip and I took off, leaving us, once again, to dance the ex-lover tango.

"Tell you one thing," Tip said, wedging her transmitter deeper into her ear. "I'm glad that woman is on our side."

"Delta? Please tell me you weren't reading her."

She shook her head. "No need to. You don't have to be a super to see she's fiercely competitive. When you look into those eyes, you are seeing her authentic self."

"You should meet her partners."

Tip stared at me.

"Her lover and her business partner. They're

all pretty damn butch and very good at what they do. Connie Rivera's computer skills may even surpass the boys from the Bat Cave."

"Wow. That's high praise indeed." Tip smiled at me. "I'm glad you have them then and I take back all the shitty things I said about them. I guess it must be really different training supers away from the bayou."

"You have no idea. It has its challenges to be sure. People like Delta make it easier, though. Her people are real experts."

Tip stood in front of me and held my hands in hers. "You know I'll get over this, someday, right? I just need time. I need—"

"Tip—"

"No, let me finish. Watching Mel slowly wither away is the worst possible torture for me. There's nothing I can do except be there for her. And to be honest, her not being here scares the hell out of me. I wake up every day wondering if today will be her last. I live in constant fear of the inevitable. It's killing me, Echo. It's tearing my heart out of my chest."

Wrapping my arms around her, I pulled her to me. "I wish there was something I could do. I wish you'd let me back in."

Crushing me to her, she whispered, "It's so hard, love. It's like I'm losing Mel and you all at once and it's all I can do to tread water."

"You've not lost me, and you never will. As surprised as I am that you came, I am also so very happy."

"I never realized how badly I needed to get away until that plane took off." She pulled away and searched my face. "Or how much I needed to see you. I've really missed you, Echo. I miss the bayou, I miss my dog, I miss a lot of things. Some days, I feel like a rudderless ship. Some days, it feels like I am walking around in someone else's skin. But not today. For the first time in a long time, I feel…okay."

Okay was not her first or second choice, but just the safer choice. I was pretty certain she was going to say it felt like home.

I knew because I felt that calm, settled feeling the moment I hugged her. She was my ground wire, my level bubble in an uneven world. "Thank you for coming."

"Thanks for asking. I'm sorry I didn't agree when you called. I was being an ass." She puffed up her cheeks and blew out a breath. "That seems to be a hat I am overly fond of wearing these days. Thank God Bailey called me. She's a good second for you."

"I'm sure that was a conversation that burned your ear drum."

Tip chuckled. "Oh yeah. She gave me an earful all right." She stepped away. "I've seldom had to worry about you as long as she and Dani are around."

"You're not Danica's favorite person, you know?" I picked a stray hair from her shoulder.

"Can you blame her? I'm the only person to hurt you and still live to tell about it."

I couldn't argue that. "We are going to need each other when Mel passes, Tip. I need you to know, to really know that I will be here for you."

She nodded, tears forming once again. "Thank you for that. In the meantime, I'll get changed and we'll see you down at the tournament. Trust me. Whatever this pudwhacker is doing will be peeled back like a banana. There's no Indie alive with the power to block me out. He'll be completely open in order to read everyone else's cards. Trust me. His information will leak from his mind like a sieve."

"You going to be okay?"

She looked at me before wiping her eyes. "I'm not sure I'll ever be okay again, but at least I know you're not leaving me, too." With that, Tip headed for the playing room.

That was the moment I knew the real truth behind her anger. She felt like me leaving the bayou was me leaving *her*. It made perfect sense now. Tip's anger wasn't from Alaska or anything that I'd said or done. She was afraid she was being left in the dust. Without Mel, and with Bailey being my second in command, Tip had…nothing and no one. No wonder she was so upset.

I left, putting my dime-sized transmitter in my ear. Already, Danica and Bailey were working it, trying it out by attempting the *Who's on First* routine.

"Will you two hush," I said, just to make sure mine worked.

"Ten-four good buddy."

Shaking my head, I made my way to the Bellagio, praying everything would indeed, be ten-four.

☙☙❧❧

Everything was ten-four at the fountains because Townsend no-showed. I wasn't surprised. The man behind the curtain was a coward.

Grabbing a coffee on my way to the tournament, I checked in with everyone. Bailey had already spotted Joy, who had no shields built at all. Typical. Danica was at Nick's with Max, but Nick wasn't there. He'd left to do some business errands before meeting Delta in the security room at the Pentagon. Delta was already there waiting in the security room for him. She said his head of security was balking at the idea of a "civilian" having a peek at the banks of monitors, but that she understood why.

Then I called the boys, who said Townsend Briggs was definitely on the move. He'd placed several calls from his cell—a phone we now could monitor through some high level GPS technology the boys were developing. Every time he used his phone, they were able to pinpoint his location on a digital map. The rest was Greek to me. All I wanted to know was whether or not he was in Vegas, and he was.

So were a lot of folks. This tournament had attracted people from all over the world. You could tell the high rolling Texans by their plate-sized belt buckles. Californians and Floridians wore deep tans and light colors. Midwesterners were inappropriately dressed for hot weather, and locals were calmly chatting with waitresses they'd probably known forever. In short, the place was packed.

As the poker players took their seats, some were chatting with their neighbors while others surveyed their opponents. Vince was in the latter group. I could have spotted him even without my powers—arrogant, haughty, gazing at his opponents with palpable contempt. He wasn't just a super, he was a super with a superiority complex, and he openly disdained his fellow competitors.

As the crowd grew, I realized I might have underestimated him. He would need a tremendous amount of focus to read the other players amidst the cacophony of the casino. He would have to use so much energy to retrieve, he would, no doubt, have no walls up—if, in fact, he even knew how to construct them. I was certain he could construct the most rudimentary shield; otherwise, he'd have gone nuts a long time ago hearing every thought happening around him.

"*That's him.*"

"Hard to miss him, huh?" I could clearly see Tip from my vantage point at the slots. She was an amazingly handsome woman with her dark red skin, long dark hair that looked like melted licorice, and shoulders that said she'd been a linebacker in another life. I warmed inside having her in my head once again.

"*He's an asshole. You can tell just by looking at him.*"

"Don't underestimate him, Tip."

"*Roger that, darlin'. Not to worry there.*"

"When will you extract his info?"

"*After the game starts. I want him to have made enough money that walking away from it is out of the question. This takes the flight response out of the fight or flight equation.*"

And there it was: the reason she'd been such a good collector. She knew people. "Has anyone told you lately that you're brilliant?"

"*Not recently, but it's always good to hear.*"

"That's *him*." It was Delta in my ear.

"We know, Storm. Tip's got it—"

"No. I mean *that's* the prick who beat the crap out of me!"

I stopped in my tracks. "Vince? *He's* the guy?" I thought about the bruises on Ricky's cheek. "Delta? Aren't you right handed?"

"Nope. Southpaw all the way. Why?"

Whoever hit Ricky was right handed. It wasn't Delta at all. "Did you land any rights?"

"Only to his body. Why?"

"Not important. If Vince took you out, that means he's also a lower level mover, which explains why he was going to finish you off with a knife. I'll bet he ran out of power."

I had to leave my slot machine to check on Bailey, only eight feet from Joy, who was stacking and re-stacking her chips.

I was a good fifteen feet away. "You ready, Bailey?" I said softly.

She nodded. "Let the games begin, baby."

Moving back to the slot area, I asked for Delta. "Nick there yet?"

There was a lot of verbal ruckus in the background before she answered. "Uh…his guys have no idea where he is. He's not answering his cell."

"They worried?"

"Understatement. He missed an appointment this afternoon."

"Shit."

"This little maneuver is called diversion interference, Echo. It's a brilliant move because it breaks up our focus and concentration. With Nick missing, they're sending us a big message: Back off or else. Now is so not the time to panic."

"We don't know that supers have taken him."

Delta breathed heavily into the mic. "No, but it would be a safe bet."

"I need your eyes up there, Delta. I need to see what you're seeing and make sure there are no surprises."

"Nick being gone is already quite a surprise, dontcha think?"

I did, and feared for his safety. "What do your

years of experience tell you about this?"

"I think we have to assume he is still alive. Dead pawns are no good to trade with. My guess is they know his men will scatter to find him, as will we. They're probably expecting Danica to join the hunt. They are counting on us to panic and go looking for him. That would be ill-advised."

"Dani? Did you hear that?"

"They don't know us very well, Clark, if they think I'd leave you to look for Nick. He's a big boy with a lot of friends. If you ask me, your Indies just made the dumbest mistake in the book."

I was more than relieved to hear that.

"We'll soon find out," Delta replied. "Okay ladies, looks like the show's about to begin. We've got our eyes in the sky here, though these boys aren't very happy about it."

"Because Nick isn't there?"

She chuckled. "Because there's estrogen in the house."

We went silent as the casino manager announced that the tournament had begun.

My insides were churning as the hands were dealt. One, two, three, four hands of poker in which Vince won two. He was overly calm, more polished than I had expected. He looked older than the kids we'd sent packing, twenty-four, twenty-five, maybe. "Slick" would be how Danica would describe him.

At the thought of her name, she spoke in my ear. "Max is returning to the stage. The replacement act got sick. Bad oysters or something. What do you want me to do?"

Distraction interference, I thought. Maybe with Max in the open, Townsend Briggs would surface more clearly. They were herding us. "He's aware it's not safe, right? That he could be stepping into muddy water?"

"The guy's tired of hiding like a yellow-bellied lizard. He wants his life back. Can't say I blame him. This place would feel like a fortress after a while. He's just doing what we asked him to do."

"What time is the show?"

"Ten."

I looked at my watch. Plenty of time. "Go for it, but stay close to him. And for God's sake, don't shoot anyone."

"Aww man, you ruin all the fun."

"Dani? Please be careful."

"Always, Clark."

As I watched Tip win her first hand, I noticed a change over her. When she'd arrived, she had appeared tired and worn. Now, there was that twinkle in her eye—a twinkle I had really missed seeing. Away from Mel's imminent death, away from the dashed hopes and failed experimental drugs, Tip's cheeks were flushed, her keen eyes sharp, her demeanor relaxed, and her aura light green. She was having a ball.

And I was awashed in emotions that surprised the hell out of me.

Then I thought about how warmly she'd greeted Delta. Not the least bit threatened by a woman of equal strength, Tip continued to amaze me with her grace and poise. Had she always been so confident and self-possessed? I suppose she had. One thing I knew for sure was how happy I was to have her here with us now. Ever since Mel's diagnosis, we'd both been treading water on different continents. She'd collected the triplets in Russia and made a beeline back to Mel before whisking her off to Europe for experimental treatment. I wondered if Mel knew the toll this was taking on her.

I knew the toll it was taking on me.

I also wondered what had happened to the girlfriend she'd brought back with her. She hadn't mentioned her once. I wasn't about to remind her she had one.

"He's won half the hands. When he loses, it's barely enough to make a dent. I'm going to give him a run at the next hand and see how he reacts. While he's off-balance, I'll read what I can."

"Perfect."

"How's Bailey?"

"Let me check." Walking over to the roulette area, I was stunned by the amount of chips Joy had amassed.

"She's won all that?" Tip was in my mind, seeing what I saw.

"Yep," Bailey said softly, turning from the table. Joy was flirting with a large black man playing next to her, so she wasn't paying any attention to Bailey. "She put something like two or three grand on double zero green. That ball was jumping all over the place, but the moment green came up, it landed and stayed. The pit boss examined the ball and tossed out another. Nothing subtle about the way she wins. Wins big, loses small."

"Ladies," It was Delta. "They've run that tape back three times. If you're afraid of people knowing about your kind, Echo, you're doing the right thing in getting them out of Vegas. That ball just stopped. Dead. It wasn't even a good try."

"What did they say?"

"They sent a guy down to make sure there are no electronic or magnetic devices in the area but, trust me...they're not fooled. They just don't know who or how."

"Then we need to take her out first if she's that obvious. Bailey?"

"I say wait until the break. I'll get her then."

"Good."

"While you're all chitty-chatting," Danica piped in, "Max is preparing to go on. He is dedicating this show to Hannah. He's nervous as hell, but wants to do this."

"Good. Stay close."

The buzz died down and I went back to the slots. One quick read of Vince told me all I needed to know. Tip had stymied him and he couldn't figure out how she did it.

"He's flustered," I said. *"Go for it."*

"Will do. Oh, and Echo? You're a great leader. Trust in that." Then she was gone—dumpster diving into the trashcan of Vince's brain.

I knew what she would do. She would peel back the layers of his mind. A telepath can really only read the thoughts in the front of the mind, but Tip was no ordinary telepath. She was capable of going behind the front of the mind and into the short-term memory. She would skim through data and material, weeding through facts and fiction alike like a computer. She would cull through his mind to give us what we needed. I was counting on that.

Watching her, I couldn't help but warm all over. She was an amazing woman and it was as if I was seeing her with fresh eyes. Her calm comportment, her confident demeanor, the way she understood the situation...I'd missed that. I needed to face it. I missed *her*. As I stood there and watched her, a slow smile spread across my face. She never ceased to amaze me. The power of that woman was unlike anything I'd ever seen.

And that was when I saw the truth of my failed relationship with Finn. All along, I had thought the great divide between us was my secret—my truth, but I'd so easily told Delta Stevens, hadn't I? I wasn't afraid of the truth. It was a *different* truth I was afraid of, and suddenly, there it was, in my face, big as day.

I loved Tiponi Redhawk, probably more than I had ever loved another. There wasn't anything wrong with Finn; she was an incredible woman as well.

She just wasn't Tip.

And right now, Tip was at the top of her game and in that love, in that moment, when she looked up at me, everything made perfect sense.

She was *the one* and I had lost her. That loss had created an imbalance in me that no amount of work could fix.

How could I have been so stupid?

"Earth to Echo. You with me here?"

"More than you know. Whatcha got?"

"He's much stronger than what I expected. No shield, though. Stays under the radar, but wins too much not to be noticed. He's good.

"Who's his boss?"

"In his mind he refers to him as T.B. Looks like he plays whatever role he's given but doesn't really have many of the other parts to the puzzle. Does his job, gets his cut, end of story."

"Then it's time you and he had a little conversation. Let him know how this is going to go down, that you want all the names of the rest of the Indies who are in Vegas."

"And if he refuses?"
"Hurt him."
"I like the way you think."
"Just enough to let him know you mean business."
"Right. Stay tuned, darlin'."

I stayed tuned in, inching closer to the action should Tip need my help. I seriously doubted it. These newbies were no match for the likes of her. I'd seen her practically melt someone's brain in their head.

"He's a little pencil-dick dweeb, Echo."

I tried not to smile. She seldom minced words. "What did he say?"

"Shorthand version? He said 'you people don't scare me'."

"And you said?"

"We oughtta. I left it at that for now. He's good at cards and flying low. I'll give him that much."

"Did he ask what you were doing there?"

"Oh yes. He was shocked shitless. Thought I was there for the tournament. I told him I came to keep an eye out on him. Know what he said? 'Eat my dick, Injun'."

The smile dropped from my face. I felt my blood run cold. "He didn't."

"Oh yes he did. He has no idea I could fry his brain inside his pinhead. Just give me the word."

"Thank you for not doing it. We need more info."

"I did find Hannah's name in there, but no attachment to it. He's going for a big win, the half a million dollar purse, then my guess is he'll take that back to Atlantic City. That's what they do. The funds travel back and forth."

"Anything else in there?"

"Yeah. A pair of angry emerald green eyes."

"Delta."

"Yep. He is afraid of her."

"He should be. Let him play on for now. Keep bugging him. Push him. Piss him off, but don't let him off the hook."

"Affirmative."

Bailey's voice came on. "Joy's winning big. She's not subtle at all now. She's betting like a pro, but that ball is moving unnaturally. My guess is they'll shut the table down."

"It's almost time for a break. Once her ass leaves that stool, escort her out. Separate her from the crowd. We need Tip to peel her."

"Gotcha. E?"

"Yeah?"

"These kids have no qualms about what they're doing and they sure as shit aren't afraid of us."

I wondered if there was a piece I was missing. How could these kids *not* be afraid of us? Or even slightly intimidated? What did they know that we didn't?"

Just then, my Vidbook vibrated. It was Sal, so I stepped outside, telling everyone I had a call from home.

"Hi Sal. What's up?"

Her reddish hair stuck out from under her military ball cap like straw. "Know you're busy, but wanted to update you on a few things going on."

"Okay."

"Someone has been checking out the secured perimeter. We've had two hits in the last two days."

"What? Everyone all right?"

"There was no breach of the systems but someone's been checking it out. I wanted to know what you want us to do? Taylor's double-checked every camera and every fence, but I wondered if you wanted to call in reinforcements."

"Where's Cinder?"

Sal smiled. "She's stepping up and taking charge of the younger ones. Film doesn't show any people outside the perimeter, but it's all been scanned. William said I needed to call you and see what you want to do."

Diversion interference. Was this part of it? My heart started racing. I needed to wrap this up and get home. "Tell William to call in back-up. He'll know what to do. I'm sending Bailey and Danica home tomorrow. Move William into the main house. Set him up in the front guest room."

"He's already packing his gear. I'm not real concerned yet, Echo, but I figured you needed to know. Could be something, could be nothing."

"I appreciate it, Sal. What about Con?"

"She's made a few calls. There will be patrols out here just to make sure. We're doing everything we can to keep everyone safe."

"Keep me posted."

Sal looked closer into the camera. "You okay?"

"Things are heating up. I've gotta get back into the casino. Thank you, Sal." Flipping the Vidbook closed, I started back into the casino. I was just rounding the corner when I saw Bailey being blown back against a wall.

"What the fuck?" Before I could move, the crowd seemed to multiply as security moved in quickly. As I squeezed through the crowd, Joy made eye contact with me. I stopped, even though the crowd hadn't. Everyone wanted to see what happened to the tall blonde woman who had been slammed against the wall. I was sure they all thought she was drunk. I read Bailey quickly and knew she was woozy and dazed, but otherwise unharmed. So I turned my attention back to Joy.

Raising her hand as if to scratch behind her ear, Joy prepared to deliver a similar blow to me.

But I was ready for her.

She tried to push her energy out at me, but I'd already built a shield around me when the crowd started squeezing me in. Good thing, too, because Joy was tossing a lot at me. It slid around my shield like water off a duck's back. The look on her face was priceless. She knew who I was and she was gunning for me anyway, but I wasn't about to let this little twit get to me.

Eyes locked onto her, I moved closer. The security guys were helping Bailey to her feet, so I kept moving toward Joy.

"Is that commotion from you?" Tip asked.

"Joy attacked Bailey."

"Shit. We need to take them down, Echo. Now."

"I'm all over it. I just need to get to—" then came the sound of shouting in my earpiece, followed by the sound of a scuffle. Knowing it wasn't coming from the roulette area, I started for the poker table. I heard, "Son of a bitch!" in my ear.

It was Delta.

As I rounded the corner, four of Nick's security guards approached Tip. One made the mistake of grabbing her arm and when she dropped him in his tracks, two of them zapped her with a stun gun. She was on the ground doing the funky chicken by the tables.

"Delta, what the hell is going on?"

"We saw her cheat, Echo," she whispered. "There

was no doubt about it. I saw it as well."

"Who, *Tip?*"

Delta was right in my ear. "Yeah. Clearly, obviously cheat."

That's when I knew. Townsend Briggs had finally entered the game. Tip hadn't cheated. With her powers, she didn't need to. Briggs had made the security unit see what he wanted them to see, effectively removing Tip from the game. That's what an illusionist did: made you see things that weren't there.

"Can you see Townsend?"

"Um, I can't see jack. They've handcuffed me to a chair. With their boss missing and Tip's apparent cheating, they're not feeling too friendly."

"They got Tip."

"Stay away from her...what? No one. I'm praying you all come to your senses. Nick is gonna be pissed when he hears how you goons treated his guest."

I nodded in silent understanding. "Hold tight, Del. Ask them to rewind the tapes. Whatever you saw won't be on the tapes." Leaving the poker arena, I started back toward Bailey, who was sitting against the wall while two guards knelt down next to her.

"I'm coming, Bailey," I whispered, slicing through the crowd. When I finally reached her, the two large men were helping her stand.

I cut my eyes over to Joy, who gave me a finger wave that might as well have been just the finger. When I reached Bailey, I grabbed her elbow. "I'm sorry, fellas, but my friend is epileptic and I bet she forgot her meds."

"Ma'am, this is a tournament, and drunk and disorderly conduct—"

I didn't hear the rest. I couldn't. I had to do

something fast before everyone was out of commission. With one hand on Bailey, I turned to Joy and smiled. Hers wavered a little right before I pushed my offensive shield out, scattering her massive pile of chips everywhere. The crowd was like piranhas in a feeding frenzy, diving on the floor for chips, pushing, shoving. It was total mayhem. Seeing the chaos, the security team turned their attention away from us long enough for us to make our way out of the casino.

"Holy crap, Batman," Bailey said when we sat on the first bench we came to. "That little bitch packs a punch."

"You okay?"

She nodded, feeling the back of her head. "Got an egg-sized knot on my head, but I'll live. What in the hell is going on?"

"Townsend Briggs is back in play. He made the security box see Tip cheating, so they zapped her."

"And Delta? I could barely hear her. Why was she whispering?"

"They handcuffed her to a chair. With Nick missing and all these weird things happening—"

"Yeah. Why did Joy attack you?"

"She had a big bet on the table. Her biggest yet, and I managed to push the ball out of the winning number at the very last minute. It was all I had left. She's too strong for my tertiary skill to make a dent."

"But she didn't know that, otherwise she wouldn't have smacked you."

Bailey looked at me, her eyes still a bit glassy. "You know, E, I don't think that's why. I'm pretty sure she did it just because she could. There's something not right about her. Have you read her? I mean, *really* read her?"

Then came Delta's whispered voice. "You guys need to get outta here. The goons are looking for Bailey."

We both rose, but Bailey shook her head "You gotta read her energy, E. I'll grab this chair and get my wits about me."

Danica piped in. "Be careful, Clark. Cornered animals are the most dangerous."

After Bailey folded onto the bench, I made my way back into the casino. Things were still hectic, and I realized the roulette area had been emptied.

"What's going on?" I asked a bystander.

"They're moving the game to a new table, so they're taking an early break."

I scanned the crowd, looking for any sign of Joy. I couldn't see her through the dense mass of bodies, so I said 'screw it' and started to leave. As I turned around, I ran right into her.

"You and your friends have become a giant, ugly hemmie on our asses," she said. Her eyes were cold, her pupils pinpricks.

"You people are dangerous to the rest of us and it's going to end." I let my energy build up and I could feel it surge through my body. The air around me was electrified.

She sneered. "No it's not. Not by the likes of you. You're weak...and old. You don't get that we're not hurting anyone here. God gave us these powers and there's nothing wrong with us using them. Better us than the casinos getting the money."

I lowered my shields. "That's just it. You *did* harm someone. You killed Hannah Sinclair and beat up a friend of mine."

She waved her hand in the air. "Do you even know why?"

Her chillingly clipped question told me what I'd feared: Joy was one of the killers. "Humor me. Why?"

"Hannah was trying to convert the young ones. The ones you sent packing with their tails between their legs. She wanted them to take the higher road." She barked a laugh that bordered on insane. "Ha! We *are* the higher road. Just like Michael Jordan made more money because of a skill he possessed, so should we. Who the fuck was *she* to turn them against us? She deserved what she got."

"So you just killed her? Like that?"

She rolled her eyes. "We warned them. All of them. This isn't about the magic show, though Townsend seems obsessed with fame. He has the fortune, thanks to us, but what he desires most is fame. We're going to get him that fame and he is getting us the fortune. It all evens out in the end." She looked at me with intense eyes. "You can't win this one, hon. We've got God on our side."

God? Was she kidding? Her aura was a dark brown, and her personality was borderline. This one wasn't playing with both oars in the water. *That* was what Bailey wanted me to see.

That, and so much more that it made me shudder.

"Why not just kill Max? Wouldn't that have been easier?"

"Not with Hannah alive, no. She'd have gone to the cops or done something stupid. No, she had to go. She'd already costed Townsend three of his team."

I caught the word 'costed' and realized I was dealing with an uneducated, immoral super who thought nothing of using her powers to get what she wanted. Very dangerous, indeed.

"Enough jibber-jabber," she said, her voice

changing so rapidly, it sounded like someone else's. "If you and your friends don't leave me alone, the next time I see you, I'll embed your fucking ass into the wall. Go save someone else, but leave us the fuck alone."

Oh, now she'd really crossed the line. I stepped closer and looked down into her face. She had no fear whatsoever. That was disconcerting. "Joy, if you so much as raise a finger toward me—"

She moved right into my space, unafraid. "You won't do jack shit, lady. You think Townsend didn't do his homework on you? Of course he did. You're some fucked up goody-goody out to save us or some shit like that. You aren't about hurting us, and as much as you'd wanna sock me right now, you'd never do it. You're so fucking afraid someone will find out about us? Well, who gives a shit? Let them find out!" She barked another laugh. "Besides, we both know my powers are way better'n yours, so if you wanna piece a me, take your best shot."

In my ear I heard Danica. "Fucking take that snotty bitch out, Clark."

I couldn't. There were too many cameras and too much going on, and she knew that. The little punk knew that.

"See? Even now you're outgunned. So move along, little doggie," she said, making shooing motions. "And let me get back to carving some of the meat from the casino bones. No one wants or needs to be saved by the likes of you." With that, she returned to the roulette table, her back confidently facing me.

There was nothing I could do with so many people around but watch her walk away. If I were Tip, I would have blown her brains out her ears.

But I wasn't. That didn't mean I wasn't beginning

to see the error of my pacifistic ways. This little nobody had just schooled me on how to thumb your nose up at authority.

"E?"

"On my way, Bailey."

I made it back to her in under five minutes. Her coloring was on the rebound as she sat on a bus bench, eyes closed, taking deep breaths. "Well? Batshit crazy that girl is."

"Bipolar, for sure. Manic. Violent tendencies. I didn't ask if she killed Hannah, didn't need to. She was almost proud of it."

"Yeah, that's one crazy ass bitch. When she looked over at me just before she fired on me, there was this freakin' weird look on her face. Weird, like she couldn't wait to blast me...like she was going to relish smacking me around."

"How are you feeling?"

"Like shit, but who cares? What the fuck is going on? What happened to Tip?"

I told her about Tip and Delta.

"These little fuckers are going on the aggressive? Oh hell no. Tell me you have a plan. Tell me you're not going to let them get away with this. Tell me I can call my little buddies to do some damage."

"Not yet. I'm waiting for Tip to come to. I'm not making a move until I know she's okay."

"Little fuckers."

I leaned closer and examined her eyes. "You sure you don't have a concussion?"

"Of course I'm sure. I'm a shaman, and right now I'm one super pissed off shaman!"

"Okay, look. Townsend has to be nearby. No doubt he's behind the stage pulling all the strings. He made Nick's men think Tip was cheating. They were on her like white on rice. Once Tip is back up, we'll figure out how to get her out of there."

"She oughtta blast their brains out the backs of their heads, fucking asswipes."

"Uh uh. Nick's men are only doing what they're being manipulated to do. We can't hurt them."

"Well shit. Who can we hurt? Come on, E, you can't let these mental retards get the drop on us. We keep dropping back to punt and we're gonna lose the whole damn game."

I tried not to smile as she slowly returned to herself. "Trust me, Bailey, we are far past push coming to shove, but right now, our best player is doing the funky chicken on the floor. We need to regroup."

Suddenly, Danica was in my ear. "Max is on stage, and let me tell you…mad skills. You alright? I can be there in—"

"We're fine. You hang tight. Stay close. Keep me posted."

"I'd rather be hanging tight with you. Sounds like you could use a little muscle."

"We can't leave him out to dry, Dani. Stay put."

She muttered expletives in my ear.

"Well, this has gone to hell in a hand basket," Bailey uttered. "Brazen little bitches."

I nodded as I examined the egg on the back of her head. "I never expected them to take Nick."

"Think he's dead?"

I shook my head. "I prefer to think that Nick's too well-connected for anyone to do something that stupid."

Danica popped back on. "They've signed their death warrants, Clark. You know that, right? Nick's men won't let this slide. *You* might, but they're out for blood. It's over for them now. Dead or alive, his guys will finish the deal."

"I realize that."

"Death warrant, Clark. There's no other way these people know how to operate, and there isn't anything you can do to stop it. Once they took Nick, this stopped being about supers, so any ideas you have about ending this peacefully need to be thrown out the window. It's time you upped the ante. They are counting on you being the kind-hearted mentor of fledgling supers. Show them the bitch. Make them pay, or you'll spend the rest of your life putting out these petty ass fires."

I didn't respond. I didn't need to. She was right. This was no longer an issue about out-of-control supers. With naturals thrown into the mix, this had the potential of creating a war neither side could win. Nick's men would hunt the Indies down and, one-by-one, pick them off or be killed themselves. The Indies would be forced to use their powers, revealing themselves in the process. This was spiraling out of control in so many ways, it made my head spin.

"What are we going to do, E?" Bailey asked.

I leveled my gaze at her. "We're going to do what we set out to do: Stop the Indies and send them home."

"You weren't listening, Clark," Danica whispered. "There's no place you can send them that Nick or his people won't find them. It's a pipe dream I—holy *crap*, mother fucker."

I sat up. "What?"

"That bitch is here! She's actually here!"

"Jasmine?"

"Uh huh. She's sitting near the back."

"She's there alone?"

"No idea. Just know she's sitting alone. Not a coincidence, Clark. I'm moving in."

"Can you get Max out of there?"

"Only if I can jump on stage and talk to him before his many thick-necked body guards can get to me. No, I'm going after that bitch."

"Then keep an eye on her, Dani. Don't let her out of your sight."

"Will do. I'm moving closer to her in case she DD's out of here. If she does, I'm taking her down, Clark. And hard."

Looking at Bailey, I felt like these inexperienced supers had outplayed me. My team was in shambles, my plan on the floor in pieces and—

"Oh God, oh God, oh God," came Danica's voice.

"What? What is it?"

"It's…it's Max."

I could hear screaming in the background of Danica's earpiece, and chaos like people caught in a burning building. "Dani, what is it?"

"He…he was…oh my God, Clark. I think he's dead!"

"What? Tell me what's going on!" I waited, but all I could hear was Danica breathing as if she was running. People were screaming and there was some sort of announcement, but I couldn't make out what they were saying.

"After…Jasmine…" Danica said breathlessly. "Max…fell one hundred feet…landed on his head. Blood…everywhere…chasing…the…bitch."

Bailey and I were on our feet. The Bellagio was just a few blocks away, but I wasn't sure she could hoof it. "Stay here. Handle Joy any way you can. Take her down. I'm going after Dani."

Bailey rose. "Ten four."

"Not without me you aren't." The voice was not Bailey's, and turning abruptly, I was face-to-face with Storm Stevens.

I understood her nickname now. Understood why she garnered so much respect in her world. Her emerald eyes were on fire, and it was as if her entire being had transformed into an action figure ready to kick some ass. At this moment, I was very glad to have her on my side.

"Gotta love the GPS in these things," she said, clutching her Vidbook.

My mouth dropped open. "How did you—"

She produced a handcuff key. "Never leave home without one. Can you keep up with my long legs?"

I nodded. "I ran track in college."

"Then let's go. What about Tip?" Delta asked.

"Trust me, Delta. When Tip comes to, those goons will wish they'd never laid eyes on her."

With that, Delta and I took off for the Bellagio.

"Talk to me, Dani." I could hear her breathing, the sound of the crowd replaced by her labored breaths.

"Goddamn it," I growled, jumping over a curb. Delta may have been taller than I, but that woman could run like a cheetah.

"Side...exit...by...Caesar's..." Danica said in my ear.

"We've got you on GPS, Dani, stay with Jazz." Delta spoke calmly, as if she was standing still while I, like Dani, was sucking wind.

"E, what do you want us to do about Vince?" It was Bailey in my ear.

As my legs churned in order to keep up with

Delta's long stride, I thought about the cold-hearted and brutal death of Hannah. I thought how effortlessly Joy had shoved Bailey against the wall. Then, it occurred to me why my plan had failed. I was trying to lead using *Melika's* model; her template, as it were, because that model had kept us all safe. That model had allowed us all to live with our powers in whatever way we saw fit. That model also worked because we lived on the bayou away from civilization.

But that model was antiquated now. It didn't fit either me or the times. If I was going to lead, I needed to do it *my* way. I needed to give myself permission to lead in a way that suited not only me, but my people, and right now my people were getting their asses kicked.

"E?"

"Tell Tip…tell her the gloves are off. She'll know what that means."

"Gotcha."

Suddenly, I could hear Danica and Jasmine fighting. There was swearing and name-calling, and horrible sounds like fists on faces, knuckles into flesh. It was like a movie with my eyes closed.

"Fucking bitch. Oh hell no," came Danica's ghetto voice. Jasmine was in for a world of hurt now. Tip was right about two point two seconds: Danica had gone ghetto.

Delta was leaping over hedges and dodging tourists like an Olympian, and I was barely able to keep up. Every now and then, she glanced at the Vidbook and adjusted her trajectory.

Then I heard it so clearly, I was certain it was Danica's Glock. A loud crashing sound followed what sounded like a cannon, and then silence.

My blood froze.

"Dani? Say something, Goddamn it." And now, I was ten feet ahead of Delta, adrenaline coursing through my veins, fear my co-pilot.

"Mothah fuckah," Dani groaned. "Coach window...not the Goddamned GPS. Don't...follow... GPS."

"You're at the Coach window?"

"Not *at*. In. The fucking bitch...pushed me through...the store window. I'm afraid to move because of all the glass."

Onlookers told us where she was, and people were filming it with their cell phones. I didn't see one person using them to call for help.

Delta held up her wallet that had a badge in it.

A badge?

"Just a prank gone wrong, people. Move on," she said in a voice I'd never heard from her.

Kneeling down, I saw blood on Danica's shoulder and a cut on her ear. "Don't move," I said.

"This was my favorite Donna Karan. That sistah is gonna pay big time for this. Her and her little TK ass-wiping, butt licking, mother fucker."

As I gingerly helped Danica to her feet, I could see a few places where the glass had found its mark like porcupine quills.

"Hold still."

"We don't have time for this, Clark. I am *not* going to the hospital."

"Nobody said you were, but you're sportin' some glass shards here and there. Can you walk okay?"

"Walk? I'll fucking run like the wind to get that cow back for ruining my outfit."

And that was Danica, back in rare form.

"We gotta jam, ladies, before LVPD arrives."

Delta whistled for a cab and helped me get Danica into the car, glass and all. She was bleeding in several places, and her outfit was destined for the trash.

Delta looked down at her Vidbook and shook it. "Shit. Must be busted. This has you moving north."

Danica plucked a piece of glass from her hair, a sardonic grin creeping across her face. "Not me. Jasmine. Before her goon jettisoned me into a plate glass window, I dropped my Vidbook into her purse."

I kissed her forehead. "You really are a genius."

"That's been proven."

"She's with a TK?"

Danica nodded. "The TK was waiting in the car. When I caught up to Jasmine, I grabbed her purse handle. You can grab anything on a sister and live to tell about it except for two things: Her purse and her hair. I went for the purse." Danica flicked the glass out the window. "That was when her bodyguard blasted me. Where we going, anyway?"

"Back to the Pentagon, where the car is. We need wheels to follow wheels."

When we got back to the Pentagon, Mario was pacing outside the Navigator, cussing in Spanish.

"Get in!" Delta ordered, jumping into the front passenger seat and rattling off directions in Spanish.

"She fucking speaks Spanish, too? I thought Mario was Italian." Danica said, wincing as she pulled a piece of glass from the back of her thigh. "Is there a tall building around? I have a theory."

"Keep it down back there," Delta said, not unkindly before giving more directions to Mario. "Last name Gonzalez. Do the math."

"Anything from Tip yet?" Danica asked me.

I was beginning to worry. How long *did* a double dose of taser knock you out for? "Not yet. Bailey, whatcha got?"

"They won't let me near the tournament because they think I'm drunk. All I can see from where I am is the back of Joy's head. Is it true? Is Max dead?"

"At the moment, we are going to assume so. Don't let Joy out of your sight. If you have to...let the dogs out."

"Gladly."

As Mario zoomed through the strip having an extended conversation with Delta in Spanish, I checked Danica for any more slivers of glass.

"Poor Max," Danica said softly. "One minute, he was suspended high above the stage—the next, he was plummeting head first onto it. It was...horrific. His assistants freaked out. There was blood everywhere. It was awful."

"And you think Jasmine did it?"

"Who else? She was there. She had to have some part in it, especially the way she bolted."

"I'm so sorry you had to see that."

"I've seen worse, Clark. I just...he seemed like a really nice guy. Genuine. He deserved a better fate, and I sort of feel responsible for him."

"Yes, he did. All we can do for him now is level some justice."

Delta turned to us. "Justice? Be careful there, Echo. Justice is a boomerang that hurts upon return."

"This one isn't returning, and if it does, I'll deal with it then, but this bullshit is stopping tonight." I leaned forward and looked over Delta's shoulder at the GPS. "How close?"

"Another four miles. They're leaving the strip

and heading for the desert."

"Good."

"Good?"

I nodded. "No windows in the desert."

≈≈≈≈

We traveled into the desert for less than a half mile before Mario quietly said something to Delta.

"Hang onto someone!" She ordered, as Mario stomped the pedal down and we hit what felt like mach five turbo.

"He wants to head them off and knows this area really well," Delta said, holding onto the safety bar. "Sorry, Dani, but it's gonna be a bumpy ride."

Pushing myself forward, I could see we were not parallel to the green dot, but nowhere I looked could I see headlights.

"*Well that was unpleasant,*" came Tip's voice in my head. "*Where are you?*"

I heaved a thankful sigh and told her we were speeding across the desert after Jasmine.

"*Gonna take Jasmine down?*"

"*Jasmine and everyone else tied to her.*"

"*You can't kill her, Echo. I know you want to. I know you think you should, but you can't.*"

"*I know. I want to. I really do, but that's just bad business and I would have a hard time explaining it to the Others. What are you going to do?*"

"*Well, I'm going to make a couple overzealous thugs pay for electrifying me and then I'm going to get the hell out of here.*"

"*What about Vince?*"

"Oh, I'm not done with Vince, but he'll see me away from the casino, away from cameras, away from prying eyes. I'll wait until the time is right and then he's mine. He's the one who beat Delta up, and I think a dose of his own medicine is the best way to go. Are you okay? How's Bailey? God, it feels like I was out forever."

"We're fine," I said, my ass leaving the seat as Mario flew over bumps. "You still have your earpiece?"

"No. It came out when I was doing the funky chicken on the floor."

"Max is dead."

"Oh no. Babe, I am so sorry."

"This has spun out of control, Tip. I'm, not even sure who to go after any more."

"Sure you are. Look, you have everyone in place. So they threw a few curves at us? So what? In the end, we will crush them. I promise. Keep me posted. Please be careful."

"You, too. And Tip? I'm really sorry you got zapped."

"Not as sorry as Vince is going to be. Stay in touch, darlin'."

"...I'll drop you off and then block the road," Mario said as we careened through the darkness. "Once they stop, they'll hit it in reverse or fight. No one drives off-road here, especially at night."

"*You* did!" Danica said.

"Because I know this area. Trust me. They'll hit reverse and try to swing it around."

Danica pulled her Glock out. "Not if I have anything to say about it."

Delta withdrew a huge gun as well. Her .357 looked like something John Wayne or Clint Eastwood sported.

"Ladies, this isn't the wild west," I reminded them.

"Actually, Miss Echo, it is. Everyone packs here," Mario quipped.

Delta and Danica grinned at each other.

"Please don't shoot anyone."

Delta frowned. "Tires, Echo. Once we disable the car, they ain't going anywhere."

Mario gunned it, and when he swung around, he stopped the Navigator. "Wait here, out of the glare of the headlights. When you see brake lights, take out the tires. Go, go, go!"

We jumped out of the SUV and got off to the side of the road when Mario turned his lights out. It was almost too dark to see anything and I wondered how they intended on finding the tires, let alone shoot them out.

"You two scare the shit out of me," I said, standing in between them. "I'm not so sure I like you hanging out together."

Delta chuckled. "Let's see. Danica was pushed through a window without being touched. I got my ass kicked by air, and *you* are afraid of *us*?"

Danica and Delta laughed.

"I'm gonna give you something to be scared about in a minute."

"Shh. Here they come."

In the darkness of the night, the desert is blacker than black. So when the headlights appeared down the road, they were so easy to see as they lit up the road before them. Behind us was pitch dark. To our left was a black hole. Suddenly, I wondered how in the hell we got here. How did this get so out of control? What should I have done differently?

"Clark?"

"Yeah?"

"Back up. The Glock is loud, but Delta's ancient bad boy 357 will pop an eardrum." She said fifty like fitty. Ghetto.

Stepping back, I watched as the lights got closer. "Okay. First things first. Jasmine."

"Oh hell yeah. Then bring her little friend to me."

Before I could respond, Mario turned his lights on and the approaching vehicle slammed on its brakes and skidded to a halt.

I jumped when both guns cracked through the warm night air. Not once, but several times. I don't know who hit it, but the left rear tire blew out, followed by the left front tire.

That didn't stop them. Jamming it into reverse, they backed up and swung the car around.

"Uh uh," Delta said, running for the car as it spun around. Jumping on the running boards, she smashed her gun into the driver's side window like some crazed action figure.

My jaw dropped. The woman was fearless. She also didn't completely know what she was up against.

"Delta, no!"

The energy ball from inside the car hit Delta square on the chest, tossing her twenty feet into the darkness, where she landed in the sand with a dull thud.

Mario came out of his car and suffered the same fate, only the blast blew him over the hood of the Navigator and into a pile of rocks.

As the car spun around, Danica emptied the Glock into the engine, dropped the clip, and slammed another one home. The car steamed, sputtered, and came to a stop. The desert became deathly quiet…as if it was holding its breath, waiting.

"Make the call, Clark." Danica held her Glock out in front of her pointed at the car.

"They're going to come out of that car swinging. It's us or them, Dani."

Danica raised the Glock in both hands. "Delta and Mario?"

I lowered my shields and read them. "Fine, but this round is up to us."

"Gotcha. Cover me."

I threw a shield in front of her so the TK's energy couldn't toss her like it had the other two.

Danica knelt on one knee. "Get the fuck out of the car, assholes!"

There was no movement from the car.

"There's three," I said. "Driver, Jasmine, and Bronwen, the TK. Driver is a precog, so no powers there. Bronwen is the only one who can hurt us."

A gunshot rang out from their car.

"Fuck!" Danica said, squeezing off a dozen rounds, taking out their headlights. The only light showing now was from Mario's car, but we were just outside of it, standing in the shadows of darkness. "Someone's got a fucking gun in that car."

"Yeah, but they're not you, are they? You just shot out the headlights."

"Wasted a bunch of ammo doing it. It's dark as shit out here."

I made another reading. "Jasmine has the gun. They're trying to figure out what to do." I looked over at Danica and knew we had only one real option. "Take your best shot."

"What?"

"Shoot the window out."

"The window? To what end? I could hit one of them."

"Better them than us." Laying my hand on her shoulder, I said the words I never thought I'd utter. "Kill them if they get out of that car."

Nodding once, Danica held her gun, exhaled slowly, and shot the window twice. The sound was chilling as the glass shattered. The moment the window blew, I sent my strongest offensive weapon into the car. The rest was much like a sonic boom. The irony was that the first time I even knew I had this ability was when I first came to Vegas. In a confined space, I am capable of blowing out eardrums. From this distance, however, it was more disorienting, like someone clapping both your ears with an open hand.

Danica was on them in an instant, shoving her Glock through the open space and commanding everyone to get out.

I could feel Delta's return to consciousness and was glad for it. Two supers against a natural wasn't really even odds, especially when they had no compunction about killing us.

They dropped out of the vehicle holding their heads. When Bronwen fell to her hands and knees, Danica ordered her to stay there.

"Keep your hands on the ground and I *might* not kill you," Danica growled, keeping the Glock pointed at Bronwen. "And yeah, I've killed before, and I'm mother fucking crazy as shit, so don't fucking test out any other theory."

As Jasmine rose to her feet, she tried shaking off the effects of the boom.

"Driver, on your goddamned hands and knees as well. Jasmine, put your fuckin' hands behind your fuckin back."

Ghetto.

"I'm a necromancer, you dolt. I can't—"

Danica moved so quickly, it surprised even me. The Glock was pressed right into Jasmine's cheek so fast we were all stunned. "I am so not fuckin' around here, necromancer. Do what I fuckin' tell you or I'm bustin' a cap right in your big mouth." Jasmine put her hands behind her and Danica backed off, keeping the gun trained on Bronwen. "Ruin, my favorite suit you fuckin' bitch."

Jasmine looked up at me in the dim light. "Echo, I'm sorry. I'm so—"

I held my hands up to silence her. "Everyone told me you were a bad seed, but I just wouldn't listen. I kept giving reasons why you couldn't be the one, but you are, aren't you? Supers killing supers doesn't sit well with me or the Others, and yet, here we are on the opposite side of the coin, and for what? What's this all about, Jasmine? I can't be for revenge. There are far easier ways to go after Bailey. So why the hell are we standing in the damn desert?"

"I haven't killed anyone, Echo. I swear."

"So Max just fell?"

She blinked. "I swear to God, I had nothing to do with that."

"Your words mean jackshit. What about Hannah? Are you blood-free there as well?"

"This isn't what you think. Hannah was...an accident."

I shook my head. "Slipping on stairs is an accident. Seventeen stab wounds is overkill."

"Not to mention what a bitch you were to Bailey in the past. Is this about that, you petty ass mother fucker?" This came from Danica.

The air around Jasmine suddenly changed and I could feel the cold, unafraid posture in her. "Look at my face, Danica, and then tell me who's the bitch. She had *them* tattoo my face. My *face*, Echo! I'd rather she had just killed me. She took my dreams and chucked them out the window."

"That can still be arranged," Danica muttered.

"So, you used the Indies to get to me. You knew I'd come down here and bring Bailey. You set this whole thing up, and for what? Vengeance?"

"Nothing so…petty. She cursed my dreams and ruined my life, and I thought I would never have a chance to be famous. Then I met Townsend, and he proved me wrong."

"You took her lover and tried to have her killed. If the Others could have proven it, you'd probably be dead. A tattoo on your face is a small price to pay for what you did and attempted to do. Do have any idea how powerful Bailey truly is? She could have killed you at any time in any number of ways, but she didn't. She let you live. And this…this is how you wanted this to play out? You used the Indie situation as camouflage to take Bailey out?"

"You'd never understand, Echo. You have everything you could ever want. I work as a fucking florist with my face marked forever."

"Boo hoo," Danica said. "I have half a mind to shoot you in the head just to stop your whining."

"Townsend's like some guru to those lost kids. He came to me and told me if I helped him make it to the stage here, he would return the favor."

That was when the light went on. "Hannah was your way of dragging us down here. You had her killed, went to the Others in hopes they would send me. Me. Because I am soft and merciful."

"You because you always bring your pit bulls with you, and I knew Bailey would come if she thought I was involved. If I helped Townsend get his act on stage, he was going to help me take Bailey out."

"What were the rest of us? Collateral damage?"

Jasmine shook her head. "Taking you two out was just a sweet, sweet bonus."

Danica backhanded her so hard with her free hand, Jasmine landed face first in the sand. "Watch your mouth, or the next time you land in the fucking sand will be your last."

Slowly, Jasmine rose and wiped her cut lip. "You two wouldn't have a clue what it's like to be a circus freak all because I loved someone I shouldn't have."

I shook my head and wondered who the real nutjob was. I was done listening to this. Studying her in the harsh glare of the Navigator headlights, I tried figuring out what to do here. I couldn't kill her, no matter what she'd done. Tip was right about that. I wanted to, yes, but I couldn't just kill her in cold blood. That would make me no better than her, and I *was* better than that. I could send her back to the Others, but I felt they had become weak and ineffective. I had come down here to help Cinder, but now I realized I had simply been manipulated by just about everyone. I had to send a message to the rest of the supernatural world what happened if you messed with me.

"Here's how this is going to play out. I want to know two things. You lie, I'll know it, and we'll leave your bodies here in the desert for the buzzards. Are we clear?"

Jasmine looked from me to Danica and back.

"Yes."

"How come I didn't read you correctly in the flower store?"

She shrugged. "I have a ghost who hangs around. She ran interference. You read her, not me."

I nodded. "Where were you planning on meeting Townsend?"

She looked surprised. "How did—"

"Answer the fucking question," Danica growled. "You are getting on my every last nerve."

"Tomorrow morning, six a.m., at Russell's Diner off the strip."

That was the truth.

"And where is Nick Harper?" I feared for the answer, afraid she had made a huge error that couldn't be undone. I feared for Jasmine, because if he was dead, Danica would shoot her right here. Right now.

"At a storage unit off First Street."

Danica raised the Glock higher now, aiming it at Jasmine's face. "If he's dead, so are you. Ask her, Clark."

Jasmine raised her hand in surrender "He's alive! I swear to God! She knows I'm telling the truth! Tell her, Echo. Tell her you know it's true!"

I nodded. "It's true, Dani. What number?"

"Two-ten. We just needed him out of the way for the tournament. Townsend wanted to kill him, and it took some convincing for him to believe that would be grabbing a tiger by the tail. He finally agreed just to hold him there until we could collect and get on with our plan. We weren't expecting that natural you brought with you. She's been a thorn in our side all week,"

Shaking my head sadly, I inhaled a deep breath and considered my options. "I don't know who's worse.

You or the Indies."

"Townsend's kids are raw, I know, but why not make money, make a living with our skills, Echo? What's the difference between making money gambling and reading palms? I've been struggling for years. I was *this close* to a local TV gig, and then *she* fucked it up for me."

"You're not a victim here, Jasmine. You started this ugly ball rolling." Danica's weapon did not waver.

"One provides a service, Jasmine, the other is cheating. Besides, you know the money isn't the reason. It's careless. It puts the rest of us in danger. It's irresponsible, and I can't let it continue." Stepping next to Danica, I kept my eyes on Jasmine. "I'll tie up Bronwen's hands, Dani, after you get Jasmine to the car."

Danica stared at me. "You're letting her go?"

"I told you. We can't kill her."

"*You* can't, but *I* sure as hell can. The Others can just rub their sore spot."

I lightly touched her arm. "Stand down, Dani. Her judgment is not in our h—"

Just then, a shot rang out and Jasmine's head rocked backwards as a bullet smashed into her forehead and blew out the back.

Danica and I both whirled around to find Mario lowering his gun. Delta was slowly getting to her feet as well.

"You're right, Miss Echo. Her judgment *wasn't* yours. Our guys are on the way to the storage unit. If he is still alive, I won't kill these two unless you want me to, but they gonna pay somehow. No one manhandles my boss. This is Vegas, man. You got any idea how many dead bodies are dumped out here every year?"

I leaned over to the other driver and whispered, "How did you not see this coming?" Rising, I turned to Mario. "I'm going to have to answer for that."

He shrugged. "Not my problem. Western justice, Miss Echo. I told you. Wild West, man. Wild West."

"Mobster justice," Delta muttered, rubbing her lower back. "Take a page from his book, Echo. Leave the living with a very clear picture of what happens when someone comes at you."

Looking from Delta to Mario and then down at Jasmine's corpse, I sighed. I would have to answer for this, but I wasn't taking the heat for it. "Take us back to the tournament, then drop these two out in the desert somewhere."

Mario grinned; Danica and Delta looked surprised.

Kneeling down next to Bronwen, I whispered, "If you live, and that is highly unlikely, you need to tell every Indie, every natural, every Tom, Dick, and fucking Harry, what happens to people who attack *my* people. If you ever even *think* about raising your hands at anyone I care about again, I won't vouch for your safety, and powers or no, I will tear your head off and spit down your throat. Now stand up and put your hands behind your back."

Once we secured them both and had them in the car, I walked over to Jasmine's lifeless body and stared down at it. It was such a shame. She had been a good necromancer once.

"She got what she deserved," Danica said, standing next to me.

"Oh no she hasn't, yet. Trust me. When Jacob Marley is through with her, she'll wish she'd gone straight to Hell."

༄ ༄ ༄ ༄

We decided Mario was safer if we remained with him while he dropped them off in the darkness of the desert. Delta had secured Bronwen's hands with cable ties from a tool chest in the back of the Navigator. No one needed to ask Mario why he carried cable ties.

With Bronwen secured, we dropped them off in the desert, stopping long enough for Mario to work his gangster magic.

When he had Jasmine out of the Navigator, he made the other driver and Bronwen kneel down next to her. He made the driver hold up the hang-ten sign with both hands. He ordered them both to smile. Then he took a pic with his cell and told us to do the same.

Ah yes, the fine art of blackmail.

"If it was up to me, I'd shitcan the both of yous and be done wid it. But in case Miss Echo didn't make it plain to yas," Mario knelt down and pressed the muzzle of his gun between Bronwen's eyes. "They's friends of mine and my boss. Ain't nowhere yous can hide dat we won't find you, skin you alive, cut off yer fingers, cut off yer toes, burn yer eyeballs out, rip out yer tongue, and finally feed you to the dogs one piece atta time. So if you like living, if you'd like to have an old age, you'll forget you ever met any of us and go on yer merry way. *Capisce*?"

"Yes," Bronwen said, too afraid to move. The driver nodded, too afraid to speak.

"Good. There's some really shitty ways to die and you'll be lookin' at some if I ever sees yous again."

Rising, Mario nodded to me. "Say yer piece, then we gotta go. The boss is pretty fuckin' fired up and heads is gonna roll."

I wasn't going to say anything more to Bronwen, but I realized there was more I needed to know.

"Sit," I said, pushing them both back on their asses with a small bit of energy. "It didn't have to end this way, you know? She burned Bailey once and she gave her a chance to redeem herself. And what did she do with it? Wasted it and her life. And for what? Fame? Tell me, Bronwen, what is it Townsend Briggs offered you all that would make you choose this path?"

She stared at me a long time before answering. "Easy money. Community. Support. We're not like you, Echo. We see no problem reaping the benefits of being born special."

"How many of you came to Vegas?"

"A dozen."

The truth.

"How many are back in Atlantic City?"

She shrugged. "Not many. Twenty, maybe?"

"So you were all going to run up the bucks here and then go back to Atlantic City with the winnings in order to triple or quadruple it?"

"Pretty much."

I nodded. "And what made you follow him? A magician? An illusionist?"

She let out a soft chuckle. "Sounds so stupid now."

"Humor me."

"Six of us are in a band. He promised to get us to the right people in Hollywood."

I blinked. "A band? You killed Hannah so you could be in a *band* in Hollywood?" I didn't know whether to laugh or cry. It was all so futile the way the younger generation covets fame.

"Hannah wasn't supposed to be killed, Echo. I'm serious. I don't know what went wrong, but that part wasn't supposed to happen. I swear."

Again, the truth. "Then what happened? You don't accidentally stab someone seventeen times."

She shook her head. "You'd have to ask Vinnie. He was the one with that job."

Shaking my head in disgust, I walked away. If there was more I needed to know, I just didn't think I could stomach it.

"Echo?"

"What?" I said sharply.

"You're fighting a losing battle. There will come a day when the world will realize we exist and that we are superior to everyone else."

"And when that day happens, Bronwen, may God help us all."

※※※※

Leaving them in the desert was really easy to do, and I marveled at how thick my skin was becoming. As we made our way back into town, Danica spoke to Nick, who was fuming more about getting wrangled by a "bunch of girls and some hippie," than anything else. She said she would explain everything later, but he told her that later wasn't going to help those two in the tournament, which was almost over for the night.

"Can I ask yous what da fuck happened back there? One minute, I was comin' outta da car, and da next, I'm flyin' over da Goddamn hood."

"She shot at you, and you were like Superman, Mario, you *leapt* over the hood. It was so awesome." Danica explained. "You rocked it."

Mario beamed. "No shit? Man, I was, like, flyin'?"

"You must have amazingly strong legs." Ever the male manipulator, Danica winked at me.

"Well, I *do* run every day."

"It shows. You flew over that hood like a high jumper. You must have hit your head on a rock or something."

And that was that.

Bailey was in my ear and quietly told me what needed to happen next. Told me. She made it clear she was not asking permission.

This was a first for her.

I agreed, even though I wasn't sure it was the best thing to do. Sometimes, a leader has to let her second in command make the hard calls. Bailey was making it with or without me.

Then we pulled up in front of the Pentagon where Bailey was waiting.

"You sure?" Delta asked her as we all piled out.

Bailey met us and nodded as she slid into the passenger seat. "Oh, I'm sure. Under no circumstances are those two gamblers to leave the Pentagon unassisted." She motioned to the main entrance with her chin. "Joy'll be out first, escorted by Nick's burliest men. She doesn't know why, just that it's for her safety because she won so much."

"Where are you?" Tip asked.

"Just outside the front entrance, waiting for Joy. You?"

"Once security gave me the all-clear, I came back inside. That little nobody isn't getting away from me."

"Good. You keep an eye on him while we take care of Joy first."

"Should I wave goodbye to her?"

I smiled. "Didn't you hear it?"

"What?"

"Pretty sure it's the fat lady singing."

"Stay light on your feet, darlin'. This thing ain't over yet."

Bailey gave me a wave as she closed the door and had Mario take her around the block.

"Where's she going?" Delta asked.

"Backup."

"I thought *we* were her backup."

"Not the right kind." I looked down at my Vidbook at the photo of Jasmine and the two supers and deleted it. I had half a mind to go get them, but their banishment wasn't my call and I sure as hell didn't need to be on Nick Harper's bad side. Besides, we'd been more than generous in giving them a chance to make it back. It was nighttime, not scorching hot, and they were only ten, maybe fifteen miles into the desert. Surely they would get back, right?

"Don't count on it, darlin'. The night desert is like a giant maze. You can start walking in circles and never know it. Don't second guess yourself, Echo. Once word gets out that you're not someone to fuck with, you won't have to play these stupid games. You're doing the right thing. Trust me."

I did. Maybe even more than she knew. It wasn't just about trust, though. It was something else—something much deeper. Maybe it had taken distance for me to get some perspective, and maybe she'd just changed enough to make me realize how very different my life was whenever she was around. She gave me confidence I didn't know I possessed. Her belief in me was like an adrenaline rush. I would need that when Melika was gone.

"You okay?" Danica asked, sidling up next to me.

"Yeah. Just working on the 'No Regrets' theory in life."

"How's that working for you?"

"Not sure yet. This mentor thing is a helluva lot tougher than I realized. I'm so not the hard ass kind of person, but I'm beginning to see where that reputation might come in handy."

"You're up to the task, Clark...especially...ah... never mind."

"No. Say it."

She tilted her head to the side. "Especially with the Big Injun around. I hate to say it, and I'll deny it if questioned, but her presence makes you...calmer. That's not something that Officer Hunky Pants ever made happen. I'm just sayin'."

I nodded and watched ex-officer Stevens scanning the streets and sidewalks. Once a cop always a cop.

"I swear to God she's like no one I've ever met. You know...it's too bad she's in love with Megan, because you two would make a great couple."

"Hush."

"I'm not kidding. She's gorgeous, strong, independent, and doesn't care that you can leap tall buildings in a single bound."

"So can she."

Danica squeezed my hand. "I'll just bet she can."

Still holding her hand, I faced her. "Thank you for not blowing Bronwen's brains out. I know you wanted to."

She smiled and shrugged. "Overkill, you know? Besides, I get what you're doing, and I think it's brilliant. Putting the rest of the supernatural world on notice is the best gift you could give those kids. I get it."

The doors swooshed open and I felt Joy's energy before I saw her. Every muscle in my body tensed.

Confident, cock-sure, untouchable. I was sure she'd made quite a killing at the roulette wheel. One thing these youngsters hadn't fully realized was who they were stealing from. If they thought the gangland mentality of old was gone, they had another thing coming. There were still plenty of mob roots growing in Vegas soil. The difference was it was legitimate now. They'd gone from being thugs to businessmen, and these businessmen did not appreciate someone coming into their casinos and stealing from them. Win legitimately? Sure. Steal? Not unless you had a death wish. While it was true most Vegas casinos were now corporate-owned, that didn't mean much had changed in the way cheaters were dealt with. Card counters had their photos handed from casino manager to casino manager as a way to stop them before they got started. Technology now gave security teams a clearer eye-in-the-sky. But there were still bookies who would break your legs, sharks who would bite them off, and owners who would make sure your body was never found.

"Here she comes," Danica said, stepping aside so Joy could see me.

When she did, she didn't even hesitate. Smiling at me, she made her last mistake. "This is *our* town, Echo. You need to take your people and go back to the sticks where you belong."

Danica started after her. "Oh hell no."

Stepping in between them, I barely managed to stop Danica before she took a swing at Joy.

"Oh come on, Clark, this little bitch has it coming."

Joy looked around and started to raise her hands, but the bodyguards did not release their grip. Without her hands, Joy was as normal as a natural.

"You've overplayed your hand, honey," I said, as the Navigator pulled up. Delta stepped behind Joy, and held her wrist at her side. Danica stepped to her other side, essentially boxing her in. When the Navigator door opened, there sat Bailey with the two enormous Dobermans I'd seen at Nick's.

Backup.

"Get in the fucking car," Bailey ordered, sliding out. Both dogs bared their teeth and Joy started to raise her hands, but she couldn't. As Danica and Delta held each arm, the goons pushed her toward Bailey, who waited in front of the open passenger door.

Bailey walked right up to Joy and hugged her, whispering, "Get in the fucking car or you'll die right here in the gutter where you belong. Raise your hands and those two dogs will eat them for lunch. Nod if you understand what I just said." Backing away, Bailey made room for a nodding Joy, who slid slowly across the seat, her eyes glued to the two big dogs.

"P-Please...don't. I'll give the money back. It was...we were..." Suddenly, Joy cried out before slumping down in the seat.

"I couldn't listen to that one more second," Tip said, putting Joy out for a bit.

"She's all yours." Slamming the door, Bailey finger-waved as Mario and his canine backup drove away.

"What did Mario think about the dogs?"

Bailey laughed. "I told him I was the sister of the real dog whisperer."

"You didn't."

"I did."

I couldn't help but smile. "You are so wrong in so many ways."

"What do you think will happen to her?" Bailey asked as we settled on a bench outside the main gate. "I wanted the dogs to tear her to shreds, but Dani said Nick had other things in mind."

"I shudder to consider the possibilities."

"Nick's pissed off about the whole thing," Danica said, putting her long arms around us both. "He'll give a whole new meaning to 'make an example out of her.' You just don't come to Vegas thinking you can cheat the house."

"Or kidnap its owner," Bailey said, shaking her head. "Can I be the first to say let's never come back here?"

I smiled slightly. "Putting out fires is what we do now, Bailey. If there's a fire in the desert, we'll come here to put it out."

On cue, a siren could be heard in the distance.

"I didn't really think the mob was alive and well down here," Bailey whispered. "And, quite frankly, they scare the bejesus out of me."

"I hear you. Those guys mean business."

"That ambulance is for Vince, darlin', so stay out of the way."

"Oh crap," I said aloud.

"What?"

I pointed to the ambulance coming toward us. "I think Vince has played his last hand."

Danica chuckled. "Bad idea, that. He killed Hannah and fucked with Tip? He's lucky if she doesn't skin him alive."

"Yeah," I said, wondering how badly she'd hurt him. "She doesn't mess around. She skips the warnings and pre-hostile stages and goes right for the throat... or mind."

"It's the warrior in her," Bailey explained. "Once she let Vinnie know who she was, the decision to stay and keep playing was a purely stupid and painful one for him to make."

We watched in silence as the paramedics unfolded the stretcher and charged inside. Half a minute later, Tip sauntered out, hands stuffed in her jean pockets. Her brown eyes sparkled.

"That is one stupid kid," she said, sitting next to Bailey.

"What happened?"

"Well, since I couldn't get close to the table, I started fucking with his mind, you know, are you sure that's an eight? It looks like a six. He called me a fucking has-been dyke, and I said, why don't you say that out loud you fucking pencil-dick?"

"Oh nooo, he didn't."

Tip nodded. "He leaned across the table and yelled, 'You're a Goddamned, rug munchin' dyke'."

The oohs got much louder.

"The cowboy sitting next to him told him to watch his mouth, to which Vinnie replied, 'Blow me, Billy Bob'." Well, I waited for Billy Bob to bounce one off Vinnie's chin, which he did, and at that moment, I squeezed Vince's brain in a vise so hard, I can't be sure he'll ever come out of it."

Danica clapped. "More western justice."

"The kid wasn't going to back off, Echo. Someone, somewhere, gave them all a false sense of security. I know you feel like this should be someone else's problem, but it's not. You did the right thing by coming down here. They had to be stopped."

"And Vince?"

Tip shrugged. "Probably a drooling bag of brain damage. I hit him pretty hard."

Danica stood and reached for Bailey's hand. "Let's go watch him being loaded into the ambulance."

Bailey shook her head and then caught a look from Danica. "Oh. Yeah. Sure. We'll be right back."

When they left, Tip chuckled softly. "Could they have been any more obvious?"

"I'm surprised at Danica. You're not one of her favorite people."

"Maybe I've changed."

I looked at her. "Have you?"

Staring down at her hands folded in her lap, she nodded. "How could I not? The only woman I've ever thought of as mother is fighting a battle she can't win. Watching her shriveling away into nothingness is like a Chinese water torture, but Mel, she still gets up every day and says what a gorgeous day it is to be alive. She amazes me."

"She's pretty amazing. There isn't a day that goes by that I don't miss her deeply." I laid my hand on top of her folded ones. "When will you be going back?"

A long, protracted moment plodded by before she quietly answered, "I'm not."

"What? I thought—"

"She wants to die on the bayou. Malecon is bringing her home soon. They're tired of Europe and she's done being poked and prodded."

"Oh God, Tip. Does that mean—"

"It won't be long, no."

Silence hung between us like a dark cloud. "So you'll go back to New Orleans?"

Another long pause. "I'll go wherever Mel wants me to be." She looked over at me with damp eyes. "You should see him with her, Echo. As much as I hated that man, I can't even remember a time when he wasn't this way with her. God, he makes her laugh. They're like two little kids, sharing secrets, telling stories, reminiscing about their odd childhood. She loves him for what he did for her, and he adores her for everything else."

"So you've said your goodbyes?"

"Not yet. She's drawing up some docs for me to sign, giving me the property."

I cocked my head. "Why not Malecon?"

"He said he could never stay there without her. He wants to retire in the French Quarter, or maybe Paris."

The doors busted open and the paramedics came out with Vince strapped to the gurney. We watched in silence as they worked on him, lifting him into the ambulance. That was when I saw the blood coming from both ears. Yeah, he would never recover from that.

"Call me a Goddamned dyke?" Tip shook her head. "There was no call for that."

When the ambulance pulled away from the curb, she turned to me and forced a smile. "That's Goddamned *powerful* dyke to you, little boy."

We managed to catch a few winks in our room before our surprise meeting with Townsend Briggs. Tip crashed with me and we were out in less than five minutes. When the alarm went off, I opened my eyes and realized Tip was spooning me, both arms wrapped so tightly around me I couldn't reach for the alarm.

"Tip?" I wriggled some and she tightened her grip.

"Tip, the alarm."

"Leave it." Pulling me closer, she threw her leg over me like she used to do when we were lovers. That seemed like a lifetime ago. Maybe it was. "I forgot how wonderful this feels." Since I couldn't reach the clock, I used a little energy to depress the buttons.

"Remember when we'd stay in bed for hours and watch movies in your dorm room? I miss that little bed."

It was so unlike her to wax poetic or be nostalgic that I turned in her arms. Our noses were less than an inch apart.

"All these years and it never dawned on me until now that you *need* me. That's why you jumped on a plane so fast, isn't it?"

Brushing my hair from my face with one finger, she smiled softly. "You never really got it. You never really understood how very much I do. These last few months..." she paused here, her eyes tearing up. "Have been so hard. So very hard. I wanted to call you when Mel first did chemo. I wanted to call you the first time I saw the Swiss Alps. There were a million and one times I wanted to call you, but I was just so angry. So pigheaded." She waited for me to agree with her. When I didn't, she continued. "I was angry for all the wrong reasons at all the wrong people. I've never felt such helplessness in my life. It's not easy playing on the team you know is going to lose."

"I knew you'd come to your senses eventually. I just didn't know how long it would take."

Tip kissed the tip of my nose. "I'm so sorry."

"Shh. We've had far too many of those. Maybe it's time we started off with a clean slate. Cut a lot of this baggage loose. Start fresh."

"I'd like that. We're both so different now. We aren't anything like we were when you were in college. I've changed a lot, darlin'. So have you. We need to stop revisiting reruns."

I grinned. "Well put."

Leaning on her elbow, Tip sighed. "I've tried so hard to give you space to live your life. I just want you to be happy, Echo. More than anything, I just want you to be happy."

"I *am* happy, Tip. I love living in the compound. I love having the kids around."

She chuckled.

"What?"

"The compound."

"That's what Dani calls it."

She nodded. "And Bailey. Is she happy?"

"She's in love, I think, so yes. Very happy. She and Taylor seem quite smitten with each other."

She blinked several times and nodded. "Then you've all settled into your new lives?"

I don't know if it was the way she asked or the look in her eyes, but I understood that Tip was floundering because everything she knew, everything she was about, was gone. There were no more students in the bayou. No more collections at the behest of Melika. No more teaching people what came naturally to her.

Tiponi Redhawk was as displaced as the Louisianans were after Katrina. She was rootless.

Except for me.

No wonder she had so quickly come to my aid. She needed contact with the only other person who grounded her.

Laying my palm on her cheek, I stared hard into her eyes. There was something hiding just behind them, peeking around, not wanting me to see her vulnerability.

It was fear.

"What are you afraid of, Tip? What has so scared you that you would flee Melika and come help me?"

When the tears finally fell from her eyes, I pulled her to me and stroked her head. She cried hard into my shoulder, her guard dropping so much I could feel her raw emotions…and they were very raw. She was tortured.

"Shhh." Stroking her hair, I gently rocked her in my arms. "I gotcha, Tip. It's all going to be okay." Pulling her closer, I checked my watch. Plenty of time.

"She's…she's not going to be here much longer… and I don't know how to be. I don't know what my life looks like without her…without you. I just…don't know. I feel so lost…like any minute now I'm going to become unhinged."

Pulling away, I gently wiped her eyes. "Maybe knowing isn't important right now. Maybe you just need to be still. Just be. Maybe it's time for a new chapter in your life. You know…time to reinvent yourself."

"I don't know where to begin."

"Sure you do. Don't force it. Just feel your feelings, and don't apologize for them. It's all going to be okay, Tip. I promise."

"I hope you're right because I don't have a clue what the future holds for me."

"You and your new woman will return to the bayou to start a new life." I looked at her. "You've not mentioned her once."

Tip shrugged. "It is what it is. Let's leave it at that, okay?"

We lay there a few minutes longer before she got up, her walls up once more. "You're a good one, darlin'. Thank you for letting me boo-hoo on your shoulder."

"It's not boo-hooing, Tip, to show your feelings. Truth be told, it's nice to see you emote."

She smiled. "Emote?" Holding her hand out, she pulled me off the bed. "Well, emote or not, thank you. You're the best. I guess I really needed to let some of that sadness out. Some days, it feels as if the sorrow is eating me alive."

We got dressed and headed for the dining room, where Bailey, Danica, and Delta were already drinking coffee.

"How did you guys sleep?"

"Short," I said, taking the offered coffee from Danica.

"God, no kidding. I don't know if it's all the smoke or lack of sleep, but I feel like a Mac truck slammed into me."

Tip and I sat down and Delta leaned right in.

"Okay, this Townsend Briggs fellow probably won't show up alone. We can be certain of that. I'm a little nervous that you don't want the gangsters involved."

I found that fascinating and said as much.

Delta waved her earlier doubts and fears away.

"I just want you all protected, and if it takes thugs and hoodlums to do it, so be it."

"We need to keep a lid on this now. I need more information from Townsend Briggs—info I don't need Nick's men to hear. I also don't want him killed." I sipped my coffee. "I'm done with all this killing and, quite frankly, it's made my heart hurt."

"He deserves it," Danica said. "He's an asshole who deserves to die."

"I understand that, but the Others have asked for me to deliver him to them. I am pretty sure they didn't mean in a body bag." I turned to Danica. "Any word about Max?"

She shook her head. "The papers just reported that it was a trick gone wrong and he died instantly. The casino did its best to keep the details on the down low."

The table went quiet.

"When did the Others tell you about bringing him in? This is news to me."

"After Delta was hurt, I received a call from them. Injuring a natural is strictly forbidden. The Others want to make an impact on both Atlantic City, Vegas, and beyond. I think they want people to know they are still alive and kicking. I guess they have their own plans for TB."

"So they're pissed, huh?"

I nodded. "That would be an understatement. Let's just say, I wouldn't want to be someone used as an example."

"Why him and not Jasmine?" Delta asked.

I sipped my coffee before answering. "Jasmine was *my* example. I gave her a second chance and this was how she chose to treat me? Treat us? Uh uh. I realized along this rocky road that other supers toed the line because they feared Tip. That fear kept a lot of riff-raff in line. Well, Bailey had Jasmine's face tattooed and that didn't stop her from trying to exact revenge. Clearly, both she and Townsend used each other for a foothold here where they could make a butt load of money. This, of course, doesn't leave this room."

"Won't need to," Tip said softly. "The ripple effect from her disappearance will create quite a wave in the community. I think the flares you're shooting up are not only smart, but important." She looked intently at me. "Especially for you."

I smiled at her. "I am aware."

"Mario had Joy call Townsend to confirm the meeting. Those dogs scared the crap out of her. I guess she offered him bills and blow jobs, to which he replied he'd rather lick a cow's ass."

"So Townsend is expecting her?"

"As well as Jasmine, yeah. I'm sure he believes Vince is in the hospital because Billy Bob punched his lights out. That was great cover, by the way."

Tip nodded. "Ain't my first rodeo, love."

"So what's our plan?" Bailey asked, rubbing her hands together. "Because mama is ready to kick some ass."

"Down girl. We've had to restructure a bit." I told them about my earlier call from Sal, and that I wanted the chateau gone over with a fine tooth comb, "Tip and I will handle Townsend. I'm sending you three home this morning to deal with whatever the hell is going on at the compound."

"Oh hell no," Bailey said. "If *they* want Townsend so bad, let *them* go after him, right guys?" She looked around for support that wasn't coming.

"I don't like the idea of someone, *anyone*, sniffing around Cinder," Danica said, flipping open her Vidbook, "...and, quite frankly, am a little pissed off you didn't mention it sooner." It was five in the morning, but I knew who she was calling.

"I'm pretty sure it was a diversion to split our forces."

"Yo, Boss, it's still oh dark thirty, man." Roger's face was creased from sleep.

"I need satellite footage of the compound for the last forty-eight hours. If you can get it for the last seventy-two, even better. This is important. Get crackin'." Then she closed the Vidbook.

We all just stared.

"Satellite?"

She shrugged. "You asked for the best security system and Sal had remarked that satellite was the best way to go. So I went."

"Wait. How—"

Danica's eyes smiled but her face did not. "Slept with a NASA guy a few years back at a tech convention. Nice guy. Long story. Short of it is he lost a bet to me. I called in the marker."

I could only shake my head. "Do I want to know how many times you've bartered with sex?"

"No. Moving on."

Delta chuckled. "Megan's gonna love that story."

"Anyway, Tip and I will wrap it up here. The Others are sending a collector to get TB. You guys make sure everything is secure at the chateau. Plane leaves in an hour and you three will be on it. I want the compound secured before I get back. Sal is lead and she'll get you up to speed."

Danica was already on her feet. "You think it

could be *them*?"

"Genesys? No idea. I don't want to jump to conclusions. It could very well have been Townsend's people trying to distract us or get us off our game."

Delta cocked her head. "Wow."

"What?"

"Impressive is all. I know how much those kids mean to you all. To stay the course means—"

"I trust your people, Delta. One thing I learned from Melika is that you either trust your own or you don't. I wasn't going to split us up, nor was I ready to walk away from this. But now, Tip and I will put the finishing touches on this shit down here. You three make sure everything is safe and secure at the chateau."

Danica was already up and stuffing her things into her bag. "Let's get a move on, people."

As everyone got to it, she came up to me, her eyes smoldering. She was livid and trying very hard to keep a lid on it. "You should have told me."

I knew her concern was Cinder. In all our years together, I'd never seen Danica care more for anyone—besides me, of course—than she did for Cinder. I don't know if Cinder reminded her of me when we first met or what, but their bond was unshakable, and right now, Danica was shaking.

"There's nothing to tell yet. Sal said someone had attempted to breach the system, not that they had."

"Semantics don't become you, Clark." Danica checked the clip on her Glock.

"See? Right there, John Wayne. That's *precisely* why. I didn't need you hitting the ground running like a crazy lady shooting the place up."

She stood still. "You're not worried?"

"Not yet. The kids are safe and Sal and Taylor

are busy checking the perimeter. Will is staying in the chateau just to be on the safe side. We're just taking extra precautions."

Danica studied me a moment. "What aren't you telling me?"

"I've told you everything I know, but I would feel better knowing you guys are at there to batten down the hatches."

She nodded. "I don't like the idea of leaving you here alone."

"I won't be alone."

"You know what I mean."

I smiled. "She's the strongest thinker I know, and these guys aren't strong enough to keep her out."

"So, a few Vulcan mind-melds and you guys'll come home?"

I nodded. "What are you worried about? Tip?"

"Just worried, in general. I don't like that we can't trust your people anymore. That's new for me. I don't like it. It's like a safety net was just pulled away, you know? Like now I need to stay on high alert."

Standing in front of her, I laid my hands on her shoulders and steadied my gaze at her. "Who are you foolin'? You're always on high alert. And while I appreciate that more than you know, I need you to go back and take care of business any way you know how."

She nodded, never taking her eyes off mine. "If someone *is* snooping around, we'll be sure to take out the trash. When will you and Tip be back?"

"As soon as we shut this entire operation down. You'll get dropped off and Sal will return for us. We'll be right behind you."

"Promise?"

"Promise. You go home and take care of Cinder

and the others. Keep her with you. Sit down with Will and go over everything he's done so far. Get up to speed. Stay in touch."

Danica nodded, pulling herself to her full height. "You realize, don't you, if it was someone and they *were* after Cinder, there isn't anything you or anyone could do to keep me at bay. I'll turn over every rock on the planet until I find them. If it's Genesys, then—"

"Then we'll wait until we have a trained group of older supers before we take them on. That plan hasn't changed."

Danica didn't miss a beat. "You're thinking of joining with Kristy's crowd, aren't you?"

She knew me so well. "Thinking about it, yes, but I haven't made any decisions. One step at a time. Let's secure the kids first and see what Sal and company have discovered."

"Don't trust your sister, Clark. Not yet. Just because you got cozy at lunch doesn't mean jack. Her being here—" She shook her head. "Doesn't add up."

Tilting my head, I said, "Been sitting on this long?"

"I don't believe in coincidences, Clark. You know that. Showing up here and saving the day? Uh uh. Too convenient for my gut. Too…pat. Just be careful."

"You, too."

"I'll be waiting at the chateau for you, so hustle along."

And hustle we did. Tip and I hugged everyone goodbye. They tried to convince us to keep Delta, but I wasn't buying. I needed Delta to get together with her people. She could do more good for us at the command center than here in Vegas. This would be done today or I would wash my hands of it. I had my own family to take care of.

With Mario and Nick's minions chasing down the few Indies who remained, Tip and I took a cab to the diner.

Holding my hand, Tip turned to me. "Melika's always said one of your greatest strengths is that you surround yourself with outstanding people—people with integrity, with courage. She said I needn't worry about you because of that. Those three women would take a bullet for you. They're awesome. You done good."

Squeezing her hand, I nodded. "I had some good teachers, and right now, I'm going to rely on those lessons learned."

"Take Townsend out quietly?"

"Yes. Cut off the head of the snake. He won't be alone. He's a coward. If we can take him down, they'll scatter. The collector should arrive shortly after we do."

"I've only dealt with one illusionist before and it wasn't pleasant. As long as you keep your shields up, he has no play."

"If he has an offensive weapon with him, we'll need to take it out first. Once we've secured Townsend, I couldn't care less where his minions go."

"You just want to go back, huh?"

I nodded. "I do. And I'd really love for you to see it. It's absolutely gorgeous." I waited for her to respond in the affirmative, but she didn't. Instead, she cocked her head to the side, as if listening for something.

"Right here is fine," she said, tossing a twenty onto the front seat.

I was out the door in a nano with Tip hot on my heels.

"What is it?"

"Lower your shields."

I did, and instantly raised them again. "Holy shit, what did he do? Raise an army?" The amount of supernatural energy filling the air made it feel like electromagnetic energy. Tip had heard it long before I felt it.

We had been dropped off three blocks before the diner, which sat on a corner at the very edge of town. I remembered it because it reminded me of that painting with Monroe, Elvis, and James Dean sitting at a diner. I think that's who they were. I wasn't sure.

"I'm thinking easily ten," Tip said as we wound our way through dark alleys away from the lights on the strip.

"But why? If he was meeting Jasmine here, why bring the troops?"

"Maybe he's expecting payoff from the tournament. Maybe he doesn't trust her. Who knows what transpired between them."

"And maybe he knows she's dead?"

Tip shook her head. "He'd know that only if your desert walkers already made it back, and I seriously doubt that. Walking in a dark desert is a fool's mission, and I guarantee they walked."

"Why wouldn't they?"

She chuffed. "The smart thing to do would be to wait until daylight and then assess your surroundings. Find a road. Anything is wiser than walking around in the dark. You could walk past a road three feet from you and never know it was there. No, Townsend Briggs brought his team for a reason and I think I know what it is." Tip stopped at a corner and peered around it. "He was planning on double-crossing his new partner."

"But why?" Then I thought of the destruction of

the front of Jasmine's store.

"He'd used her up. She'd done her job by killing Max. He had no further use for her. That's what the Indies do, Echo. They use people and then dispose of them when they have outlived their usefulness. They used each other. She wanted Bailey; he wanted Max dead and tons of money. They both stood to gain."

"Then killing Bailey was just her own little peccadillo?"

"Well, darlin', she *did* have the woman's face tattooed." She chuckled as she rounded the first corner. "And I have to say, bravo to Bailey for that punishment. Very clever."

I reached for her arm. "Tell me the truth. *You'd* have killed her, huh?"

Tip locked eyes with me, and even in the semi-darkness of the side street, I could see their fire. "Absolutely. Sometimes, love, the needs of the many truly do outweigh the needs of the few. If Bailey had dispatched Jasmine for attempting to take her life, maybe none of this would have happened. Bailey is no killer, though, and that's why your team is stronger with Danica. She might be a crazy ass bitch, but she'll pull the trigger when she has to. I appreciate that about her." She shrugged and continued walking. "Sometimes, darlin', you have to make the tough decisions. Right now is one of those times."

"What do you mean?"

"Well, let's take stock. We're outnumbered ten or eleven to two. We can try to take them. We can call on the gangsters for natural help, or we could walk away and figure we've done the best we can and call it a day. Get on that plane with your people and let the Others sort all this out. It's your call."

The idea of letting Townsend Briggs go did not at all sit well with me. After all, look at what a mess of things Jasmine had made when Bailey let *her* go. "The Others want Townsend. I'm planning on delivering. I need to show them I am capable of making those tough decisions."

She nodded. "See? That wasn't so hard. So, what's the plan?"

I have to admit, while I was thrilled she deferred to me, I wished she would have just thrown down a plan like she had when we were together.

"He's expecting Jasmine. He won't be expecting you."

"You want me to go in, sit down, and tell him the jig is up and he needs to leave quietly?"

"Too easy?"

She grinned. "Remember, those Indies think their shit doesn't stink. That makes them dangerous. Separating is a bad idea. If I go in, you need to come with me. I'm sure I can incapacitate him, but then we have to get him out of there. That's the tough part. It's not like we can just carry him out."

"Then we tell him the truth. We tell him if he doesn't come with us, we'll be forced to take drastic measures."

She stopped so fast I ran into her. "Drastic measures?" She laughed. "You're kidding me, right?"

"Well, I'm not planning on *killing* him."

"But *he* doesn't know that. Look Echo, if you're going to play the heavy, be heavy."

"And if he doesn't agree to come peacefully?"

She looked at me. "Darlin', you've been watching way too much TV. If he doesn't agree to leave with us, I'll make him wish he had."

"And the others? How dangerous are they to us? I don't have a great deal of offensive weaponry at our disposal." I suddenly wished Danica was with us.

"Well, we know they're good at flinging knives, so you'll want to take care they don't have that chance."

I nodded. "I'll be our defense then."

"There's the diner. You ready?"

I wasn't. "Tip, do you have a better plan?"

This amused her. "Of course I do. I'm just waiting for you to ask."

I did, and once she laid it out to me, I could see the superior design of it.

We walked out to the front of the diner. The sun had yet to peek up over the mountains, but you could see the early risers drinking coffee.

"Ready?"

"As ready as I'll ever be."

As we walked through the parking lot, a silver Lincoln Town Car rolled its window down and a gray-haired man leaned out. "Send him to us and we'll take care of the rest." The window rolled back up.

The Others' collector had arrived.

※ ※ ※ ※

Tip and I walked into the diner, the little bell hanging from the handle ringing as we entered. I spotted Townsend sitting at a corner booth. Two young women who could have been pole dancers for the attire they wore flanked him. Both were supers. The one on the left, wearing a red midriff Minnie Mouse tee shirt, was a TK. Rare; female TKs are few and far between. The one on the right, wearing her blonde hair in two ponytails, was a combination of sorts. She was part empath, part something else...something I hadn't ever felt before, and that worried me.

"Tip—"

"I know...she's a pusher. Like an illusionist, only she can push thoughts and ideas into your mind. We don't have to worry. She's not strong enough to breach our walls."

When Tip came to the booth, she slid in on one side and I on the other.

"Hello, Townsend," Tip said, motioning the waitress over and ordering us both coffee.

"Who the hell—" Then his eyes registered recognition: Of Tip, not me. "This doesn't concern you, Redhawk."

"You see, that's where you're wrong. Your people attacked Echo twice and beat up a friend of ours. I don't take lightly to assholes who disrespect my people and come after Melika's heir apparent. That was a very, very bad decision."

Minnie Mouse started to move her hand from her lap, but I put a vice grip on her wrist. "Uh uh," I whispered. "Unless your powers can stop bullets, you best keep your hands in your lap."

Minnie blinked and then looked at Townsend, who nodded once.

"Where's Jasmine?" He asked.

Tip smiled at the waitress as she brought the coffee over. "You see, that's why messing with friends who have friends in low places is a really dumb idea. Last we saw of her, she was heading out to the desert with some...unsavory friends of ours. These friends have your name. All I have to do is drop a dime on you and you won't get one mile off the strip before these big black SUV's and Hummers track your ass down and give you a one-way ticket to cactus land. You and your little pack of Indies will be breathing in sand." Tip leaned toward him. "*Nobody* comes after our people and lives to tell about it, asshole."

I could sense Townsend's fear and indecision—a combustible mixture for sure.

"So here's the way I see it. You can walk out that door and get in the silver Lincoln with the tinted windows and possibly save your people from getting hurt or worse, or you can be an asshole and try to take us on and the semi-automatics they're packing. It's your call."

Townsend looked at both women, weighing his options. He wanted to run—but that wasn't one of them.

"They'll kill me."

"You have our word they won't." I said. "You can't go around attacking our people and think there won't be some sort of consequence. The Others won't kill you. We will. So, what's it gonna be? You going to walk out of this diner and straight to that silver Lincoln, or are people going to die today?"

Townsend slowly looked at every face before settling back on Tip's. Everything about his energy changed…and not in our favor. "Any idea how many of *my* people are nearby?"

Tip leaned forward, her voice soft and chilling. "Do I look like I give a shit? Can any of them stop the bullets of an M-16 automatic? Because if they can't, you're going to be responsible for quite a few deaths. Is that what you want?"

"What if you're bluffing?"

"What if we're not?"

No one moved.

"Stand and tell them we're through then."
I did.

Minnie started to rise and Tip sent her a little energy present that made her grab her head.

"You don't want to mess with us, Townsend," I said, leaning on the table, arms straight, eyes glaring. "You've hurt enough people and now it's time to pay the piper. Get in the Goddamned car."

On cue, Tip sent so much force into Minnie's head she slumped against the wall.

"What the fuck?" Ponytail said, looking helplessly at Townsend.

"The fuck is the power of we, who have been *trained,* have approximately ten times your feeble power. I could scramble your brains right here, honey, and you'd never even know your own name after I got through with you. Your friend Vince is one good example."

"You? You did that to him?"

"So what do you say?" I interrupted. "Live to conjure another day or go out in a blaze of glory?"

Townsend looked out the window at the silver Town Car. "I have your word they won't kill me?"

I offered him my hand. "You have my word. No one is going to kill you."

Townsend hesitated before shaking my hand. "If they do, my kids will hunt you down and—" Townsend grabbed his forehead in both hands.

Tip leaned closer. *"Nobody* threatens her, *ever,* Briggs. Understand?"

He nodded as he threw a fifty out on the table, shaking the pain from his head. "She's dead, isn't she?"

"Who?"

"Jasmine."

"I have no idea what happened to her. Right now, you need to worry about your own neck. Go straight to the Lincoln. Make any gestures or sudden moves—"

"I got it. Jesus. You people are so serious."

Before I knew what happened, Tip had pinned him by the throat, her face inches from his. I quickly shoved Ponytail back into the booth, where Minnie was coming to.

"You tried coming after us, Dickweed. I'd say that's pretty serious business."

Townsend sputtered, his face turning red. Tip would have kept squeezing if I hadn't stopped her.

Releasing him, she shook her head. "FYI, we're not playing around here. Get in the car."

Townsend nodded and started for the door with Tip hot on his heels. That was when I felt it.

Whirling around, I locked eyes with Ponytail, and sure enough, there it was: Overconfidence and a bravado that shouldn't have been there.

"Ti—" I started to yell, but Ponytail flung herself at me, where we went to the floor of the diner. She was all arms and legs, scratching, clawing. She'd probably have bitten me if I hadn't blasted her off me. The energy was so powerful she landed on her back on the table, breaking plates and sending silverware flying to the floor. She was knocked completely out.

Scrambling to my feet, I raced to the door in time to see Townsend's head as he climbed into the sedan. Tip stood in the near empty lot as the sun peeked over the mountains. Ten Indies closed ranks around her.

"Stay back, love," Tip ordered, looking at each super as they formed a ring around her. Townsend may have gotten in the car, but he did not order is troops to back down. Each was about fifteen to twenty feet away and many had some sort of wry grin on their faces. It was eerie how they acted. Creepy. Like they had the whole situation under control.

To my utter astonishment, the sedan pulled away, leaving me and Tip against a dozen baby rattlers.

Ignoring her command, I joined her and pressed my back to hers. "Since when did I ever listen to you?" I asked.

"No kidding."

"We can take them, right?"

"Oh hell yeah. Them and their brothers and sisters."

Good old, reliable Tip. She would never believe a dozen other supers were strong enough to take her on. She'd never surrender to the likes of these rookies; never believe Indies could ever have the upper hand...

Unless they had guns.

And they did. Big ones.

"Fuck," Tip muttered as a young black kid pointed a gun at her, gangster-style. "Stay behind me, Echo."

I looked at the girl directly in front of me who also wielded a handgun and I knew we were in deep shit. We couldn't stop them all. I knew it. Tip knew it. They knew it.

"Shield up, Echo." Tip was going to attempt the impossible: she was going to try to buy us time by sending out her energy in ten different directions.

I knew she was strong, but I was pretty certain even she couldn't do that.

"Ready, Tip. Go for it. Hurry, she's going to sh—"

All at once, everything collided.

When they talk about your life flashing before your eyes, they never mention that it doesn't flash as much as it rolls in slow motion. We were now in that slow motion, as the girl pulled the trigger at the same time Tip let out the most crushing energy she possessed—an energy that saved my life.

The girl's hand dropped slightly as she pulled the trigger, sending the bullet burning through my side and out through Tip's leather jacket.

Seven of them went down on one or both knees, clutching their heads. Two weaker Indies immediately had nosebleeds and passed out.

I fell forward, clutching my side, feeling the warmth of my blood as it flowed through my shirt and onto my fingers. It was warm and sticky and there wasn't as much pain as one would expect from getting shot—just a burning sensation where the bullet had entered.

When I went down on one knee, Tip felt my pain as surely as if she had been shot herself, and did the one thing I had never seen her do.

She panicked.

Whirling around, she was immediately at my side, releasing the energy vise so she could focus on me and make sure that I was okay.

It was the worst mistake she could have made.

"I'm...fine," I said, not feeling fine at all. "Protect us...God...damn it."

Tip hesitated and I knew, at that moment, it would cost her her life.

As the edges of darkness crept around my consciousness, everything moved in even slower motion. Tip straightened up and hit my shooter with so much force the girl was dead before she hit the ground, blood streaming from her nose and ears. As Tip turned back toward the male shooter, we both knew she was too late. He fired three quick shots at her.

Boom. Boom. Boom.

They were aimed right at her heart, and in this bizarre moment of clarity, I could actually see all three bullets as they cut through the air toward her.

I could actually *see* them.

I'm not quite sure what happened next, but I heard my voice cry out, "No!" and I reached out, not toward Tip, not even toward the shooter, but toward the bullets I shouldn't have been able to see. I reach out and felt this energy travel like the chills down my arms.

There they were—three in a row, all moving toward Tip's chest in such slow motion that when I raised my hand toward them, a strange oval-like mirror that looked like shimmering silver nitrate appeared before them in front of Tip. The weird oval flickered for one second before the bullets disappeared into it. The iridescent air vanished as quickly as it came, taking the bullets with it.

When the bullets disappeared, time returned to normal speed and Tip looked down at her chest for a moment.

No one moved as they stared at the space where bullets should have entered her body.

Realizing she was not hit, she blasted the male shooter with mental energy I could feel from my place on the asphalt.

He, too, was dead before he hit the ground, his brains scrambled by her power, but we both knew it was not enough. There were too many and Tip had lost her focus. We were screwed.

As his weapon clattered to the pavement, one of the other Indies made a move for it. That was when something equally as strange happened. At first, I thought it was my gunshot wound-induced lightheadedness that made me see Tip standing there holding a machine gun of some sort. I mean, where did she get that...and...before I could find the answer, the darkness flowed over me like the blood over my fingers. The last thing I remember was hearing Tip say to me, "Hang on, baby. I gotcha."

※※※※

I came to in a hospital room too white for my eyes. Tip sat by the bed holding my hand in a death grip. As my eyes focused on her worried face, I smiled softly. "Dani's gonna kill me."

Tip smiled back, her eyes filling with tears. "Yes, she is. She's on her way back. I'm pretty sure she's going to kick my ass first." Bringing my hand to her lips, she kissed the back of it. "You scared the shit out of me."

I thought she was talking about the disappearing bullets. "I scared the shit out of me, too."

Shaking her head, she tenderly brushed my hair from my forehead—a gesture she had done for half of my life. "I meant getting shot."

"Oh. That. You disrupted their aim, Tip. You saved me."

"Uh uh. *You* did all the saving...but—"

I asked for some water, and she poured me a glass.

"But what?" I asked, sipping it. My side felt like it was on fire.

A nurse came in to check on me. Then a doctor entered and explained that the bullet had gone cleanly through my right side, just missing my hipbone. He said I'd lost blood, but would be able to leave in the morning. Then he said the police would need to file a report. I nodded, holding Tip's hand tighter, thankful she wasn't trying to speak in my head. I just didn't have the energy.

When the doctor left, Tip scooted closer. "I told the cops those two kids were shooting at each other, and we just got caught in the crossfire."

"No time for a cleanup crew?"

She shook her head. "Someone in the diner called nine-one-one when you blasted that girl inside."

Nodding, I closed my eyes. I was so tired.

"You rest. I'll tell you how it all ended later." As she rose to leave, I held tightly.

"Uh uh. Stay. Please."

Sitting back down, she stroked my cheek with the back of her hand. Tears suddenly sprung to her eyes. "I don't know if I can live my life without you, Echo. That...that was the worst moment of my life. The. Worst."

I released her hand and pulled her head to my lap and ran my hand gently over her long hair while she wept. I couldn't remember many times where I had seen her cry, but I knew it was something she really needed to do. Between Melika's cancer and nearly losing me, Tip was emotionally spent. This worst moment was soon to receive an encore. It was coming at us slowly...like those bullets. We could see it coming and had nothing to stop it.

"You can't get rid of me that easily," I whispered, caressing her head. "I'm thinking you might be stuck with me for a really long time."

Tip cried and cried, until finally there were no more tears to shed. She wiped her eyes on her sleeve and blew her nose on a Kleenex before regaining her composure.

"I love you, Echo Branson. You know that, right?"

Smiling into her eyes, I nodded. "I've always known it."

"I know everything has changed between us, but that never will. Women will come and go, but you are the only one with the key."

I closed my eyes and swallowed hard. We had an enduring love but had never managed to keep it together. Epic failure.

"I need to know something." Her dark eyes focused like an eagle's. "What in the hell *was* that?"

"Honestly, Tip, I have no clue. I've...I've never done that before. I'm not even sure what *it* was."

Bringing my hand to her cheek, she pressed her face into it. "I was a dead woman standing, Echo. Dead. He had me. Whatever you did saved my life, and whatever that was, we need to know." She shook her head. "It was...I don't even have the words. It was like—"

"It was almost as amazing as you producing a machine gun. How the hell did you do *that*?"

"*She* didn't. I did."

Looking up, I saw Max standing in the doorway. "Max?"

He nodded and came up to the other side of the bed. He didn't look like a guy whose head had splattered on a stage floor like a watermelon dropped from a fifth story window.

"I'm so sorry I didn't get to you guys in time," he said.

I looked at Tip. "Get. To. Us?"

She nodded. "I wasn't holding a weapon, Echo.

Max created an illusion the Indies believed and they scattered for the hills. It was the strangest...well, one of the strangest things I've ever seen."

"Or not seen, as the case was," Max added. "Tip's shields prevented her from seeing it—all she saw was everyone taking off, but you had lowered yours to do whatever the hell it was you did, so you saw it."

"But now...you...Danica saw—"

"They *all* saw what I wanted everyone to see. That's why I went on in the first place. I needed to carve out some breathing room. No one hunts down a dead man, and I knew I needed to be dead so Townsend would leave me alone. Sorry I didn't wait for you guys to do your mojo, but he wasn't going to stop until he got what he wanted."

"How?"

"The audience *saw* me fall to my death. The ambulance guys saw a dead man on a stretcher, and the coroner saw a corpse on a slab. Everyone saw what I wanted them to see. Then I got out. By then, though, I'd used so much energy I was weak and needed to recuperate. I was out of commission for a bit. I apologize for that or I would have let you know."

"No need for apologies Max. You came in the nick of time, and we appreciate that. Really."

"Appreciate it enough to let me in?"

"In?"

"Your school. I understand you might be able to show me how to...be better."

I nodded. "I sure can try. You are welcome to join us in Marin and see if our school suits you."

He glanced over at Tip before nodding. "I'd like that."

"But what about your show?"

"I'm wasting my powers entertaining people. Let Angel and Copperfield do that. Me? I'm done."

Suddenly feeling very worn out, I closed my eyes and tried to find a reserve of energy. Sensing this, Tip jerked her head toward the door, and Max made his way to it.

Before he could leave, I opened my eyes and said, "Max? What were you doing out there anyway?"

I saw a rise of blush in his cheeks. "Following you guys. I...uh...I hope you feel better." Shaking his head, he left my room.

I looked into Tip's red rimmed eyes. "What was that really about, Tip?"

"Guilt. He feels badly that he couldn't prevent you from being hurt. Now, he wants you to train him. He doesn't want to be just a magician anymore. He doesn't want anything more to do with Vegas."

"Can't say I blame him." I closed my eyes and blew out a deep breath that made my side feel like someone had a hot poker up to it. Tip was on her feet in an instant.

"Shh. Sit down," I whispered, opening my eyes. "It's a little tender is all." I held her hand as she sat. "Tell Max to pack up. He is more than welcome after saving our lives."

"He's a good guy with a lot of mad skills." Kissing the back of my hand, she held it between both of hers. "We didn't tell the kids about this, about you being hurt. Only Danica and Bailey know, and Bailey was none too happy about staying behind to hold down the fort. That girl thinks the world of you."

I nodded. "I love her to death. Bailey is one of the coolest people I know. I'm lucky to have her." I could sense Tip's discomfort. "No, not like that. We've become really close. She was a good choice for my right hand, but she is madly in love with Taylor."

"From what I've seen, she'd walk on hot coals for you."

"Yes, I know she would." Forcing my eyelids up one last time, I ran my fingertips down her jawline. "So would you. Thank you."

"Close your eyes, love. I'll stay until you fall asleep, then I'm grabbing our things and taking you back." Leaning over, she kissed my forehead, letting her lips linger there. "I've noticed one thing. You never call Marin home."

"No?" I was fading fast.

"No. Home is where your heart is. I love you."

As I faded into the comfort of the drugs dripping into my system, I remembered one last thing I needed to tell her.

"Oh, and Tip? Jacob Marley says hello."

༄༄༄༄

I felt someone standing over my bed and thought maybe it was Jacob Marley again, but when I felt the pain in my side, I knew it wasn't a dream.

"Shhh."

Peering through the darkness, I didn't need to lower my shields to know who had snuck into my room. "Kristy?" I shot a look over at the chair Tip had been in and out of, and was shocked to find her asleep. "Did you do something to her?"

Kristy shook her head as she gingerly sat on the edge of my hospital bed. "I didn't, but one of my people did. Sorry, but I'm not her favorite person and I wasn't letting her or anyone else keep me from my sister."

"Is she just asleep?"

"Don't worry about her, she's fine. Tell me about you. How are you feeling? Are you okay? They say you were shot."

The worry in her eyes took me aback. "Better. Tired. Sore. All of the above. I thought you were going to Los Angeles?"

"I did. I was. I heard about the shooting and beat a hasty retreat back here. I'm sorry I didn't stay here. I thought—"

"You saved my bacon once, and I really appreciate it. I didn't expect you to stay around and babysit me."

She smiled and for the first time I realized how pretty she was and how much she looked like our mother. "Charlie...when they called and told me..." Tears filled her eyes. "Something happened...you know?" She looked away as she wiped her eyes. "It was like I realized for the first time that I had a sister...that I have a family and I walked away when you needed me most."

I was stunned. I didn't even know what to say.

"I thought you could handle it, so I went on with my life. I'm so sorry. I have been such an ass." Her voice was tinged with such sadness and remorse, I found myself consoling her.

"Kristy, you've spent your whole life without a sister, without a mother, without a family. Just because I've suddenly popped up in your life doesn't mean you're supposed to just accept it and be one with it. Me being alive is a lot to take in."

Tears fell from her eyes and ran swiftly down her face. "You have no idea. When I first saw you, it turned everything I thought I knew about my life and my memories upside down. You might have been erased, Charlie, but *my* memories, and those repressed ones all came jumping to life: Times we went to the beach with Harmon and our mother. Movie night with popcorn and caramel apples in the winter. I might have been just three when our lives fell apart, but that little girl remembered her big sister. Those memories have been flooding back for the last six months, shaking me to the bone at times." Slowly shaking her head, she wiped her eyes. "Then to realize we were on different sides of this war with Genesys...I was so much more disappointed than you could have known. I was so bummed...and angry. I'd spent my whole life pushing the memories of some other little girl away from my mind, that when she...you...were finally real, I...I just felt angry and ripped off. It wasn't until I thought I'd lost you that I realized how stupid I'd been. I think I drove a hundred the whole way back."

The pain in my side traveled to my heart as Kristy's pain pushed hard against my shields. "Tell you what—let's start with a clean slate. No regrets. No more apologies. You saved my life and—"

"And I should have done so again."

I held her hand. "Kristy...it's okay. We've both been through a hell of a lot. Let's try starting again as sisters. Just sisters. Not supers, not enemies. Sisters."

She sniffed and nodded. "I'd like that. Now, how are you, sis?"

"Good. The bullet went clean through. The shooter—"

"Is dead, yeah I heard that. Good going Redhawk. I want you to know his pack of hoodlums are also dead."

I stared at her.

"My people work fast, Charlie. By the time I made

it back here, my people had found the fuckers who did this and took care of it. Let's just say, regardless of what your old folks want you to do, the loudest message one can send arrives in a body bag with a toe-tag. Those asshole Indies won't be bothering you anymore."

I tried not to grin, but I did anyway. "Thank you...I think. The Others won't be thrilled."

"Tough shit. They're nothing to me. Shooting my sister means you aren't going to live to tell about it." She chuckled and shook her head. "My sister. It sounds so...foreign to my ears, and even stranger saying it."

"Well, that makes two of us. Thank you for coming back."

"I've had a long talk with my bosses and explained to them that you and I have been at cross purposes for no real reason other than my pigheadedness. We don't have to be on opposite sides of the same coin, Charlie. Life's not that black and white. I may have been, but that doesn't mean I have to stay that way. I know you won't come work for us...and believe it or not, I understand that. I have a deal of sorts. Maybe we can come to an agreement."

I leaned back. "I'm all ears."

"You provide a valuable service for young supers. I apologize if I made it seem like I didn't think it worthy. I do. It's just...my people collect soldiers and you collect students."

I did not disagree.

"But sometimes, my soldiers need to be students first, and sometimes, your students might choose to be soldiers after leaving your tutelage."

I barely nodded. "Okay."

"So here's the deal. Let's not fight over supers anymore. If I collect a kid who needs your help first,

I'll bring him to you."

"In exchange for what?"

"In exchange for you letting him or her know that joining STOP is an option. And when you collect supers, you let them know we exist and that we can be a choice when they leave the school. We're really on the same side, you know?"

I felt a huge grin light up my face. "Well, I've always thought so. I have to say, this piece of news thrills me to death, Kristy. It's a deal. Thank you so much."

She pressed my hand between hers. "You're my sister, Charlie. A sister I remember and want to get to know."

Pulling her to me, I hugged her as tightly as my wound would let me. "I'd so love that." Pulling away, I looked into her blue eyes. "The rest of the Indies?"

Kristy rose when Tip adjusted in her chair. "Dust in the wind, baby. Those we let live have been…well… we call it hobbled. I don't think we'll see those Indies for a long time."

I didn't want to know what hobbled meant, but I had a pretty good idea.

When Tip turned again, Kristy moved away from the bed. "I applaud what you do, Charlie, working with those kids who obviously love you to death. I almost envy you the family you've created."

"You don't have to be apart from that, Kristy. You are my family, too."

She shook her head sadly. "Oh yes I do. Things happened to me in those labs. That kind of pain changes a person forever. It's almost as if I have no soul. I am not a kind person, Charlie, and until I can burn Genesys to the ground once and for all, I pretty much have one single goal in my life...and that is death. It is almost as if someone has programmed my DNA to hunt them." She held up her hand to stop me. "I've heard it all before. I know it doesn't have to be that way, but *that's* the way it is...and I am okay with that."

"And what then?"

She came back to the bed. "Then maybe I'll have a normal life. Until then, I'll keep on keeping on and doing my thing."

Tip stirred again, and Kristy stepped back. "I better go. Your girlfriend sees me here, her first thought will be to put my brains on opposite walls."

"She's not my girlfriend."

Kristy looked at Tip. "Too bad. She's smokin' hot and she'd die for you, this one. You may not be her girlfriend, but she sure as shit is yours." Giving my wrist a quick squeeze, she leaned over and whispered, "You keep people like Tiponi Redhawk close by regardless of your relationship. Stay safe, Charlie."

She was gone in an instant, and when Tip stirred a moment before going back to sleep, I eased back down under the covers.

I had a real sister.

That was worth a bullet any day.

※※※※

It was dark out when I opened my eyes again to find Danica reading *Vogue* by the side of my bed. Tip was not in the room.

"If you weren't feeling so bad, I would kick your ever-lovin' ass into next week. I *knew* I should have stayed."

I smiled at her. Bravado was Danica's defense mechanism when what she really wanted to do was cry. "I'm going to be fine. Where's Tip?"

"Went to grab a coffee and a shower." She rose and paced across the floor, pretending to look out the window. "That...call..." She hesitated, a catch in her voice. "Was a dagger in my gut, Jane." Turning, tears ran down her cheeks. The last time I'd seen her cry was when her mother died, nearly ten years ago. "Goddamn it, don't *do* that to me."

Slowly sitting up, I rubbed the sleep from my eyes. "Do what, Dani?"

"Scare me! The whole flight down here, I could barely breathe thinking what if I got here and you were...were—"

For the second time in twelve hours, I, the gunshot victim, had to console one of my people.

"Come here."

"I'm so fucking mad at you." The tears were really coming now. "And at myself. I knew I should have stayed. I wrestled with getting on that plane. Next time, I am going to listen to myself."

I patted the bed. "Please."

She did, and melted into my arms, sobbing almost as hard as Tip had.

"I never expected supers to be carrying guns," I said softly.

"Yeah, well, so do we. This won't happen again. I promise," Danica said, trying to pull it together.

"It's not your fault. The world has changed. Supers are changing. We'll be better prepared next time."

"Hell yeah we will." Pulling away, Dani wiped her face with my sheets. "I'm all for hunting those assholes down and giving them a piece of my action. Just say the word."

I shook my head, appreciating the sentiment anyway. "Kristy's people took care of it." I held up a hand to stop her next question. "Can I just please go home?"

"Absolutely. After the doctor has checked on you. Tip's got everything in the plane. All we need is the A-OK and we're out of here. Can I get you something? Anything?"

"I'd love a sandwich or something. I'm starving."

Danica stood by my bed and looked down at me for a really long time. "That day at the creek, when you pushed me through the fence to keep Todd from getting to me. I never told you...never shared the promise I made to myself the moment the cops whisked you away." She impatiently wiped her tears away. "We were fourteen and I swore I would do everything in my power to protect you—to keep you safe. Always. You always wondered how it was so easy for me to kill that asshole in the Superdome? Well, that's why. You mean more to me than just being my best friend. You're my family and you always will be. And I'd kill again if it meant making sure you were safe. It was a promise I made myself that I intend on keeping. Always." With that, she leaned forward and kissed my forehead just as Tip had done. "Don't leave me in this life by myself, Clark. I wouldn't know how to get through a single day."

"Sure you would. Fortunately, you won't have to."

"Better not. You don't want to be on this planet if that happens." Grabbing her purse, she wiped her face. "I'm going to go get us some real breakfast."

When she left, Tip returned shortly after.

"Did she tear you a new one?" I asked, as she handed me a Starbucks.

"Actually, she surprised me by fighting back her tears. That girl loves you more than life itself. She's fashioned herself as your bodyguard and feels a little like she's failed you. How you feeling?" Tip sat on the bed and played with my hair.

"Sore. You should have told me bullet wounds get sore."

"Mine didn't, but I had Bailey's poultice, remember? Man's medicine pales next to nature's. Other than that, how are you feeling?"

"Like I just want to go back. Home. Back home."

She nodded and suppressed a grin. "The second you get a release, you are out of here. Plane is on standby. Thank God Dani bought that damn thing. She's known for a long time what her role is in your life and she's certainly come through." Tip leaned closer until I thought she was going to kiss me. "What is it you haven't shared with me, darlin' What is it you're keeping from me?"

I didn't bother trying to hide from her. I had no energy for anything but the most rudimentary of shields.

"I saw Jacob Marley."

Tip swallowed loudly. "Oh?"

Nodding, I sipped my coffee. Why is it warm drinks are so soothing? "He came to me somewhere between the ambulance and the hospital."

Tip shook her head. "You know, I've dealt with a lot of paranormal activity in my life, but not once have I been approached by the dead. What did he want?"

I felt tears burn my eyes. "He came to fight

Death."

Tip wiped my falling tears with her thumb as they fell.

"Really?"

"Really. He said it wasn't my time but that sometimes the body doesn't understand that and shuts down anyway. He told me there was so much more I needed to do—so many more lives I needed to touch."

"So he yelled at you."

I chuckled, and it hurt. "Yeah. I guess he did."

"I don't know what it is about you, darlin', that makes people want to protect you, but that kid…he'd have eaten glass for you."

Two more tears rolled down my cheeks, but this time, I got them. "I miss him so much."

"I know you do."

"He told me that Cinder, more than anyone else, needs me and that this little adventure was just a practice run for what's coming."

"That little bastard was always so cryptic. Did he bother to tell you what that is?"

I shook my head. "He's not allowed. Besides, he can't actually see into the future. I'm not quite sure of the parameters involved and, quite frankly, I don't care. I just loved seeing him."

"Well, not like that."

"I never thought I was going to die."

"No, but it *is* nice to know that even in death, Jacob Marley has your back."

"That he does."

Tip stood and poured me some water. Hospitals always made her nervous. Like a panther in a cage, she'd pace back and forth, and I was sure she was tired of all the doctors poking Melika.

"I didn't tell her." Tip said softly. "She'd only worry."

"Good call. I'm sure she's better off not worrying."

Just then, Danica returned, empty-handed.

"No sandwich?"

She chuckled. "I ordered delivery. There's some old guy sitting out in the waiting room who's bugging the shit out of me. I don't think he speaks English."

Tip closed the door and leaned against it. They both looked as tired as I felt. "That's Harry. He's deaf. He's one the Others sent here to protect Echo."

Danica was incredulous. "Protect her? It's a little late for that, isn't it? Where were they when those assholes were pulling out the heat? Where were they when she was in harm's way? I have half a mind to pay those assholes a visit and give them a piece of my mind."

"Dani—"

"He's good because he's invisible. No one ever sees Harry."

"They sent a deaf guy as protection? Jesus H., Tiponi, what's wrong with those geriatrics anyway?"

"Harry's special, Danica. He's a unique empath. He not only feels negative emotions, he can turn your own emotions against you."

"And that's helpful how?"

"If someone were to come after Echo, they would do harm to themselves."

Danica grinned. "Oh. Oh, I *like* that. I like that a lot."

Tip grinned. "It keeps us out of it, know what I mean?"

When the food arrived, it was enough for an army, so I invited Harry in for some.

"Dani, this is a butt load of food."

"I wasn't sure what you wanted. I'll take the rest of these sandwiches to the nurse's station when we're done."

When Harry came in, I could see what Tip meant about him being invisible. He looked like a little old Jewish man in his grey sweater vest and pleated slacks.

"Is it safe to talk?" he asked in perfect enunciation.

I looked over at Tip, who nodded.

"I thought you said he was deaf," Danica said.

He turned to Danica and scowled. "Naturals see so little."

"Hey!"

"Dani, please. Clearly Harry uses a different sense to hear us. Right?"

He turned and grinned at me. "Exactamundo. Now, I just wanted to let you know that Townsend is being given the option of leaving the country or staying on the island, the latter of which means our version of rehabilitation. We think he'll leave the country."

"They should have killed the asshole," Danica said.

"We don't play judge and jury," he said, not taking his eyes from mine. "And we frown upon those who do. The council would like a word with you before you return home."

I held my hand up to silence both Tip and Dani, who seldom saw anything eye-to-eye. "I'm afraid that's not possible. My students need us to return home first. Tell the council I will see them in a week and only if I'm feeling up to it."

Harry slowly grinned. "They said you weren't one to do as you were told."

"My priorities are in California. I'm not trying to

be adversarial."

"Very well then. I shall let them know." He started for the door when Danica moved for it.

"You can also tell them we don't appreciate the way they bailed on her at the diner. For Christ's sake, why didn't they *do* anything to help?"

Harry ignored Danica and turned to me, weathered hand on the door. "I know it's often hard to understand, Echo, but we really are on the same team. All your questions will be answered when you come to the island." With that, Harry left.

"They just piss me the hell off," Danica growled.

"Theirs is not an easy job, Danica," Tip replied. "I suggest you go to the island as soon as you are up to it and let them know how you feel about all of it. You came down here to help and they left us hanging. I agree with Danica on that point."

"Fine." Suddenly, I felt incredibly weary. "I'll go see them when I feel up to it. Right now, I think I'd best get some sleep. Tomorrow at this time, I want to be in my own bed."

And, true to Tip and Dani's word, I was.

⁂

I'd never been happier to be home than I was when I walked through the door of the chateau. It had been a warm homecoming, with Cinder and her puppy in the lead. She hugged my neck so hard it took everything I had not to grimace. The triplets seemed to have grown overnight, and they, too, hugged me tightly in a crowd of youngsters. Tack held back a little before joining the group hug. As the newest member of our family, he was still working things out.

Then came the adults—Sal, Connie, Delta, Taylor, and Megan, and of course, Bailey, who couldn't stop crying. Thankfully, Danica had taken the kids upstairs to give them the little mementos I'd brought back from Vegas, or they would have wondered at Bailey's emotional state. I'd never seen her cry so hard.

"I'm fine, Bailey," I said as she held me to her. "I really am."

She pulled slightly away and whispered, "Townsend is a dead man and I don't give a shit what the Others say."

Looking into her eyes, I realized right at that moment how tight knit my new family had become. Supers and naturals alike had gathered to welcome me home, and the short little party we had together was just what I needed, though it tired me out something fierce. I had no idea getting shot took so much out of a person.

When everyone had gone or returned to work, over Tip and Danica's reservations, I met with Sal in the Security Room. "Did you locate the breach?"

Sal shook her head before tucking her red hair behind her ears. "There was no breach, Echo. What it was is someone took a photo from something like a hang glider or parachute, or small aircraft. See, the sensors we have placed all around are set up to detect any sort of irregular electrical activity. Usually reserved for larger items like cars or cell phones, it still registers energy in the area. It took me and Taylor a long time to figure out where it came from."

"And you're certain it came from some sort of photography?"

She nodded as she fiddled with her elaborate instrument panel. "Want me to show you?"

I shook my head. "Just give me the upshot."

"The upshot is someone took anywhere from twenty to a hundred photos from various overhead positions of the compound in a five-minute period. We are working now on a scrambling device that will disrupt any satellite or other overhead photo in the future."

"We?"

She grinned. "Me and the boys. They are over-the-top awesome. Working with geniuses of their caliber is the second best part of this job."

"And the first best part?"

She smiled softly. "The kids. That Tack kid is a great student. So eager."

"Excellent work, Sal. So can we rest easier?"

"For the moment. You'll need to talk to Bailey, though. She and William have been going at it."

"Oh?"

"Yeah. Bailey wants a living sentry system and he said no way."

"Meaning dogs?"

Sal laughed. "Worse. Wolves."

I blinked. "Wolves? Bailey wants wolves around the perimeter?"

"Hey, it's her idea, not mine."

"You're our security expert, Sal, what do *you* think?"

"Honestly? She made a believer out of me. Should all else fail, a living sentry that can tear a man's throat out is the next best thing."

"I'll think about it. Right now, I'm too tired to commit."

"You look a little pale, Echo. Maybe you've overdone it for the day."

There was no maybe about it. I was exhausted.

When I finished with Sal, I went in and sat with each one of the kids and asked them about their week and what they had learned. I saved Cinder for last, but when I looked in her room, she wasn't there. I found her waiting on my bed with Shila fast asleep.

"*You look tired,*" she said.

"I am. It's good to be back."

Back.

There. I'd said it just like Tip said I did. How weird was that? And what did it really mean? Danica had just dropped millions on this place. It's not like I could leave it. Besides, where would I go?

"How's the puppy training going?" I asked aloud. Cinder had signed up for puppy training courses at the local pet store. Danica was correct about the responsibility piece...I shouldn't have been surprised: Danica was always right (But I'd never tell *her* that).

"Awesome! *Shila is the smartest dog in the class.*"

"Of course she is. Have you met anyone there?"

She scrunched up her face at me. "*You mean kids my age?*"

I nodded. "Or anyone else."

"*There's this fat lady with a pug who's really nice. She laughs all the time and loves her little puppy like it was a baby. I don't know if it's cute or disgusting.*"

"Good. How are the rest of the kids doing?"

"*Much better. Will is a good teacher. Not as good as you, but he really cares. He expects them to reach their potential.*"

"Good."

Cinder tilted her head as she studied me, her left hand playing with Shila's ear. The dog was sound asleep. "*Is Tip staying?*"

The question surprised me, and the truth was, I

didn't know. "I'm not sure kiddo. Why do you ask?"

She shrugged. *"She loves you. You love her. You belong together. Like Shila belongs with me."*

I looked at the puppy ensconced between Cinder's legs. "She's adorable."

"She's so awesome, Echo. I don't think I've ever loved anything so hard in my life."

"That's how it should be. Life without love is a waste of time."

Cinder stared at me. *"Did you almost die?"*

I looked at her, wondering how she knew. We'd all decided it was best if the kids didn't know I'd been shot, but Cinder was different. She was in between being a kid and being an adult. Killing people will mature you pretty quickly.

"How did you know?"

"Danica shot out of here after a phone call. Pushed her driver out of the car, got behind the wheel, and peeled rubber out of here. I've never seen her move so fast. So I eavesdropped on Sal's conversations until I understood what had happened." She shrugged. *"Did you?"*

"No, hon. Not even close. I was shot. Bullet went straight through. I'm fine. Really. Just a little tired."

Her eyes scanned my face. *"Someone shot you?"* She shook her head. *"Not good."*

"No, but it's over and we all arrived safely. That's what counts."

"Good. We missed you. A lot."

"Well, I missed you, too."

Nodding, Cinder rose and started for the door, Shila right on her heels as if she'd never been sleeping.

"Cinder?"

She turned.

"Thank you."

"What for?"

"For not saying the obvious."

She fought back a smile. *"That you shouldn't have left me here?"*

"Right."

Cinder walked back into my room. *"Echo, Melika pulled me aside just before I left and told me it was my job to keep you safe—to protect you. She understands that I am not a little girl anymore. You need to as well. Next time I'll do just that."*

I stared into her blue eyes and marveled at the wisdom behind them. "Yes, you will, because next time I'll take you."

When she was gone, I carefully scooted under the covers and was almost asleep when I felt someone sit on the edge of the bed.

"This place is incredible, darlin'. I mean, Danica left nothing to chance." Tip reached out and gently smoothed one of my eyebrows.

Nodding, I closed my eyes again. My side was hurting and I just wanted to sleep. "She never does anything second class."

"That vineyard is breathtaking, this house is a technological marvel, and the grounds gorgeous. I had no idea."

I nodded. "She spent a fortune, but everything is top of the line. She did everything in her power to make this home."

"It's your home now."

I felt her fingertips linger on my eyebrows. It felt soft and soothing. "It still doesn't feel like home," I said, my voice barely above a whisper. "I want it to, but it doesn't yet. You hit it on the head when you said I never call this place home. I heard myself and I hardly ever do."

"The bayou is a tough place to replicate, love. Danica's added some nice touches, like the river, but… it's not the bayou. It may look like it, it may even feel like it at times, but it will never be the bayou. It will never have bayou folks or food, or—"

Tip would never leave the river. That much I had always known. If Melika was giving her the house on the river, that meant she knew, too.

"Will you stay?" I whispered.

She looked away. "You know I can't. I belong on the river. With or without Mel, the bayou is my home."

"I mean now…tonight…will you stay?"

"As much as I'd love to, it's safer for you to be alone in your bed. I wouldn't want to bump your side accidentally. I'll stay here while you rest. Just close your eyes and your pie hole and rest. I'll be right here the whole night."

"No you won't."

I opened my eyes to find Bailey standing at the door with a bowl in her hands.

"I want to take a look at that wound. Tip said it felt hot to her. I just need to make sure we've done everything we can to settle it." Bailey made a shooing motion with her hands, shooing Tip out. "Don't need you hovering, Chief. Go on now. You can come back later, but right now, I need to check that doctor's work."

When Tip left, Bailey sat next to me and gingerly unwrapped the bandage. "Just so we're clear," she started, "we're *never* doing that again."

I nodded and tried not to wince as the bandage peeled back. "So I've been told. Under the circumstances—"

"Never. Again." Bailey gazed hard into my eyes. "It's a different world out there now, E. It's one where people covet fame even over fortune. It's one where people are enrapt by wizards, werewolves, and vampires. Enrapt now, scared shitless later if they knew for sure what we could really do. We dodged..." She stopped and shook her head as she dipped her fingers into a lavender paste. "Well, we didn't quite dodge a bullet, did we?"

I said nothing as she gently smeared the lavender paste over my wound. I jumped at its coolness against my hot wound.

Bailey peered closely at the sutures before sniffing it like an animal. "Okay, this is better than I expected. Good sutures, the skin isn't as angry as I thought it would be."

"It actually feels pretty good."

"It will feel much better tomorrow. Roll over."

Gingerly, I did, and held my pillow while she peeled the bandage back.

"I know you'd love nothing more than to make the place a Shangri-la for the kids, but like I said, these are different times. We can't afford to be caught unaware again. We can't split our offense, and we can't assume, ever again, that today's supers won't stoop to gangsterland tactics. We learned a great deal this week, E, and hopefully, that knowledge will help keep us all safe and sound."

"I know you're right, Bailey. I made a stupid tactical error by dividing my troops. It worked in Alaska, so I thought—" I hesitated. I just wanted sleep. "Believe me, it's a blunder I won't make again." The paste felt cool on my skin and suddenly, I felt my muscles go slack. "Goddamn you...what did you—"

"Shh." Bailey stroked my hair lovingly. It felt so good. "You need to rest. You need to settle your mind and let your body heal. You need to trust us to hold down the fort and take care of the kids."

My eyelids felt like concrete. "Damn you, Bailey. Damn you and your...voodoo magic."

She helped me roll over and readjusted my pillows. "Yeah, you and everyone else."

"How long?" I couldn't even keep my eyes open.

"Long enough for you to let both body and mind rest and recuperate. We'll all be here in the morning. The kids are dying to tell you all the lessons they've learned. But for now, you rest. We've got it all covered."

If she said anything else, I didn't hear it, as the drug she'd given me took over and carried me into a blissful night of near dreamless sleep.

≈≈≈≈

Jacob Marley came to me in my dreams, sitting on the edge of my bed as he always seemed to do. "What the hell were you thinking?" he asked. He was wearing a Braves baseball cap, jeans, and a black T-shirt.

"Is the cap an homage to Zack's team?"

"Of course. He's been scouting some great college players lately. The Braves are gonna be good soon." He inched closer. "Speaking of brave, taking on a bunch of gun-toting thugs is pretty courageous, if not stupid. You scared the everloving crap out of me."

I smiled and gingerly sat up in bed, glad there was no gunshot wound pain in my dream. "I never expected supers to be packing guns." Shrugging, I pulled the covers up around me. "I was wrong."

"Ya think? You took a bullet. Tip almost took three. I was so afraid for you, Echo. That could have gone south on you so quickly."

"And it didn't?"

"It went *somewhere*, that's for sure."

"And Jasmine?"

An angry grin crept across his face. "Oh that bitch is getting just what she deserves. That's all I can tell you, but just know, if she thought her life sucked, it ain't nothing compared to her death." Jacob bit on a fingernail. "Okay, I don't have much time. I just wanted you to know that not everything is as it seems. I need you to remember that, okay?"

Leaning forward, I saw something in his eyes. Was it fear? "Jacob?"

"I can't say anything else, Echo. I wish I could, but I can't. Just remember that, okay? Everything is not as it seems." Reaching for my hands, he gave them a quick squeeze. "You mean the world to me, and I wish there was something I could do to make your life easier. Watching over you is not easy when I can't do anything to stop bullets or punches."

"Oh, Jacob. I don't need you to watch over me. I just need you to be here for me."

"And I am." He looked over his shoulder and then lowered his voice. "I have to go. Remember what I said."

I nodded.

"No. Repeat it."

"Everything is not always as it seems."

He jumped off the bed. "Good. No more playing with guns, okay?"

Before I could answer, he disappeared.

I didn't wake up until after one the next afternoon. When my eyes finally focused, I could see Tip reading a book in one of the reddish brown leather high-backed chairs across the room.

"Please tell me you didn't sleep in that chair," I said, testing out my side. It was far less sore than the day before. Bailey's hands and poultices were magic.

Setting the book down, Tip and her great big grin came over to the side of the bed and sat down on it. She looked tired and unrested. "You look better, Echo. How you feeling?"

I moved a little more to see how my side felt. "Umm...it feels really good."

"Bailey has mad skills." Tip leaned over and pressed her lips to my forehead, letting them linger there. "I've been running background on Max and he checks out. Nice guy. A little old for the crowd you have here, but I think the age difference can be an asset."

"You like him."

She nodded. "I do. He's a good guy. I think he'll fit in just fine here, but I can take him to the bayou if you'd rather not take on such an old student."

I reached for her hand. "He saved my life. He is welcome here if this is where he chooses to stay."

She nodded. "That's pretty much what I told him. He's a good one, I think, but raw. He could use a hand in the shield-building department."

Looking in her eyes, I cocked my head at her. "Thank you for staying. Seems like forever since we've spent any time together."

Her eyes smiled as she nodded. "Seems like we never get the chance to just rest and hang out like when you were a kid." She shook her head. "Sorry. When you were younger."

"I'm sorry about whatever happened between you and Yvonne. I thought—"

"She didn't make it a week on the bayou. The moment she saw New Orleans, she hightailed it out of the swamp." She shrugged. "Can't say I blame her. The river's not for everyone."

"No. That it's not."

"So much has changed...even there." She looked away. "I've changed. I don't know what I was thinking bringing a woman to the bayou while dealing with all that I'm dealing with. She bolted the first chance she got. Can't say I blame her. Life has always been different there, but since Katrina, it's just not the same."

"Like Bailey said, the world's changed a helluva lot since we were kids on the bayou. Katrina changed us all."

"Yeah, she did, and I don't know that we'll ever get it back. We try. We work to try to fix that which the government won't, but we still have a long journey ahead of us." Tip shook her head. "Anyway, what can I get you? What do you need?"

"I'd like the chance to just stay in one place for awhile. Work with the kids, enjoy watching the vines ripen. I need a breather, Tip. It feels like I've been going balls to the wall for months."

"You have. Now you have time to stop and smell the roses." Tip's smile grew. "I can't even believe you own a winery."

"I don't. Dani does. She calls it 'diversifying' her portfolio."

"And you call it?"

"Payback."

She nodded sagely. "Ah yes. Her mother. Well, she outdid herself. Sal showed me the extent of your security. She's an odd little thing, isn't she? Sorta part woman, part dwarf, part lesbian."

I tried to ease myself up so I was sitting up. "I don't think she's gay."

"No? Coulda fooled me. She's a bundle of something, that's for sure." We both chuckled like we did when we were young lovers.

"Well, she's a good egg, regardless of who or what she sleeps with," I said. "We couldn't be in better hands with our security team."

"Agreed. I have to hand it to you, darlin', you really got it going on here. I'm totally impressed. You'll do good work here."

I don't know why, but that was important to me. Maybe in some weird way, I had always sought her approval. "Thanks. That means a lot coming from you."

"Mel would really approve." Releasing my hand, Tip stood. "Bailey will be coming to get you in an hour, so you might want to get dressed. I'll bring you some coffee."

When she returned, I was dressed in black sweat bottoms with a red hoodie and matching Nikes.

"When you're feeling up to it, we need to go see the Others and put a period at the end of all this."

"We?"

She nodded. "I need to talk to Bishop about Melika's condition."

I nodded. "Then I'd love to have your company."

Just then, Bailey came in with another bowl of poultice, only this one was lime green. "I know I'm early, but when I saw Tip making you a cup of Joe, I figured why not?" Bailey set the bowl on my nightstand. "While I put this on, I need you to listen to me, okay? No reply necessary. I just need you to hear me, okay?"

I waved to Tip, who set my coffee down on her way out the door. "Okay."

Once the bandage was removed, Bailey started talking. "I know you have faith in me, E, and I am thrilled to be your number two. I never expected to be, but I'm proud and privileged to do the honors." She paused as she examined the wound. "And as your second in command here, it's incumbent upon me to help you with decisions I think would be best for all involved, and I think you should ask Tip to stay."

I looked over my shoulder at her. "Ask—"

"Uh uh. Not done yet. Whatever happened between you two is water under. You're both different people now. If you don't give her some place to set her roots when Mel dies, she'll be lost. She'll be like a piece of tissue paper in the wind. She won't know where to go or what to do. We can't let her be alone when Mel dies, E. Tip deserves better than that from you...from all of us she taught. Just think about it." She put on new gauze and gently pressed the tape down. "Everything she knows will change. I, for one, think we need to be here for her."

When I gingerly rolled off the bed, I held my coffee between both hands, savoring the warmth. "I never thought of it that way."

"Where would she go, E? What the fuck will she do when Mel dies and Tip has no place to call home? You want her to go live out on the bayou by herself, with only Bones for company?"

"No. Of course not."

"Then say she can stay. Give her something to

hold onto. These are dark, dark times for her. You need to be the light to help her out of that darkness."

I tilted my head and stared at her. "She can't live here, Bailey. You know that as well as I do. She's a creature. Not like you, but she's a creature of the bayou. I can't imagine her living anywhere else."

"You can still offer it. The gesture alone is enough to give her something to hold onto."

I thought about it a moment. Yes, the day that Melika departs this earth will change everything Tiponi Redhawk has ever known. "You really like her, don't you?"

Bailey looked me right in the eyes and replied. "No, you goof. I really love her. Tip has been a great teacher, mentor, and friend. We take care of our own, E. She needs that right now. Throw her a bone."

"But what about...you know...*your* role here?"

She threw her head back and laughed. "Tip can't have that—nor, I'm guessing, would she want it. Look, when Mel dies, Tip will have to reinvent herself. Being your number two won't figure in the cards. Besides, she can't have it. It's mine. I like it and I'm good at it."

This made me laugh. "You're right. And you're also right about offering Tip a home. All I have to do is pass it through congress, and you know how she feels about Tip."

"*She's* on-board with it."

My jaw dropped. "Dani signed off on this?"

"You kidding? She knows one thing: Tiponi Redhawk would take a bullet in the head for you, and that means everything to Danica." Bailey chuckled and shook her head. "I swear to God that girl's in love with that gun. Anyway, I cleared it with her first. She's got William preparing the blue cottage for her should she choose to stay."

"Why not the main house?"

"She needs her own space. Tip's sort of a feral creature. She was on the bayou too long to assimilate, really. The blue cottage is furthest from the main house, and it sits on the river bend. It's perfect for her."

I nodded. "You're right. Thank you, thank you."

She finished dressing my wound and pulled my shirt down. "Don't take no for an answer, because you know how she gets. She'll want to be all big and strong, but you see right through it."

"Absolutely. I'll keep that in mind. Thanks. And thanks for the green stuff. It tingles."

"That's the mint. Mint tingles. It'll feel much better tomorrow. Just don't overdo it, okay? There isn't anything really pressing that can't wait. The kids are thrilled you're home and now that Tip's here—"

"She and I need to run up to the islands to see the Others."

"Oh? When?"

"As soon as we can. I need to put this whole thing behind us and move forward. I need to come to some sort of agreement with them. The sooner, the better."

Sooner came three days later, after Bailey gave me the all clear on my fast-healing wound. I had decided on the way up to ask Tip to stay. If I'd had any doubts, the last three days had convinced me. I'd never seen her more relaxed. Maybe being focused on Melika's imminent death had changed her. Here, she was lighter…free of the responsibility of caring for Mel or training any of us, which she had been doing for more than half her life. Turns out, she had no desire to be my second. She was thoroughly enjoying her free time, her lessons with the kids and, oddly enough, the wine industry fascinated her. If I couldn't find her around the house, all I had to do was call down to the barn, and there she'd be, hanging out with Will. For his part, he loved the company, and the two readers became fast friends.

But she declined my offer to stay, as I suspected she would. She told me that after we saw the Others, she would be returning to Mel until...until Mel didn't need her any more. I got that. But still, my offer rendered me speechless afterwards.

"What's going on in there?" She asked, as we flew over Portland.

"I really want you to stay." I blurted this out without even thinking. All my rehearsed words fled me. "After Mel...is gone—"

"Stay?"

"At the compound. I've...all of us have really been enjoying your company. I'd like it if you would reconsider making it your home. I know you love the bayou, but can't you give it a try?"

Tip looked out the window for a long time before turning back to me. "My home is the bayou, love. You know that."

Taking both her hands in mine, I smiled gently into her face. "Home is where your family is, Tip, and we're your family now. Me, Bailey, Danica. Hell, even Delta's gang adores you. Just tell me you'll think about it some more."

"I don't know if us being that close to each other is such a good idea. I'm still in love with you, you know? I know you don't have time for a relationship, and even if you did, wouldn't necessarily choose me, so no, I don't think it's a good idea. You have a lot of work to do here, and I..." she shook her head.

I nodded. "I know. I just thought—"

She shrugged. "You got under my skin fourteen years ago, and won't go away. But yeah, I'll think on it. I doubt I'll change my mind. Me and the bayou, we're buds."

When we landed on the San Juan Islands, two Town Cars met us. Tip was going off to see Bishop while I had a meeting with the Grand Council.

"See you in an hour," she said, kissing my forehead. I suddenly wondered when she had started doing that. I think she did it the first time she ever gave me a gift. It was an amethyst pendant that lay in my jewelry box.

"You bet. Give Bishop my love."

Ten minutes later, I was sitting in a chair facing the Grand Council. They all sat with their hands folded on the table before them.

"We wanted to give our appreciation to you in person, Echo. What you did and how you handled that whole sordid affair was noteworthy."

"Noteworthy? I was shot, a dear friend beat up, supers were killed; it was a great deal more than noteworthy." I didn't want to sound so pissed off, but I was.

Ramona held her hand up and apologized. "Forgive us for making it sound light. Clearly, it was not. We merely wish to thank you for a job well done."

"Where's Townsend?"

"Put out to pasture, so to speak. He won't be around to bother you or anyone else for a long time. You and yours are safe from him for the time being."

The last four words were like a slap in the face. "What does *that* mean?"

"It means," an elderly man by the name of Alan Swift said over his folded hands, "you're free from any repercussions from anyone in Vegas or Atlantic City. We sent a crew of cleaners who swept both cities clean with a warning that they were to stay far from you or they would deal with a wrath the likes of which they have never experienced. Without a leader, the Indies fall apart into the rag-tag group of nobodies they are."

"Did you offer to train them?"

Ramona shook her head. "Don't be absurd. Of course not. Their chances of being trained are over. They are too wild and set in their independent ways to be tamed, let alone trained. No, they will never come here, nor will they be formally taught."

"Are you saying I am not to teach them?"

"That is correct. You are not. How are *you* feeling, dear? We understand you were shot saving Tiponi."

"I'm fine. Bailey is the best healer, so I'll be back to one hundred percent in no time." I looked at each of them a moment before continuing. "We have been at odds in recent months—as you are aware—about letting naturals know about us, about who we are and what we do. After Vegas, I have come to the conclusion that you were...you *are*...correct in your views about naturals getting too close to us. Delta Stevens is a very strong woman—a warrior—and a loyal friend, yet I put her in harm's way in a situation she shouldn't have been in. As a result, I have had to tell more naturals than I am comfortable with who and what we are. While I trust this group with my life, I had no right endangering Delta to the degree I did."

Ramona tilted her head. "Oh, Echo, do you not realize every single one of us has been where you stand today? Each of us has believed *we* were the ones who could co-mingle? *We* were the ones who could change those facts? Sadly, we cannot. You endangered good people because you didn't tell them the truth and telling them the truth puts them and us in danger. It is a classic lose-lose situation."

I nodded and pressed on. "You were right on another count as well—the world isn't ready for us. Maybe it never will be." I shrugged, tears gathering in the corners of my eyes. "It's not time. No matter how much I might want it to be, it's just not time."

Ramona inched forward, her face soft, her smile genuine. "Every single one of us has had to battle that demon, Echo. We desperately wish to be a part of the world in which we live. For now though, we must remain apart from it, if for nothing else, to not endanger those who love us...both super as well as natural."

Wiping my tears, I nodded. "I realize that now. My own hubris got the best of me and I apologize. I just thought you should know where I stand on that."

"We appreciate your apology. Now, we must offer up one of our own. It appears Sonja Satre has reneged on her promise to help train Cinder, and has gone to ground."

I sat upright. "What do you mean, 'gone to ground'? Who is she hiding from?"

"This, we do not know. We have hunters out looking for her. We believe she is still in Alaska, but won't know for a week or so. It isn't uncommon for her to leap off our radar, but given her mercenary tendencies, we feel it best if you scratch her off your list as a potential mentor. You were right. She simply cannot be trusted."

I'd known that the first time I'd met her and, if I wasn't so hard up to find someone who could train Cinder better, I'd never have considered her. "Just as well. Also, it's possible Tip will be staying with me in California for a little while, but I'm not sure yet."

Ramona raised her eyebrows. "Oh?"

"She will need me and someplace to call home when Melika passes. When that happens, I ask that you give Tip time and room to grieve. No scouting, no hunting, nothing."

"We can try to honor your re—"

"It's not really a request." I rose from my chair. "Let me rephrase this. You felt I was best to mentor in Melika's place. I am. You thought I had what it takes to give these kids a chance at a new life. I do. That means I, and I alone, am responsible for my people. Tip is my people, so that call is mine to make. *I* will get in touch with *you* when she is ready for any task you might have for her. I won't have you doling out tasks for her until she's ready." I waited for the volley.

Ramona looked down the line at the other council members. "Very well. We shall place her active status on hold until the unfortunate day your mentor passes."

"Thank you. Is there anything else?"

"Actually, there is. You've taken Max Rhodes under your tutelage?"

"I have."

"Good. He can be quite an asset, as you've seen."

"He's a very sweet guy as well. It will be good for him to be around good people and away from Vegas."

"How are the triplets progressing?" Swift asked.

"You'll receive a report on them by the end of next week when I've had a chance to fully evaluate them. Tack, however, is doing remarkably well since I hooked him up with my security specialist."

Eric tossed out, "You have a *natural* mentoring him?"

"Tack can better utilize his skills if he understands how electricity and technology work. So yes, I do."

They muttered to each other as I waited.

"Very well. We would like to meet this young man in the near future. Perhaps we can send a team down to meet them all."

I nodded. "One more thing. Have you heard about any movement from Genesys? We had a slight security breach, but are unsure of its origins."

Consulting some notes, Ramona said, "Since Alaska, we've heard nothing. There has been little to no movement from them. No young supers snatched, no dead bodies found. You put the fear of God into them, Echo."

"Oh I doubt that. A bear is most dangerous when it emerges from hibernation. I would appreciate a heads up if you hear of anything."

We talked for another fifteen minutes about everyone's training and other goings on in the paranormal world, until it was time for me to go. After saying my goodbyes, I walked out to find my driver replaced by Tip's limo. When the door opened, there sat Tip and Bishop.

"Bishop!" I reached in and hugged the tiny woman. "How are you? You look great."

She smiled and patted the seat next to her. When I was in, the door closed and the limo pulled away. "There's much to say, my dear, and not so much time to say it." Her voice was thin with suspense and intrigue.

I looked over at Tip, who sat facing us. She

offered no clue.

"Tiponi explained to me what happened the other day in Las Vegas…during the…shooting. That was information no one here had heard."

I nodded, unclear what this was about since so much had happened.

"When that kid shot at me," Tip said softly. "The…oval thingie."

Bishop nodded. "Tiponi tells me a shimmering portal opened and swallowed up the bullets. Does that sum it up?"

I nodded. "Pretty much, though 'portal' is her word. I have no words for what happened."

Bishop patted my hand. "No, but I do." She adjusted herself so she was completely facing me now. "When you first came to us, my daughter realized you were so much more than an empath. Your empathic skills were merely the first of your powers to show themselves, so she focused on those, always waiting to see who you truly are. Then, we discovered you have selective telepathy with Tip and Cinder. Then there came that psionic blast of energy in close quarters."

"How did you—"

She held up her hand. "Little of what you do gets by me unnoticed. The origin of those bursts is a reserve energy battery of sorts that you are capable of reaching and unleashing when your emotions are out of balance. You know how naturals will get fatigued or irritable when under stress? Your response is much different. You are able to reach down, as it were, and flip on a switch to these reserves, which burst like a mini-sonic boom."

"So I have control over it?"

She shook her head. "Not really. You can access

and harness the energy, but you cannot control the volume."

"It acts like a percussion grenade in the military, Echo," Tip explained. "It can knock people out or blow their brains to bits. It all depends on the location and the volume."

"Great. Just what I need, a power I can't control."

"Can't right now," Bishop continued, "but we are making some calls. There's a rumor of a young percussionist in Europe somewhere. Our people are on top of it. Once we find her, we'll see if she can come here or we can send you there."

I drank this information in. I was in no mood to travel away from my kids.

"Now," Bishop inhaled deeply. "About this other power. I do not wish to alarm you, but several of us have seen this power. None of us knew from whom it emanated, but it is clear now what you truly are, my dear, and you are no mere empath. You are far more than even Melika, who, as we all know, is one of the most powerful supers in the country."

I looked over at Tip, who nodded solemnly. "What am I?"

Bishop took my hands in hers and stared into my face, no trace of a smile anywhere. "You, my dear child, are a space bender."

※ ※ ※ ※

"A what?"

"A space bender. We just call them benders. You are capable of bending space and perhaps even time. We won't know until we see it in action, but what we do know for sure is that you are a bender. You opened up a seam in space those bullets went through, saving Tip's life."

My hand raised to my mouth. "I bent space?"

She nodded. "You opened a portal—like a seam, a slit, a window, whatever you wish to call it—and the bullets went into it."

"Where did they go?"

Bishop unfolded a newspaper and handed it to me. "Read this."

I read a short article about two hunters in the woods of Wisconsin. As they were hiding behind a tree, three bullets embedded in the trunk of the tree, inches away from one man's head. Thinking some inexperienced hunter had taken a shot at them, they dug the bullets from the tree and took them to the local police department, where it was discovered the bullets had come from a .38 automatic handgun.

I dropped the paper on my lap. "Jesus."

Bishop nodded. "Even Jesus couldn't do that. It seems you have quite the rare gift. I've got calls in to all of my global connections, but there has only been one other known bender and she disappeared somewhere in South America over ten years ago, but we've heard she is still alive. Nevertheless, once the council is made aware of your power, we will actively search for her in the event she is still alive. You are going to need help that is well beyond even our collective capabilities."

Tip took my other hand. "As you can see, love, like all our powers, it's not without its drawbacks."

I stared at the tiny article. "So we don't know how or why the bullets ended up in Wisconsin?"

"We can only speculate right now. That's why we must locate this woman and see if she has anything she can teach you."

"What's her name?"

"Nuku. Nuku'alofa Murch."

I glanced up at Tip, who shrugged. "Never heard of her, but if she's been hiding out for ten years, it's no surprise."

I handed Bishop the paper. "I could have killed one or both of those men."

"Yes, you could have. Had you not, Tip would be lying in a hearse right now. This is a cautionary tale, my dear child. There will come a day when you will have to choose your kind over the naturals, when you will have to be willing to sacrifice them in order to save your own. You must prepare yourself for this moment. You must recognize all that you are and all you must do to train and protect *our* people. That day is nearing, Echo, and the onset of your new, and probably true, powers heralds a new beginning." Opening up her briefcase, Bishop handed me a file. "This is all we have on Nuku and bending. There are articles by Hawking, Einstein, and others about the crossover domains of time and space. When you thought Tip was going to die, your energy was so powerful, you opened a riff in space, saving her life. Can you do that without being in emotional distress? Is it somehow tied into your percussion blasts? We don't know. But what we do know is the potential of that ability to teleport something from one space to another is astronomical. You, my dear, are an incredibly powerful supernatural and, as such, the Others will wish for you to be protected at all costs."

"I *am* protected."

"Not enough. I have asked Tiponi to escort you to South America once we pin Nuku down. Do you have any objections to this arrangement?"

I looked up at Tip. "It's entirely up to her, but I am not ready to go anywhere for awhile. I have kids to train and a life to live in California."

"But you *will* go at some point? I have done everything I can to get the Council to back off from you, but they are persistent. They want you trained."

"If you find her, sure. At some point, but when I'm ready. Not when they think I am ready. I have kids to teach, Bishop. I am not at the Council's beck and call."

Bishop clapped. "It's settled then. Melika will be pleased."

We visited a little as the limo dropped us off at the airport. We hugged her tiny, fragile frame and waved as the limo pulled away.

"Bender, huh?"

Tip nodded. "I'm pretty sure I'm afraid of you now, little bender."

I laughed. "It's a lot to process."

"At least you're not processing it from a rubber room."

"No kidding."

Just then, both our Vidbooks rang. I flipped mine open to find Danica, a look of terror on her face, staring into the camera.

"Clark? You need to come home right now."

Oh no. No. No. No. "What's happened?"

"It's Cinder. Someone took her."

About the Author

Linda Kay Silva lives in the San Francisco Bay Area and teaches American, World, British, Asian, African, and sci-fi/fantasy literature at a military university. She holds a Masters in English with an emphasis in 18th Century British as well as a Masters Degree in Ancient and Classical Civilizations. When she isn't inspiring students to contemplate the world in which they live, she's reading and writing and dreaming up more stories than she can write out long hand with her fountain pen.

On any given day, she can be found puttering in her backyard, sitting on her patio overlooking her pond or working on her next novel.

>Linda Kay is the author of:
>Man Eaters—a zombie series
>Echo Branson—paranormal series
>Across Time—time travel series
>Lucky—written as Storm
>and she is currently is working on a new series.

Linda Kay invites your comments, questions and quips, about anything ranging from writing and education to trekking the rain forest and riding Harley's. She is an avid naturalist, a Harley enthusiast, a lover of all things Celtic, a fan of author Elizabeth Peters, and a woman who wakes up every morning glad to be alive. Linda Kay plans on writing until the day she can no longer hold one of her many fountain pens.

Other books by, Linda Kay Silva

Man Eaters - ISBN- 978-0-9828608-9-2

They prey only on human flesh, and as the virus spreads and the horde of man eaters grows, firefighter, Dallas Barkley struggles hourly to keep her little band of survivors from the grasp of killers who never tire, never sleep, and never quit longing to make a meal out of them. As martial law sweeps through the country, Dallas's new family must fight off not only voracious man eaters and a deadly military containment procedure, but rogue survivors who obey no law of the land as they wantonly take from those they perceive as weaker. But Dallas and her people are far from weak. With a cowgirl named Roper and a medic called Butcher, these three women must brave the darkest hours of the bloodiest days as they work together to create a safe haven in a world destroyed by a man made plague ravaging the country and threatening their lives. Only by placing their faith, loyalty, and love in each other's hands can they hope to survive. Only by forging bonds stronger than death can they hope to beat back the hordes of undead.

In the Nick of Time - ISBN - 978-1-939062-01-7

Jessie Ferguson has her hands full. Between sending her soul to the jungles of Viet Nam and visiting the oak groves of Merlin's backyard, Jessie races against the clock to save her little brother caught in a time and body she does not know. With danger lurking around every soggy corner for American troops slogging through the bug-infested rain forest, Jessie must find who Daniel was and get to him before he becomes a casualty. If that isn't enough, she must return to the Druids and face the wrath of Morgana. Jessie has slipped through time again and again, but never has so much been at stake. Can she reach Daniel before a bullet finds him first? And does she have the power to face a foe as deadly as Morgana? As sand falls through the hourglass, can Jessie get to both In the Nick of Time?